A TALE OF WITCHCRAFT...

ALSO BY CHRIS COLFER

A Tale of Magic...

The Land of Stories series:

The Wishing Spell

The Enchantress Returns

A Grimm Warning

Beyond the Kingdoms

An Author's Odyssey

Worlds Collide

The Ultimate Book Hugger's Guide

A Treasury of Classic Fairy Tales

The Mother Goose Diaries

Queen Red Riding Hood's Guide to Royalty

The Curvy Tree

Trollbella Throws a Party

A TALE OF WITCHCRAFT

CHRIS COLFER

ILLUSTRATED BY BRANDON DORMAN

LITTLE, BROWN AND COMPANY
NEW YORK BOSTON

Little, Brown and Company
Hachette Book Group
1290 Avenue of the Americas, New York, NY 10104
Visit us at LBYR.com

First Edition: September 2020

Little, Brown and Company is a division of Hachette Book Group, Inc. The Little, Brown name and logo are trademarks of Hachette Book Group, Inc.

The publisher is not responsible for websites (or their content) that are not owned by the publisher.

Library of Congress Cataloging-in-Publication Data
Names: Colfer, Chris, 1990– author. | Dorman, Brandon, illustrator.
Title: A tale of witchcraft... / Chris Colfer ; illustrated by Brandon Dorman.
Description: First edition. | New York : Little, Brown and Company, 2020. | Series: [A tale of magic... ; 2] | Audience: Ages 8–12. | Summary: Fourteen-year-old Brystal Evergreen has secured worldwide acceptance for the magical community, but new threats arise, including the centuries-old Righteous Brotherhood, which intends to exterminate all magical life, beginning with Brystal.
Identifiers: LCCN 2020017858 (print) | LCCN 2020017859 (ebook) |
ISBN 9780316523561 (hardcover) | ISBN 9780316523530 (ebook) |
ISBN 9780316523554 (ebook other)
Subjects: CYAC: Magic—Fiction. | Witches—Fiction. | Fairies—Fiction. |
Secret societies—Fiction. | Fantasy.
Classification: LCC PZ7.C677474 Tar 2020 (print) | LCC PZ7.C677474 (ebook) |
DDC [Fic]—dc23
LC record available at https://lccn.loc.gov/2020017858

ISBNs: 978-0-316-52356-1 (hardcover), 978-0-316-52353-0 (ebook), 978-0-316-70335-2 (int'l), 978-0-316-54175-6 (large print), 978-0-316-59120-1 (Barnes & Noble), 978-0-316-59119-5 (Barnes & Noble Black Friday), 978-0-316-59220-8 (BJ's), 978-0-316-59302-1 (Scholastic)

Printed in the United States of America

LSC-H

10 9 8 7 6 5 4 3 2 1

To all the mental health professionals, advocates, and pioneers.
Thank you for spreading the light.
And to all the essential workers who recently
redefined the word heroism.

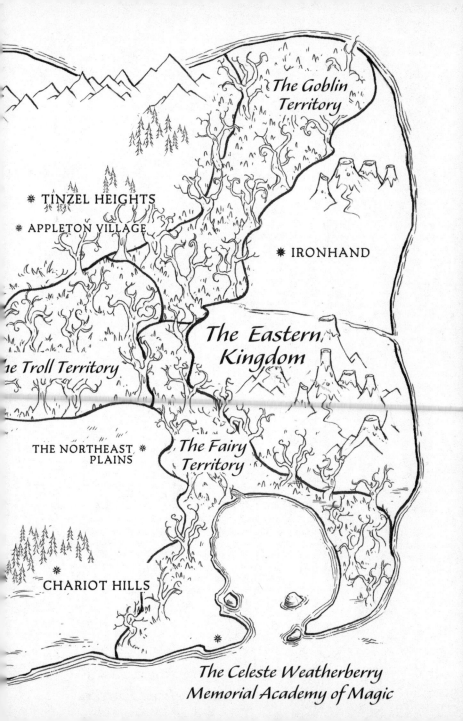

The Goblin Territory

TINZEL HEIGHTS

APPLETON VILLAGE

IRONHAND

The Eastern Kingdom

The Troll Territory

THE NORTHEAST PLAINS

The Fairy Territory

CHARIOT HILLS

The Celeste Weatherberry Memorial Academy of Magic

A RIGHTEOUS RETURN

I t began in the dead of night while the world was asleep. As soon as all the streetlamps faded and the lanterns dimmed throughout the Southern Kingdom, hundreds of men across the country—333 to be exact—suddenly emerged from their homes at precisely the same moment.

The peculiar activity hadn't been planned or rehearsed. The men never discussed it with one another or even knew the identities of their fellow participants. They were from different villages, different families, and different backgrounds, but the men were secretly united by one malevolent cause. And tonight, after a long hiatus, that cause had finally called them into action.

Each man stepped into the night wearing a pristine silver robe that practically glowed in the moonlight. Matching silver masks with two slits were draped over their heads to shield everything but their eyes, and the face of a ferocious white wolf was proudly displayed across each of their chests. The ominous uniforms made the men seem more ghostlike than human, and in many ways, they *were* ghosts.

After all, it had been centuries since the Righteous Brotherhood's last appearance.

The men left their homes and journeyed into the darkness, all heading for the same location. They traveled entirely on foot and walked so softly their footsteps didn't make a single sound. When their towns and villages were far behind them, and they were certain they hadn't been followed, the men lit torches to illuminate the road ahead. But they weren't on the paved roads for very long. Their destination was far beyond any beaten path, and it wasn't on any surviving maps.

The Brotherhood hiked over grassy hills, stomped through muddy fields, and splashed across shallow streams as they trekked through uncharted territory. They had never been to their destination or seen it with their own eyes, but the directions were so ingrained in them that every tree and boulder they passed felt as familiar as a memory.

Some men traveled greater distances than others, some moved faster or more slowly, but at two hours past midnight, the first of the 333 travelers started to arrive. And the site was exactly as they had expected.

At the southernmost point of the Southern Kingdom, at the base of a rocky mountain bordering the South Sea, were the ancient ruins of a long-forgotten fortress. From afar, the fortress looked like the carcass of an enormous creature that had washed ashore. It had jagged stone walls that were horribly cracked and chipped. Five crumbling towers stretched into the sky like the fingers of a skeletal hand, and sharp rocks hung over the drawbridge like teeth in a giant mouth.

The fortress hadn't been occupied by a single soul in over six hundred years—even the seagulls avoided it as they hovered in the night breeze—but regardless of its eerie appearance, the fortress was sacred to the Righteous Brotherhood. It was the birthplace of their clan, a temple of their beliefs, and it had served as their headquarters during the days when they imposed their Righteous Philosophy upon the kingdom.

There had come a time when the Brotherhood was so effective at enforcing the Righteous Philosophy that such a base of operations was no longer needed. So the Brotherhood boarded up their beloved fortress, hung up their uniforms, and retreated from sight. Over time, their existence became merely a rumor, the rumor became a myth, and the myth was nearly forgotten. For centuries, generation after generation of the Brotherhood sat quietly on the sidelines and relished the profound ways their ancestors had shaped the Southern Kingdom—and, by extension, the rest of the world.

But the world was changing. And the Brotherhood's time of silence was over.

Earlier that day, a series of silver flags with the images of white wolves were placed throughout the towns and villages in the Southern Kingdom. The flags were subtle and hardly noticed by most citizens, but to these 333 men, the flags conveyed an unmistakable message: *It was time for the Righteous Brotherhood to return.* And so, later that night, once their wives and children were asleep, the men quietly retrieved their uniforms from their hiding places, wrapped the silver robes around their bodies, draped the silver masks over their faces, and promptly left their homes for the fortress in the south.

The first arrivals took position on the drawbridge and guarded the entrance. As the other clansmen trickled in, they lined up one by one and recited an ancient passphrase before entering:

"Nothing can flee the three thirty-three."

Once they were permitted inside, the Brotherhood gathered in a vast courtyard at the heart of the fortress. The men stood in complete silence as they waited for the rest of the clan to arrive. They watched one another with extreme curiosity—none of them had ever seen a fellow clansman before. The men wondered if they recognized any of the eyes peering through the masks surrounding them, but they didn't dare ask. The first rule of the Righteous Brotherhood was to never disclose your identity, especially not to one another. As they saw it, the key to a successful secret society was keeping *everyone* a secret.

At five hours past midnight, all 333 members were finally present. A silver flag bearing the image of a white wolf was hoisted above the tallest tower to mark the Brotherhood's official return. Once the flag was raised, the High Commander of the clan revealed himself by placing a crown of sharp metal spikes on his head. The men bowed to their superior as he climbed to the top of a stone platform, where all 332 pairs of eyes could see him.

"Welcome, brothers," the High Commander said with open arms. " 'Tis a glorious sight to see all of you gathered here tonight. Such a meeting has not been held in over six hundred years, and our forefathers would be triumphant to know the Brotherhood has survived the test of time. For generations, the principles and responsibilities of this Brotherhood have been passed down from father to eldest son in three hundred and thirty-three of the Southern Kingdom's finest families. And on our fathers' deathbeds, we each swore an oath to devote our entire existence—this lifetime, and whatever lies beyond it—to protecting and upholding our Righteous Philosophy."

The High Commander gestured a hand to the Brotherhood, and they passionately recited the Righteous Philosophy in perfect unison:

"Mankind was meant to rule, and men to rule mankind."

"Indeed," the High Commander said. "Our philosophy is not just an opinion, it is the *natural order*. Mankind is the strongest and wisest species to ever grace this planet. We were meant to dominate, and our dominance is the key to survival itself. Without men like us, civilization would collapse and the world would return to the chaos of primitive times.

"For thousands of years, this Brotherhood has battled the dark and unnatural forces that threaten the natural order, and our ancestors have worked tirelessly to ensure mankind's rightful supremacy. They destabilized the communities of trolls, goblins, elves, dwarfs, and ogres so that the talking creatures could never organize an attack against us. They deprived women of education and opportunity to prevent the weaker sex from rising to power. And most important of all, our ancestors were the first to wage war against the blasphemy of *magic* and send its wicked practitioners into oblivion."

The clansmen raised their torches high above their heads and cheered for their ancestors' *heroic* deeds.

"Six centuries ago, this Brotherhood accomplished its greatest feat yet," the High Commander continued. "Our ancestors carried out a meticulous plan to put King Champion I on the throne of the Southern Kingdom. And then they surrounded the young king with an advisory council of High Justices, who were under the Brotherhood's control. Soon the Righteous Philosophy became the foundation of the mightiest kingdom on earth. The talking creatures were ostracized and stripped of rights, women were legally banned from reading books, and magic became a criminal offense punishable by death. For six hundred magnificent years, mankind ruled without opposition. With the Righteous Philosophy safely secured, our Brotherhood slowly faded into the shadows and enjoyed a prolonged period of rest.

"But nothing lasts forever. The Brotherhood has been reassembled tonight because a new threat has emerged that was unimaginable until now. And we must eliminate it *immediately*."

The High Commander snapped his fingers, and two clansmen hurried out of the courtyard. They returned a moment later carrying a large painting and set it on the stone platform beside their superior. The painting was a portrait of a beautiful young woman with bright blue eyes and light brown hair. She wore sparkling clothes, and white flowers adorned her long braid. Although she had a kind smile that could warm the coldest of hearts, something about the young woman made the Brotherhood uneasy.

"But it's just a *girl*," said a man in the back. "What's so threatening about that?"

"That's not just any girl," said a man in the front. "It's *her*—isn't it? The one that people are calling the *Fairy Godmother*!"

"Make no mistake, my brothers, this young woman is dangerous," the High Commander warned. "Underneath the flowers and the cheerful grin lies the greatest threat the Righteous Brotherhood has ever encountered. As we speak, this monster—this *girl*—is destroying everything our ancestors created!"

A nervous murmuring swept through the courtyard, prompting another man to step forward and address the anxious clan.

"I've learned a great deal about this Fairy Godmother," he announced. "Her real name is *Brystal*

Evergreen, and she's a criminal from Chariot Hills! Last year she was arrested for *female literacy* and *conjuring magic*! She should have been executed for her crimes, but Brystal Evergreen was spared because of her father, Justice Evergreen. The Justice used his connections to lessen her punishment, and instead of death, she was sentenced to hard labor at the Bootstrap Correctional Facility for Troubled Young Women. But Brystal Evergreen was only there for a couple of weeks before she escaped! She fled to the southeast In-Between and joined a devilish coven of fairies! She's lived there ever since, developing her sinful abilities with other heathens like her."

"I'd say her abilities are more than developed now," the High Commander chimed in. "Recently, Brystal Evergreen bewitched King Champion XIV into amending the laws of the Southern Kingdom! The In-Between was divided into territories so the talking creatures *and* the fairies would have proper homes! Women were granted permission to read and seek higher education! But worst of all, Brystal Evergreen orchestrated the worldwide *legalization of magic*! Virtually overnight, every trace of the Righteous

Philosophy was stripped from the Southern Kingdom's constitution!

"But Brystal Evergreen's reign of terror doesn't end there, my brothers. She has since opened an atrocious school of magic in the Fairy Territory and invited all members of the magical community to move there and develop their own unnatural abilities. When she's not teaching, Brystal Evergreen travels across the kingdoms with a crew of colorful degenerates known as the Fairy Council. They've captured the world's attention and affection, claiming to 'help' and 'heal' those in need, but our Brotherhood will not be fooled. The magical community's objective is the same today as it was six hundred years ago: *to brainwash the world with sorcery and enslave the human race.*"

The Brotherhood roared so loudly the ancient fortress shook.

"High Commander, I fear we're too late," said a man in the crowd. "Since the Fairy Council appeared, the public has grown fond of magic. I've overheard people discussing the surprising benefits the legalization has caused. Apparently, illnesses and diseases are on the decline, thanks to the new potions and elixirs that are sold in apothecaries. They say agriculture is thriving, thanks to the spells protecting crops from frost and insects. And people are even crediting our growing economy to the popularity of enchanted products. Every man wants a self-driving carriage, every woman wants a self-sweeping broom, and every child wants a self-swinging swing set."

"Public opinion is starting to shift about the other amendments, too," said another man in the crowd. "In fact, most of the Southern Kingdom actually *likes* the changes King Champion has made to the constitution. They say allowing women to read and pursue education has elevated discussions in our schools, causing students of all genders to think outside the box. They say splitting the In-Between into territories has made the talking creatures more civilized, and now travel and trade between kingdoms is much safer than before. All in all, the people believe the legalization of magic has sparked a new age of prosperity, and they wonder why it didn't happen sooner."

"*Their prosperity is a facade!*" the High Commander shouted. "A hydrangea may be beautiful, its scent may be pleasurable, but it is still *poisonous* when ingested! If we don't restore the Righteous Philosophy, our world will begin to rot from the inside out! Too much diplomacy will make us *weak*, too much equality will kill *initiative*, and too much magic will make us *lazy* and *incompetent*. The magical community will dominate us, the natural order will crumble, and absolute pandemonium will ensue!"

"But how do we restore the Righteous Philosophy?" a clansman asked. "King Champion is under Brystal Evergreen's influence—and we need the king to amend the law!"

"Not necessarily," the High Commander scoffed. "We need *a* king, not *the* king."

From the new creases in his mask, the Brotherhood could tell their superior was smiling.

"And now for the good news," the High Commander said. "King Champion XIV is eighty-eight years old, and it won't be long until a *new* king sits on the throne of the Southern Kingdom. And as fate would have it, the *next* king is very sympathetic to our cause. He respects the natural order, he believes in the Righteous Philosophy, and like us, he has not been fooled by the Fairy Council's displays of compassion. The next king has agreed to abolish King Champion's amendments on one condition: that we appoint him as the new leader of our Brotherhood and serve him as a *Righteous King.*"

The clansmen couldn't contain their excitement. Until now, they could never have imagined a world in which the sovereign of the Righteous Brotherhood and the sovereign of the Southern Kingdom would be one and the same. If they proceeded wisely, such an outcome could solidify the Righteous Philosophy for generations to come.

"What about the magical community?" a clansman asked. "They're more powerful and popular than ever before. Surely they'll revolt against the new king or bewitch him just as easily as the old king."

"Then we must terminate them *before* the next king takes the throne," the High Commander said.

"But how?" the clansman asked.

"The same way our Brotherhood nearly obliterated the magical community six hundred years ago. And believe me, brothers, our ancestors were armed with much more than a *philosophy.*"

The High Commander climbed down from the stone platform and then hoisted the platform up like a gigantic hatch. To the Brotherhood's surprise, what he exposed was a massive arsenal of cannons, swords, crossbows, spears, and chains. There were enough weapons to mobilize an army of a thousand men, but these weapons were unlike any the clansmen had ever seen. Instead of being made from iron or steel, all the blades, arrowheads, chains, and cannonballs were made from a red stone that glowed and flickered, as if fire were trapped inside. The crimson light flooded the colorless courtyard and mesmerized the clansmen.

"It's time for the Righteous Brotherhood to come out of the shadows!" the High Commander declared. "We must honor the oath we made to our fathers and strike before our enemies have a chance to prepare. Together, with our new Righteous King, we will preserve the natural order, restore our Righteous Philosophy, and exterminate the magical community once and for all!"

The High Commander removed a loaded crossbow from the arsenal and fired three arrows at the portrait of Brystal Evergreen—one into her head and two into her heart.

"And just like any colony of pests, first we must *kill its queen.*"

CHAPTER ONE

DAM DAMAGE

Besides a successful logging industry—and a handful of royal scandals—the Western Kingdom was best known for the iconic Western Dam in the capital city of Fort Longsworth. The landmark was over a thousand feet tall and made from over five million stone blocks, and it protected Fort Longsworth from being flooded by the Great Western Lake.

The dam was two centuries old and had taken seventy years to build, and when the construction was finally finished in the summer of 452, a national holiday was created to celebrate the historic achievement.

Dam Day was beloved by all the citizens in the Western Kingdom and a highlight of their year. People were given the day off from work, children were given the day off from school, and they all gathered together to play games, eat food, and raise a glass to the dam towering over the capital city.

Unfortunately, this year's Dam Day was expected to be a disappointment. After a series of unexpected earthquakes, the ground beneath the Western Dam had shifted and caused a large crack to spread across the structure. Water sprayed through the narrow opening and misted Fort Longsworth like a constant rain. The damage only worsened as time went on—the crack grew longer and wider, so water drenched the city more and more each day.

Immediate maintenance was required, but the kingdom's frugal sovereign, King Warworth, was reluctant to give the orders. Besides being a costly and timely endeavor, the repair would be a dangerous task, and the entire city of Fort Longsworth would have to be evacuated in the process. The king spent many sleepless nights scratching his bald head and twirling his bushy mustache, trying to think of an alternative solution.

Luckily for him (and his very, very wet citizens), new resources were at his disposal, and using them would cost him only a little of his pride. At first, the king rejected the idea, but as he watched the endless mist turn Fort Longworth's streets into small rivers, he realized he didn't have a choice. So King Warworth requested his finest parchment and his finest quill and wrote a letter asking for the one thing he hated asking for the most—*help*:

Dear Fairy Godmother,

Last year, you earned the world's gratitude after your courageous deeds in the Northern Kingdom. I, along with my subjects, can never thank you enough for sending the terrible Snow Queen into seclusion and saving the planet from the Great Blizzard of 651. Since then, you have continued to fascinate and inspire the world with profound acts of generosity. From building orphanages and shelters to feeding the hungry and healing the sick, you and the Fairy

Council have touched our hearts with your compassion and charity.

Today, I write to you with hopes that you'll consider sharing that compassion with the Western Kingdom. Recently, the Western Dam in Fort Longsworth suffered damages that must be addressed immediately. A traditional repair would take the better half of a decade and force thousands of citizens out of their homes. However, if you were willing to provide us with a magical remedy, my people would be spared from such grievances. If such a gesture is possible, the fairies would earn the Western Kingdom's eternal appreciation and give us more reason to celebrate on our beloved Dam Day.

It is no secret that the Western Kingdom, like our neighboring nations, has had a complicated history with the magical community. We cannot erase the discrimination and injustices of the past, but with your kindness, we could mark a new beginning for Western relations with magic.

I pray you'll forgive us and help us in our hour of need.

With humility,

His Excellency,
King Warworth of the Western Kingdom

The king was exhausted after all the groveling. He carefully folded the letter, stamped it with his official seal, and gave it to his fastest messenger.

The following morning, the messenger arrived at the border of the Fairy Territory, but he couldn't find a way inside. An enormous hedge grew along the perimeter and protected the territory like a leafy wall. The hedge was too tall to climb and too thick to crawl through, so the messenger searched the border and eventually found an entrance.

He was surprised to find a large group of *other* messengers lined up at the entrance, and judging by their elegant wardrobes, they were *all* delivering messages from prominent households. Even more surprising, the entrance was guarded by a terrifying knight who sat atop a massive three-headed horse. The knight was twice the size of a regular man, and antlers grew out of his helmet. Although the knight watched the messengers in complete silence, he didn't have to say anything to make one thing perfectly clear—*nothing* was getting past him.

Two mail bins were on the ground in front of the knight, one labeled REQUESTS and the other PRAISE. One at a time, the fearful messengers approached the knight, placed their messages into the appropriate box, and then hurried away as fast as they could. King Warworth's messenger waited for his turn and, with a trembling hand, dropped the king's letter into the box marked REQUESTS, then he raced back to the Western Kingdom.

Just a few hours after his letter was delivered, King Warworth received a response. While the king was enjoying dinner in the Western Castle, a unicorn suddenly burst into the dining room with a golden envelope in its mouth. The magical steed was followed by two dozen guards who had failed to stop it from entering the castle. The guards chased the unicorn in circles around the dining room, and on their fifth lap around the table, the unicorn dropped the golden envelope in the king's bowl of soup.

The unicorn left the dining room just as quickly as it had arrived. As the guards hurried after the beast, King Warworth dried the envelope with his napkin, opened it with his butter knife, and read the message inside:

Dear King Warworth,

I passed your request on to the Fairy Godmother, and she sends her deepest sympathies for your dam troubles. She, along with myself and the rest of the

Fairy Council, has agreed to help you. We will arrive in Fort Longsworth at noon on Dam Day to fix the damage.

Please let us know of any changes, conflicts, or additional information prior to our visit. Thank you and have a magical day.

Sincerely,

Emerelda Stone,
Director of Correspondence to the Fairy Godmother

PS—We apologize for meeting you on your national holiday. The Fairy Council is very busy with requests at the moment.

King Warworth was overjoyed by the good news and saw it as a personal victory. He decided to make the Fairy Council's visit a momentous occasion and ordered his staff to spread word of their upcoming engagement. Soggy banners were flown and damp flags were raised across the moist capital. A row of risers was placed at the foot of the Western Dam, and a stage was built so the king could present the council with a token of his appreciation afterward.

Such arrangements hadn't been made since King Warworth's coronation—but public interest in the Fairy Council was gravely underestimated.

On the eve of Dam Day, hundreds of thousands of citizens from all corners of the kingdom traveled to Fort Longsworth. By dawn, the risers were overflowing, and crowds formed in every part of the city with a view of the dam. Families stood on the roofs of their homes, shopkeepers stood on the roofs of their shops, and monks straddled the spires of their churches for a glimpse of the festivities. The spewing dam soaked all the spectators throughout the city; they shivered in the morning air, but their hearts were kept warm by the promise of magic.

The Western Kingdom had never hosted such a tremendous celebration. It was being called "the event of the decade," "a celebration of the century," and "a Dam Day for the history books."

But even with those expectations, no one could have predicted just how *memorable* the day would be....

· • ★ • ·

On the morning of Dam Day, Fort Longsworth was so busy it took King Warworth three hours to travel the short distance between the Western Castle and the Western Dam. His carriage squeezed through the crowded streets and arrived at the dam with only minutes to spare. Once the king was seated in a private section of the risers, an energetic presenter took to the stage and greeted the hundreds of thousands of people surrounding the landmark.

"*Helloooooo, Western Kingdom!*" he called out. "It is my great honor to welcome you to what will surely be remembered as *the best Dam Day of our lifetime!*"

The presenter's boisterous voice echoed through the congested city, and all the citizens cheered. Their enthusiastic roar was so strong it almost knocked the presenter off his feet.

"In just a few minutes, the Fairy Council will arrive in Fort Longsworth to repair the damages on the Western Dam. Such an endeavor would normally take several years to complete, but with the help of a little magic, the dam will be fixed *instantaneously* before our eyes! Of course, none of this would be happening without the swift negotiations led by our bold and brilliant

King Warworth—*go ahead, Your Excellency, give the crowd a wave!*"

The sovereign stood and waved to his adoring citizens. Their polite praise eventually died down, but King Warworth remained on his feet, basking in his own glory.

"Now prepare yourselves," the presenter went on. "At any moment, you'll be treated to a spectacle that's guaranteed to stimulate all your senses! But *how* will the Fairy Council repair the Western Dam, you ask? Perhaps they'll mend it with the fire of a thousand torches! Perhaps they'll seal it with a sheet of glittering diamonds! Or perhaps they'll stitch it together with strands of invincible ivy! We won't know until it happens! But punctuality must be part of their process, because *here they come now!*"

In the distance, traveling above the surface of the Great Western Lake, were six colorful young people who approached the city like a moving rainbow.

The group was led by an eleven-year-old girl with a beehive of bright orange hair and a dress made from dripping patches of honeycomb. She was carried through the air by a swarm of live bumblebees. The swarm dropped her off on top of the Western Dam and then took refuge inside her hair. She was followed by another eleven-year-old girl, who surfed across the Great Western Lake on a lone wave. The surfer wore a sapphire bathing suit, and instead of hair, a stream of water flowed down her body and evaporated at her feet. As her wave reached the edge of the dam, the surfer hopped out of the lake and landed beside the girl in the honeycomb dress.

"One is sassy with a stinger, and the other is the only person wetter than Fort Longsworth—please put your hands together for *Tangerina Turkin* and *Skylene Lavenders!*" the presenter said.

All of Fort Longsworth burst into applause for the first members of the Fairy Council.

Tangerina and Skylene couldn't believe their eyes—they had never seen such a massive gathering.

"Is there some sort of sale happening?" Skylene asked her friend.

"No, I think they're here to see *us*," Tangerina said.

The crowds cheered even louder as the next two members of the Fairy Council arrived. A thirteen-year-old girl with beautiful brown skin and curly black hair sailed across the Great Western Lake in a bejeweled sailboat. She wore a robe made from beaded emeralds, diamond-studded sandals, and a shimmering tiara. The girl docked her sailboat at the edge of the lake and joined Tangerina and Skylene on top of the Western Dam. She was followed by a twelve-year-old boy who shot through the sky like a rocket. The boy wore a shiny gold suit, flames covered his head and shoulders, and he was propelled through the air by two fiery blasts expelling from his feet. The blasts faded as he reached the Western Dam and landed beside the girl covered in emeralds.

"She's beautiful and tough as diamonds, and he's never afraid to play with fire—*it's Emerelda Stone and Xanthous Hayfield!*" the presenter announced.

Just like Tangerina and Skylene, Emerelda and Xanthous were amazed by the sea of people surrounding the dam. The flames on Xanthous's head and shoulders flickered with anxiety and he hid behind Emerelda.

"Look at all the protesters!" the boy cried. "Should we leave?"

"They seem a little *happy* for protesters," Skylene said.

"That's because they're not," Tangerina said. "Read their signs!"

The Fairy Council had grown accustomed to seeing groups of protesters whenever they made a public appearance. Usually, the demonstrators chanted degrading things at them and held signs with messages like GOD HATES FAIRIES, MAGIC EQUALS MAYHEM, and THE END IS NEAR. However, their visit to Fort Longsworth hadn't attracted the sort of protest they were used to. On the contrary, as the fairies looked around the crowd, they saw only positive messages like THANK GOD FOR FAIRIES, MAGIC IS BEAUTIFUL, and DON'T BE TRAGIC, THEY'RE JUST MAGIC.

"Oh," Xanthous said, and his nerves calmed down. "Sorry, I keep forgetting people actually *like* us now. Old habits die hard."

Emerelda grunted and folded her arms. "King Warworth should have mentioned there'd be an *audience*," she grumbled. "I should have known better—monarchs make a meal out of everything."

The sound of squawking filled the air as a rowdy flock of geese carried the fifth member of the Fairy Council to the Western Dam. She was a chubby fourteen-year-old who wore a bowler hat, a black jumpsuit, a pair of oversize boots, and a bottle-cap necklace. The geese dropped her next to the other fairies and she landed with a *thump* on her behind.

"Ouch!" she yelled at the birds. "You call that a landing? Meteors have softer impacts!"

"You don't want to ruffle her feathers—*say hello to Lucy Goose!*" the presenter announced.

"That's pronounced GOO-SAY!" she shouted as she climbed to her feet. "Next time do some research before you—" Lucy's mouth fell open, and she lost her train of thought when she spotted all the observers. *"Holy full house!* Look at the size of that crowd! It's even bigger than the one that watched us build the bridge in the Eastern Kingdom!"

"I'd say the entire Western Kingdom is here," Emerelda said. "Maybe more."

Lucy grinned from ear to ear as she took in the gathering. A group of children caught her eye and she became very excited. Each child was snuggling a doll that resembled a member of the Fairy Council.

"We've been *merchandised!*" Lucy declared. "Gosh, it's a real shame we do this stuff out of the goodness of our hearts. We'd make a fortune if we charged admission."

A hush fell over Fort Longsworth in anticipation of the sixth and final member of the Fairy Council. Just when the citizens started to worry she wasn't coming, a beautiful fifteen-year-old girl with bright blue eyes and light brown hair descended from the clouds in a large bubble. She wore a sparkling blue pantsuit with matching gloves and a train at the waist, and white flowers were placed in her long braid. The bubble landed gently on the Western Dam beside the other fairies, and the girl popped it with her crystal wand.

"Snow Queens beware—you're no match for our next guest!" the presenter said. "She is compassion personified and considered a goddess among men— *please give a warm Western Kingdom welcome to the one and only Faaaaairy Goooooodmother!*"

The citizens cheered so loudly the Western Dam vibrated under the Fairy Council's feet. People near the front of the dam started chanting and soon the entire city joined in.

"Fairy Godmother! Fairy Godmother! Fairy Godmother! Fairy Godmother!"

Brystal Evergreen was overwhelmed by the

passionate greeting. She had never seen so many people in one place before, and every single person was clapping, jumping, or crying tears of joy for *her*. They held paintings of her face and posters with her name written on them. Little girls (and a couple of grown men) were dressed up as her and twirled fake wands in their hands.

The Western Kingdom's admiration was an incredible honor, but for reasons Brystal couldn't explain, all the excitement made her uncomfortable. It didn't matter how enthusiastically the people cheered for her, Brystal felt undeserving of their recognition. And despite their vibrant welcome, she couldn't fight the urge to leave. Nevertheless, Brystal had a job to do. So she forced herself to smile and gave the crowd a modest wave.

The other fairies seemed to enjoy the attention much more than Brystal did, especially Lucy.

"Boy, the crowd really loves that Fairy Godmother name," Lucy said. "Aren't you glad I gave you a title?"

"I told you I didn't want one," Brystal replied. "It makes me feel like an object."

"Well, as my mother always said, if you're going to

be objectified, you might as well be objectified by family," Lucy said, and patted Brystal on the back. "Just be glad Fairy Godmother is what stuck—we've all been called a lot worse."

"Excuse me, Brystal?" Emerelda interjected. "It might be best if we make this a quick one. We've got a windmill to repair at three o'clock and a farm to defrost at five. Besides, people are starting to foam at the mouth down there."

"I couldn't agree more," Brystal said. "Let's just do what we came here to do and be done with it. There's no need to cause a bigger fuss than necessary."

Without wasting another moment, Brystal stepped to the edge of the Western Dam and waved her wand at the damage below her. The giant crack was magically filled with a golden seal, and after more than a week of constant mist, the spewing water finally stopped. To help matters even more, Brystal flicked her wand again and this time sent a powerful breeze through the city that dried all the streets, shops, and homes. The breeze knocked a couple of people to the ground and blew hats off people's heads, but they returned to their feet with completely dry clothes.

It all happened so quickly it took the citizens a

minute to realize their problems were solved. Their roar of appreciation was so powerful it was a miracle the Western Dam didn't crack again.

"Good, everyone is satisfied," Brystal said. "Now let's get going so—"

"*Astounding!*" the presenter bellowed. "With just a flick of her wrist, the Fairy Godmother has restored the Western Dam and saved Fort Longsworth from a decade of rain! And now the Fairy Council will join King Warworth onstage so he can present them with a token of our kingdom's gratitude!"

"Say *what*?" Emerelda said.

The fairies looked down and saw King Warworth was standing on the stage with a large golden trophy. Tangerina and Skylene squealed with delight.

"They want to give us an award!" Skylene said. "I *love* awards!"

"Can we stay and accept it?" Tangerina asked the others. "Pretty please?"

"Absolutely not," Emerelda said. "If King Warworth wanted to give us an award, he should have cleared it with me first. We can't let people take advantage of our time."

"Oh, lighten up, Em," Tangerina said. "We've

worked our butts off trying to gain the world's approval—and now we *finally* have it! If we don't give people a *chance* to admire us every now and then, we might *lose* their admiration!"

"I think Tangerina has a point," Xanthous said. "King Warworth may have broken the rules but his people don't know that. If they don't get the ceremony they're expecting, they'll probably blame *us*. And we shouldn't give them a reason to start hating us again."

Emerelda groaned and rolled her eyes. She pushed up the sleeve of her robe and checked the emerald sundial around her wrist.

"Fine," Emerelda said. "We'll give them another twenty minutes—but that's it."

The fairy snapped her fingers, and a long emerald slide magically appeared. It stretched from the top of the dam to the stage below. Emerelda, Xanthous, Tangerina, and Skylene slid down the slide and joined King Warworth on the stage, but Brystal paused before she followed them. She noticed Lucy hadn't said a word since the dam had been repaired, and instead, she was standing very still, watching the crowd in deep contemplation.

"Lucy, are you coming?" she asked.

"Yeah, I'll be right there," Lucy said. "I'm just thinking."

"Uh-oh," Brystal said. "It must be serious if you're missing the chance to be on a stage."

"Are we doing enough?"

Brystal was confused by the abrupt question. "Huh?"

"We fix dams, we build bridges, we help people—but is it *enough*?" Lucy elaborated. "All these people traveled here to see something spectacular, and what did we give them? Some sealant and a little wind."

"Right," Brystal said. "We gave them exactly what they *needed*."

"Yes, but not what they *wanted*," Lucy said. "If performing in the Goose Troupe taught me anything, it's the psychology of an audience. If these people go home disappointed, even slightly, they're going to be angry with us. And just like Xanthous said, we shouldn't give them *any* reason to hate us. If people start resenting the Fairy Council, then soon they'll start resenting *all* fairies and *boom!* The magical community is back to where it started. I think it'd be smart to stick around and give these folks a show."

Brystal gazed at the city as she thought about what Lucy had said. It was obvious the people were hungry for more magic—they'd been fixated on the Fairy Council since they arrived—but Brystal didn't want to indulge them. She and the others had worked so hard to get to this point. The idea of working harder just to *maintain* their position was an exhausting thought. And Brystal didn't want to think about anything—she just wanted to leave and get away from the crowd.

"We're philanthropists, Lucy, not performers," she said. "If people expect a show from us, we'll always have to give them a show, and where will it end? It'll be easier to please people and manage their expectations if we keep things simple. Now let's accept the king's award, shake a few hands, and keep it moving."

Brystal slid to the stage before Lucy had the chance to argue, but they both knew their conversation was far from over.

"On behalf of the Western Kingdom, I would like

to thank the Fairy Godmother for her grand acts of generosity," King Warworth told his citizens. "As a token of our eternal gratitude and undying appreciation, I present her with the most prestigious prize in our kingdom, the Dam Cup."

Before King Warworth could hand the trophy to Brystal, Skylene snatched the award from him and cradled it like a baby. Tangerina nudged Brystal forward, forcing her into an impromptu acceptance speech.

"Um . . . well, first I'd like to say *thank you*," Brystal said, and reminded herself to smile. "It's always a privilege to visit the Western Kingdom. The Fairy Council and I were very honored that you trusted us with such an important piece of your country, I hope from now on, whenever people look up at the Western Dam, they'll be reminded of all the potential magic has to offer. . . ."

As Brystal continued her speech, Lucy studied the citizens in the crowd. They were hanging on every word Brystal said, but Lucy worried it was only a matter of time before they lost interest—they didn't want to *hear* about magic, they wanted to *see* magic! If Brystal wasn't going to give them the spectacle they desired, then Lucy was. And she was confident her *specialty for trouble* would do the trick.

When she was certain all the eyes were on Brystal, Lucy snuck off the stage and tiptoed to the base of the Western Dam. She rubbed her hands together, placed both of her palms against the stone landmark, and summoned a little magic.

"This should spice things up," she said to herself.

Suddenly, the Western Dam started to crack like an eggshell. Chunk by chunk, the dam began to crumble, and water from the Great Western Lake sprayed through the structure. Lucy had figured something strange would happen—it always did when she used her magic—but she hadn't expected the whole dam to fall apart! She screamed and ran back to her friends as fast as she could.

"... if we leave you with anything, let it be a newfound appreciation, not just for the Fairy Council, but for magic as a whole," Brystal said as she concluded her speech. "And in the future, I hope mankind and the magical community will be so close it'll be hard to imagine a time when there was any conflict between us. Because at the end of the day, we all want the same—"

"*Brystal!*" Lucy shouted.

"Not now, Lucy, I'm finishing my speech," Brystal said without looking.

"*Dam!*"

"Lucy, watch your mouth! There are children—"

"*NO! LOOK AT THE DAM! BEHIND YOU!*"

The Fairy Council turned around just as the entire Western Dam collapsed. The Great Western Lake surged toward Fort Longsworth like a thousand-foot-tall tidal wave.

"*Lucy!*" Brystal gasped. "*What did you—*"

"*RUN FOR YOUR LIVES!*" King Warworth screamed.

Fort Longsworth was consumed with panic. The citizens pushed and shoved one another as they tried to flee, but the city was so crowded there was nowhere to go. When the tidal wave was just a few feet from colliding with its first victims, Brystal leaped into action. A wind with the power of a hundred hurricanes erupted from the tip of her wand and blocked the wave like an invisible shield. It took all of Brystal's strength to hold her wand steady, and she was able to stop the majority of the water, but there was too much to stop on her own.

"Xanthous! Emerelda!" Brystal called over her shoulder. "You two stop the water coming around the sides of my shield! Skylene, make sure the water doesn't spill over the top! Tangerina, help the people get to safety!"

"What about me?" Lucy asked. "What can I do?"

Brystal shot her a scathing look. "Nothing," she said. "You've done *enough*!"

As Lucy watched helplessly, the rest of the Fairy Council followed Brystal's commands. Xanthous ran to Brystal's left side and blasted the oncoming water with fire, causing it to steam and disappear. Emerelda created an emerald wall to block the water on Brystal's right side, but the wave was so powerful it knocked the wall down, forcing Emerelda to rebuild it over and over again. Skylene waved her hand in a large circle, and the water spilling over the top of Brystal's shield looped through the air and poured back into the Great Western Lake. While her friends blocked the water, Tangerina sent her bumblebees into the frantic crowd, and the swarm scooped up children and elderly people before they were trampled.

Although the Fairy Council put up a quick and effective barrier, Lucy knew her friends couldn't block the wave forever. She disregarded Brystal's instructions and came up with a plan to help them. Lucy whistled for her geese, and the flock swooped down and plucked her off the ground.

"Take me to the hill next to the lake!" she said. "And make it quick!"

The geese carried Lucy to the hill as fast as they could. They dropped her off on the hillside, and, once again, Lucy landed on her behind with a *thump*—but she didn't have time to scold the birds. From the hill, Lucy had a perfect view of the Fairy Council as they fought off the monstrous wave. She could tell her friends were getting tired, because the water was pushing them closer and closer to the city.

"I really hope this works," Lucy prayed.

She summoned all the magic in her body and hit the ground with a clenched fist. Suddenly, hundreds and hundreds of grand pianos appeared out of thin air and tumbled down the hillside. It caused a thunderous—not to mention *musical*—commotion. All the panicked citizens froze and watched the bizarre landslide in awe. The pianos crashed onto the ground and piled up between the Fairy Council and the enormous wave. The instruments kept coming and coming, and soon the pile grew over the fairies' heads. Within moments, a completely new dam was created, and Fort Longsworth was saved by a barrier of broken pianos.

It had been the most stressful and chaotic five minutes in the Western Kingdom's history—but the citizens had also just witnessed the most spectacular sight of their lives. They clapped and cheered so loudly the ovation was felt in neighboring kingdoms.

Lucy hurried down the hill to check on her friends. The fairies were so furious none of them could look her in the eye.

"Well, that was a doozy," Lucy said with a nervous laugh. "Are you guys all right?"

"*You walking nightmare!*" Skylene shouted.

"*What the heck were you thinking?*" Tangerina asked.

"*You could have killed us all!*" Emerelda yelled.

"*And obliterated an entire city!*" Xanthous cried.

Lucy shrugged innocently. "Hey, at least I *gave a dam*." She laughed. "Get it, guys? Get it?"

Brystal let out a long, aggravated sigh to make her anger perfectly clear. Lucy was used to infuriating the others, but she couldn't remember the last time she had disappointed Brystal. She sheepishly lowered her head and kept her hands in her pockets for the remainder of their visit.

"We'll discuss this later," Brystal told the fairies. "Right now, we need to apologize for Lucy's behavior and leave before we lose mankind's trust forever!"

The Fairy Council followed Brystal back to the stage, but they quickly realized an apology wasn't necessary. The citizens were so bewildered by all the magic they had never stopped cheering. King Warworth returned to the stage and profusely shook the fairies' hands—even *he* was spellbound by the day's events.

While the fairies were distracted by the endless praise, four wheels and six horses were covertly hooked up to the stage. The stage unexpectedly lunged forward and it was pulled through Fort Longsworth like an enormous wagon.

"What's happening?" Xanthous asked.

"Why, it's time for the parade, of course," King Warworth said.

"You never said anything about a parade!" Emerelda griped.

"Didn't I?" King Warworth played dumb. "It's a Western Kingdom tradition to give our guests of honor a parade through the capital."

Emerelda growled and flared her nostrils. "All right, that's it!" she exclaimed. "We put up with an unexpected audience, we were nice enough to accept your award, but we will absolutely not participate in a stupid—"

"Em, just let the man give us a parade," Tangerina said. "We've earned one."

"It's the least we could do after Lucy almost destroyed their city," Skylene said.

Emerelda wasn't happy about it, but her friends were right—there had been enough conflict for one day. She glared at King Warworth and aggressively stuck her finger in his face.

"Expect a letter from my office tomorrow morning," she told him. "And fair warning, it'll have some *strong language.*"

The Fairy Council was paraded down every street in Fort Longsworth, and even though the ordeal lasted much longer than they anticipated, the fairies ended up enjoying themselves. The citizens were practically buzzing with excitement, and their happiness was infectious. The fairies smiled, laughed, and occasionally blushed at the eccentric displays of affection.

"I love you, Fairy Godmother!"

"I want to be you when I grow up!"
"You look fabulous today, Fairy Godmother!"
"You're my hero!"
"Marry me, Fairy Godmother!"

Brystal smiled and waved as much as the other fairies, but on the inside, she wasn't as gleeful as her friends were. In fact, being closer to the citizens made Brystal even more uncomfortable than before. She desperately wanted the parade to end so she could get away from all the smiling faces, but still, she couldn't explain why.

The parade may have been unexpected, but it was also a huge milestone for the fairies. The cheering crowds were proof that the Fairy Council had changed the world—*the magical community was finally accepted and safe from persecution*! It didn't make sense for Brystal to feel anything but triumphant, but for whatever reason, her heart wouldn't let her.

Because none of this is real....

The voice came out of nowhere and startled Brystal. She looked around the traveling stage but couldn't find who it was coming from.

Deep down, you know this won't last....

It was as soft as a whisper, but despite the commotion of the parade, the voice was crystal clear. No matter which way Brystal turned or where she stood, it was like someone was speaking directly into both of her ears at once. And whoever they were, they sounded awfully familiar.

Their affection...

Their excitement...

Their joy...

It's only temporary.

Brystal stopped trying to find the voice and focused on what it was saying. Was mankind's affection really as fickle as the voice suggested? People's opinion of magic had changed so quickly, was it possible they'd change their minds again? Or worse, was it *inevitable*?

Not long ago, the people cheering for your parade would have cheered just as loudly for your execution....

I wonder how many fairies were dragged through these same streets before being burned at the stake....

I wonder how many were drowned in the lake you just saved the city from.

The voice made Brystal feel unsafe. As she gazed upon the crowd, she saw the citizens in a different light. There was something sinister behind their ~~smiles and~~ something primitive about their undying praise. She no longer felt like an honoree among admirers—*she was a piece of meat among predators.* But this wasn't a new epiphany. *This* was the reason Brystal had been uncomfortable from the moment she'd arrived, she just hadn't been able to articulate it until now.

Mankind may have forgotten about the horrors of history, but Brystal would never forget what they had done to witches and fairies like her in the past. And she'd never forgive them either.

They may celebrate you today ...

But eventually, they'll grow tired of celebrating you. . . .

Mankind will hate you and your friends, just as they did before.

It suddenly dawned on Brystal why the voice sounded so familiar. It wasn't coming from someone nearby, it was coming from *inside her head*. She wasn't hearing voices—these were her *own thoughts*.

History always repeats itself. . . .

The pendulum always swings. . . .

Always. . . .

You'd be wise to prepare.

The grim thoughts faded away as if a switch had been flipped, but Brystal didn't know where or what the switch was. The sensation was unlike anything she had ever experienced. She wasn't a stranger to peculiar ideas or unsettling emotions, but *this* seemed completely random and out of her control.

These thoughts had a mind of their own.

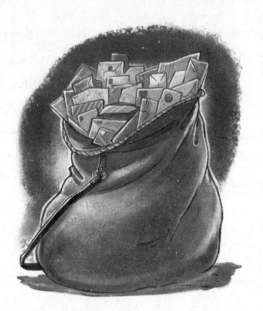

CHAPTER TWO

HAPPINESS

After a long day of energetic crowds, magical charity, and not-so-natural disasters, Brystal was looking forward to a quiet evening alone. Unfortunately, as soon as the Fairy Council returned to the Academy of Magic, she realized solitude wasn't in the cards for her.

"Brystal, can we please talk about this?" Lucy

asked. "You've been giving me the silent treatment since we left the Western Kingdom."

In all honesty, Brystal *was* furious with her, but Lucy's behavior at the Western Dam wasn't the reason for her silence. All Brystal could think about was the strange thoughts that had consumed her during the parade. The longer she dwelled on the experience, the more confusing and upsetting the thoughts became. She hoped a little downtime might help her find an explanation, but Lucy wasn't going to give her any privacy.

"Come ooooon, Brystal!" Lucy moaned. "How many times do I have to say I'm sorry?"

"Until I believe you," she said.

Brystal hurried up the front steps of the academy and climbed the floating staircase in the entrance hall, but Lucy persisted.

"Once again, I *sincerely* apologize for my behavior today," Lucy said with a dramatic bow. "What I did was childish, reckless, and downright dangerous—*buuuuut*, you have to admit, it all worked out for us in the end."

"*Worked out?*" Brystal was appalled by Lucy's choice of words. "You can't be serious!"

"Of course I am! The crowd loved it!" Lucy said. "We gave them a spectacle they'll never forget and a reason to love magic forever!"

"You almost killed us and destroyed an entire city!"

"Yes, but *then* I saved you!"

"From a situation *you* caused! That doesn't make you a hero!"

"I told you, I never meant to destroy the dam. Honestly, I didn't know what my magic was going to do; I just wanted to give the Western Kingdom a show. If you had just listened to me, none of it would have happened!"

The notion infuriated Brystal. She paused halfway up the floating steps and turned to Lucy with a nasty scowl.

"Don't you dare blame this on me!" Brystal said. "*You* put thousands of people in danger! *You* nearly destroyed one of the biggest cities in the world! *You* almost ruined the magical community's relationship with mankind! And until that sinks in, I'm sorry, Lucy, but you're *out of the Fairy Council*!"

Lucy was so stunned her jaw nearly hit the floor.

"What?! You can't kick me out of the Fairy Council!"

Brystal wasn't certain she could either. Until now, the council had never needed a protocol for bad behavior.

"Well . . . I just did," Brystal said with a confident nod. "You are hereby stripped of all council privileges until you're mature enough to take responsibility for your actions. Now, if you'll please excuse me, I have business to attend to."

Brystal left Lucy in a frozen state of shock on the floating steps and headed to her office on the second floor. She pushed through the heavy double doors and sighed with relief at the sight of an empty room.

The office was a circular and spacious chamber with bookshelves, potion cabinets, and glass furniture. It had floor-to-ceiling windows that offered a breathtaking view of the academy grounds and the sparkling ocean beyond it. Fluffy white clouds drifted through the high ceiling, and bubbles emitted from the fireplace and floated through the air.

The chamber was filled with unique objects that Brystal and her predecessor, Madame Weatherberry, had collected over the years. On the wall above the fireplace was an enlarged Map of Magic. The map was covered in thousands of twinkling lights, one for every living witch and fairy on earth. The lights showed where they were located throughout the four kingdoms and six territories.

In the back of the office, beside Brystal's glass desk, was a very special globe that showed her what the world looked like from space. It allowed Brystal to monitor hurricanes as they blew across the seas and thunderstorms as they swept across the land, but most important of all, Brystal used the globe to keep an eye on the northern lights twinkling above the Northern Mountains.

"Thank goodness," she whispered to herself. "You're still there."

Brystal was relieved to see the northern lights hadn't moved while she was away. She never told anyone *why* the lights were so important, but then again, no one ever noticed how frequently she checked on them throughout the day. It was the first thing she did in the morning and the last thing she did at night, and on the days the Fairy Council traveled, Brystal always inspected the globe before and after their trips.

The lights meant Brystal could put her mind at

ease, at least, about *one* thing. The day had provided her with plenty of other concerns—and the day wasn't over yet.

"You're making a huge mistake!" Lucy declared as she burst into the office.

For a split second, Brystal was tempted to remove Lucy with magic, but she figured it wouldn't help matters.

"And why is that?"

"Because losing a member of the band always ends in disaster!" Lucy explained. "The same thing happened with the Goblin Tenors! A few years ago, one of the goblins was kicked out of the group for eating their fans. But the decision backfired! Without a fourth member, people felt like something was missing from their show, and everyone stopped going to their performances!"

"Or maybe they stopped showing up because *people were getting eaten!*"

Lucy paused for a moment—she had never thought of that before—but she quickly waved it off and went back to her point.

"Look, I understand I messed up and deserve a

punishment, but you shouldn't put the Fairy Council at risk just to teach me a lesson," she said. "Everyone knows there are six of us—and *that's* what people expect to see! If only five of us show up to our events, people will be disappointed. And just like I said at the Western Dam, if we disappoint people, they'll start to resent us, and soon, they'll start hating *everyone* in the magical community!"

"Lucy, I sincerely doubt the fate of the magical community depends on *your* attendance."

"Not at first, but it will!" Lucy insisted. "Right now, the Fairy Council is the hottest ticket in town—but the hotter the ticket, the quicker it can fizzle out. I've seen it happen so many times I've lost count. When performers get too big too fast, they start making mistakes. They get comfortable and stop putting in the work to please people. Corners get cut, promises get broken, and audiences get taken for granted. And just when performers think they're unstoppable—*wham!*—the audience ditches them for an act that *does* meet their expectations!"

"Lucy, this isn't show business!"

"*Everything is show business!* Why don't you see that?"

Brystal took a deep breath and slid into the chair behind her glass desk.

"I'm not trying to upset you, I'm just looking out for us," Lucy said. "The magical community is safe because people love the Fairy Council, and if we want to keep the public on our side, we can't risk upsetting them. Giving people what they want, when they want it, is the best way to ensure our survival."

She's right you know....

Once again, the thought came out of nowhere, startling Brystal.

You'll never *own* mankind's approval....

You'll have to earn it over and over again, until the end of time....

Brystal heard the thoughts so clearly she had to remind herself they were only in her mind.

They may treat you like a savior, but in truth, you're nothing but a *slave*...

A *jester* in mankind's court...

A *clown* in their circus.

Brystal was disturbed by what the thoughts implied. She tried to concentrate on where the thoughts were coming from, but each one entered and left her mind so quickly, she couldn't trace them to a logical train of thought. It was like someone else was dropping the ideas into her head and then running away.

"I can tell I'm making you think," Lucy said. "I don't consider myself an expert in many fields, but for once, I definitely know what I'm talking about. It doesn't matter how much compassion and charity we give people, they won't be satisfied unless we *entertain* them in the process. And luckily, I'm the perfect person to help us do that."

She doesn't want to help you....

She only wants to help herself....

She'd betray you for an *ounce* of attention....

She'd abandon you for a *sliver* of glory.

Brystal tried to ignore the thoughts, but the harder she tried, the louder they seemed. She covered her ears to block them out, but she heard them just as clearly as before. Lucy raised an eyebrow at Brystal and took the gesture personally.

"Are you seriously covering your ears?" she asked.

"Lucy, please, I don't want to talk about this anymore," Brystal said.

"Why is it so difficult for you to listen to me?"

"There's just a lot on my mind and I—"

"This is about the Western Dam, isn't it? What will it take to get you to trust me again?"

"No, it has nothing to do with—"

"Then what's your problem? Why are you acting like this?"

Brystal sighed and sank into the chair behind her desk. Part of her wanted to tell *someone* about the distressing thoughts, but she was still so confused she didn't know what to say. Besides, it wasn't a great moment to have a heart-to-heart with Lucy.

She wouldn't understand....

No one would....

Everyone will think you're crazy....

They'll find a way to use it against you....

They've been _waiting_ for a reason to get rid of you.

Brystal didn't want to think such horrible things, but she had no control over what the thoughts said. Lucy crossed her arms and studied Brystal like she was a human riddle.

"Something is troubling you," she said. "I can sense it—_trouble_ is my specialty."

"I told you, I don't want to talk about it," Brystal said.

"Why not? I tell you everything about me!"

"Please, stop—"

"No, I won't stop! I'm not leaving this office until you tell me what's going on!"

"_Fine!_ Then _I'll_ leave!"

Brystal jumped to her feet and marched to the door, desperate for some alone time. But just as she was about to exit her office, the double doors swung open. Tangerina and Skylene skipped inside carrying the PRAISE and REQUESTS bins. Both bins were overflowing with envelopes.

"We've got more fan mail!" Tangerina announced.

"You won't believe how much we got this week!" Skylene said.

The girls were followed by the massive knight with antlers who guarded the border. The knight was dragging two enormous bags that were bulging with even more envelopes.

"What's Horence doing with the mail?" Brystal asked.

"The border's been pretty safe since the world fell in love with magic," Tangerina said. "We needed someone to manage the mail, so we gave him a new job."

"Brystal, where do you want us to put your letters?" Skylene asked.

"Some of those are for me?" Brystal asked.

Tangerina and Skylene looked at her like she was kidding.

"They're *all* for you," Tangerina said.

Brystal couldn't believe how many people had taken the time to write her. There were hundreds—maybe *thousands*—of letters and every one of them was addressed to *The Fairy Godmother.*

None of those people actually *care* about you....

They only *want* something from you....

They'll always want more and more....

They'll *never* be content.

Brystal stood as still and stoic as possible so the others wouldn't notice how much the thoughts were affecting her mood.

"Just put them by the tea table," she said. "I'll look through them later."

"We'd be happy to sort through your mail if you like!" Tangerina said.

"Sometimes people send gifts!" Skylene said.

Lucy crossed her arms and scowled at the girls.

"Do you guys mind?" she asked. "Brystal and I were in the middle of something before you interrupted."

"Actually, I was just leaving," Brystal said. "Feel free to sort through the mail and keep whatever gifts you find."

Tangerina and Skylene sat on the glass sofa and excitedly went through the mail. But once again, before Brystal reached the doors, they were pushed open by another guest. Emerelda charged into the office at a determined pace, making notes on an emerald clipboard.

"Brystal, do you have a minute?" Emerelda asked. "I've been going over our schedule for next week and I have a couple questions for you. I'm trying to iron out all the details so there aren't any surprises. I won't let another entitled royal take advantage of us again. Hoodwink us once, shame on them; hoodwink us twice, shame on me."

"Honestly, Em, right now isn't a good time," Brystal said.

"Don't worry, this won't take long," Emerelda said, and checked her clipboard. "Queen Endustria would like to name a ship after you while we're in the Eastern Kingdom next week. I told her it depends on what *type* of ship it is—I don't want anyone using the *Fairy Godmother* to harpoon whales."

"Good foresight," Brystal said, inching closer and closer to the door. "I agree—it depends on the type of ship."

"Next, King White wants to name a holiday after you," Emerelda said. "They want to commemorate the day you sent the Snow Queen into seclusion. I don't see a problem with it as long as we get to choose the name of the holiday. We should also find out what kind of *festivities* will take place on this day. We don't want people playing pin the wand on the fairy to celebrate you."

"Sounds good," Brystal said. "Is that all?"

"Not quite," Emerelda said. "King Champion XIV would like to place a statue of you in the Chariot Hills town square. If you're comfortable with that, I suggest we ask for approval over the sculptor. The last thing we want is something *abstract* that traumatizes small children."

"Tell the king I'll get back to him on that," Brystal said, and reached for the door. "Now if you'll please excuse me, I'm going to get some fresh air."

"*Brystal!*" Lucy said. "Are you seriously going to leave before we finish talking?"

"*Brystal!*" Tangerina said. "Someone from the

Northern Kingdom sent you the most beautiful bracelet! It looks gorgeous on me!"

"*Brystal!*" Skylene said. "Someone from the Southern Kingdom sent you a dead caterpillar! Oh wait, the letter says it was supposed to be a butterfly by the time you opened it. Well, that's a shame."

As Brystal opened the door, a bubbly old woman entered the office. She had violet hair and a purple apron and was very glad to see Brystal—but Brystal groaned at *another* visitor.

"Oh good, you're here!" the old woman said. "You're a difficult person to track down. Either you're incredibly busy or incredibly good at avoiding me! HA-HA!"

"Hi, Mrs. Vee," Brystal said. "What can I do for you?"

"I was wondering if you made a decision about the request I sent you?" Mrs. Vee asked.

"Um . . . I'm sure I did," Brystal said. "Remind me what your request was again?"

"I want to knock down a wall and expand my kitchen," Mrs. Vee said. "We have a lot more mouths to feed than we used to. One picture may paint a thousand words, but one oven does not cook for thousands of people! HA-HA!"

"Of course you can expand your kitchen, Mrs. Vee," Brystal said. "My apologies for not giving you an answer sooner. The council's been really busy."

As Brystal squeezed past Mrs. Vee in the doorway, Xanthous came running and blocked her escape.

"Brystal! I just came from the southwest wing of the academy!" He panted.

"Why? What happened?" she asked.

"A spell went horribly wrong during lessons this afternoon!" Xanthous said. "All the fairies on the fifth floor were shrunk to the size of pixies!"

"And they need me to change them back?"

"Actually, they want your permission to stay small. They mentioned the *benefits of downsizing*, but I didn't understand the appeal. Anyway, they wanted to get an answer before they get their hopes up—or *down*, I should say."

Brystal groaned and rolled her eyes.

"Sure! Whatever they want! I don't care!"

Brystal pushed past Xanthous and stomped down the hall. She was used to making decisions and finding solutions, but today she felt like she was drowning in all the requests and questions.

It's all too much....

There are too many decisions to make....

It shouldn't be on your shoulders.

For once, Brystal agreed with the strange thoughts. All she wanted was a few moments alone; all she needed was a few moments of quiet, but it seemed like an impossibility.

Your friends will never know what it's like....

They would snap from all the pressure....

They'd be crushed by the responsibility.

The thoughts made Brystal's heart rate rise more and more. If she didn't get away from the others, she was afraid she might explode. Unfortunately, as Brystal proceeded down the hall, her friends followed her.

"*Brystal!* Would you like to send a thank-you note for my bracelet?"

"*Brystal!* King Champion needs an answer by tomorrow."

"*Brystal!* Should the small fairies be worried about gryphons?"

"*Brystal!* Do you know a fairy with a specialty for renovations? HA-HA!"

"*Brystal!* Should we have a service for the caterpillar?"

"*Brystal!* When are we going to finish our conversation?"

"*EVERYONE SHUT UP!*"

Brystal's outburst stunned the fairies, but no one was more surprised than Brystal herself. She was ashamed of raising her voice, but for the first time all day, she finally had *silence*—inside *and* outside her head.

"I'm...I'm...I'm so sorry," she said. "I didn't mean to shout.... It's just been a long day and I want to be alone.... *Please*, just leave me alone...."

Brystal raced down the hall before her friends could respond. The fairies respected her request and didn't chase after her.

"What's gotten into her?" Tangerina whispered to the others.

Lucy watched Brystal leave with a determined gaze.

"I have no idea," she whispered back. "But I'm going to find out."

· · ★ · ·

Brystal took a long walk to clear her head, and thankfully the unpleasant thoughts didn't follow her. She was desperate to find out how and why they were happening, but unfortunately, the peace and quiet didn't provide any answers. The thoughts left her in a worse mood each time they occurred, and the more she tried to understand them, the more frustrated she became.

She strolled through the Fairy Territory, hoping the picturesque grounds would put her in a better mood. As she walked, Brystal focused on all the positivity around her, and she reminded herself of all the reasons she had to be *happy*.

Over the past year, the Celeste Weatherberry Memorial Academy of Magic had changed so much it was almost unrecognizable. The castle had expanded to nearly ten times its original size to accommodate all the fairies who had moved there. Its shimmering towers stood over thirty stories high and its golden walls stretched over ten acres. And every time a new fairy arrived, the castle grew a little bit bigger.

The unicorns, the gryphons, and the pixies were no longer endangered species, and they roamed across the property in healthy-size flocks and herds. The animals helped fertilize the land, allowing even more colorful flowers and vibrant trees to flourish than before.

Everywhere Brystal looked, she saw fairies practicing magic and teaching newcomers how to develop their abilities. The fairies waved and bowed to Brystal as she walked by, and she could feel the gratitude radiating from their hearts. Thanks to her, Madame Weatherberry's small academy had transformed into the Fairy Territory, and for the first time in history, the magical community had a safe environment where they could live peacefully and thrive.

All the fairies knew Brystal was responsible for their happiness, but despite the joy she created for others, Brystal couldn't seem to muster any for herself.

At dusk, Brystal walked down the cliff to the beach below the academy. She sat on a stone bench and watched the sunset. The evening sky was full of pink clouds, and the ocean sparkled as the sun sank into the horizon. It was a breathtaking sight—one of the most spectacular sunsets Brystal had seen at the Fairy Territory—but even *that* didn't lift Brystal's spirits.

"Just be happy...," Brystal told herself. "Be happy.... Be happy.... Be happy...."

Sadly, no matter how many times she repeated the command, her heart didn't listen.

"Who are you talking to?"

Brystal looked over her shoulder and saw an eight-year-old girl standing on the beach behind her. The girl had big brown eyes and short messy hair, and she wore stretchable clothing made from tree sap. Although she had grown a foot in the last year, to Brystal, she'd always be the tiny girl she met at the Bootstrap Correctional Facility.

"Hi, Pip," Brystal said. "Sorry, you caught me talking to myself."

"No judgments here," Pip said. "Some of my best conversations are with myself. Do you want some company?"

More *company* was the last thing Brystal wanted, but since the alone time wasn't as helpful as she'd hoped, Brystal welcomed a distraction. She patted the stone bench, and Pip took a seat beside her.

"How are your lessons coming along?" Brystal asked.

"Good," Pip said. "I've completed my improvement, rehabilitation, and manifestation lessons, and tomorrow, I start working on imagination."

"That's wonderful. Have you been working on your specialty, too?"

"I have—watch this!"

Pip removed a ring from her pocket and showed Brystal how she could squeeze her entire arm through it, as if her limb were made of clay.

"Very impressive," Brystal said.

"Yesterday I squeezed my whole body into a pickle jar," Pip said. "Unfortunately, I was stuck in it for three hours. Getting into things is much easier than getting out of them, but I guess that's life for you."

"I wish I was there to help you. The Fairy Council has been so busy I barely get a moment to myself anymore."

"Everyone's talking about your visit to the Western Kingdom. I heard it was a smash."

"It was a little too eventful for my taste, but we still

helped a lot of people and made them very happy in the process. I guess that's all that matters."

"You don't *look* very happy, though," Pip noticed. "Is something bothering you?"

Brystal faced the sunset and sighed—she didn't have the strength to hide it anymore.

"Happiness is difficult for me at the moment," she confessed. "Don't get me wrong, I *want* to be happy. There is so much to be grateful for, but for some reason, I can't stop having negative thoughts about everything. It feels like I'm stuck in a pickle jar of my own."

"Are you sure you're being negative?" Pip asked. "I know from experience, there's a thin line between negativity and just being realistic. When I was living at Bootstrap, there were days I would wake up thinking, *Wow, I'm going to be here forever*, and other days I would wake up thinking, *Dang, I'm going to be here forever*—but they were very different points of view."

"No, I'm definitely being negative," Brystal said. "My thoughts put me in a horrible mood and they make me feel restless and paranoid. Gosh, I wish Madame Weatherberry was still here—she'd know exactly how to help me."

"If she was, what would she tell you?" Pip asked.

Brystal closed her eyes and imagined Madame Weatherberry was sitting beside her. A bittersweet smile came to her face as she remembered her mentor's bright violet eyes and the soft touch of her gloved hands.

"She'd probably encourage me to get to the root of the problem," Brystal said. "Honestly, I think being the Fairy Godmother is just taking a toll on me. I knew it would be a lot of responsibility, but there's an emotional component I never expected."

"Really?" Pip asked. "How so?"

Brystal went quiet as she thought about it. The feeling was difficult to explain to herself, let alone someone else.

"The world knows and loves me for a quality I used to hide and hate myself for," she said. "And even though I know I have nothing to fear or be ashamed of, deep down, I'm still carrying that fear and shame with me. Somewhere along the line, I got so busy changing the world I forgot to change myself with it. And now I think those old feelings are starting to play tricks on me."

The fresh insight didn't solve her problems, but it made Brystal feel a little better. Pip looked across the ocean with a somber gaze, as if she knew *exactly* what Brystal was talking about.

"I think I understand," she said. "When I was at

Bootstrap, I never felt like I belonged there—*I mean, it would have been weird if I did.* But even though I live in the Fairy Territory now, the emptiness has stayed with me. It's like, since no one taught me how to *belong* somewhere, I just feel hollow everywhere I go. I suppose I'm carrying around old feelings, too."

Brystal felt sorry for Pip and wished she was in a better state of mind to help her.

"Maybe *belonging* can't be taught," she said. "Maybe it's just something we have to practice."

Pip nodded. "Maybe *happiness* is, too," she said.

The girls exchanged half-hearted smiles and watched the rest of the sunset in silence. The tranquility was interrupted shortly after by the sound of whispering.

"Oh, look! There she is!"

"Shhh! Don't make any sudden movements!"

Brystal turned around and saw Tangerina and Skylene on the beach behind her.

"It's all right," she said. "I'm not going to yell at you again."

"Sorry, we know you wanted to be alone," Tangerina said.

"It's just—um—something came in the mail that you should see," Skylene said.

"Who is it from?" Brystal asked.

Tangerina and Skylene glanced at each other with concern.

"Your *family*," they said.

Brystal's heart suddenly sank into the pit of her stomach. She hadn't spoken to anyone in her family in over a year—it must have been important if they were reaching out to her. Brystal jumped up from the bench and Tangerina handed her a square envelope. Unlike the other letters, this envelope was addressed to *Brystal Evergreen* instead of *The Fairy Godmother*, and her family's home was listed as the return address. Brystal opened the envelope and found a thick card with cheerful lettering inside:

You Are Cordially Invited to

The Wedding of

Deputy Justice Barrie Evergreen
&
Lady Penny Charming

Champvember 16th
At Five o'clock in the Afternoon

The Evergreen Residence
481 East Countryside Road
Chariot Hills
The Southern Kingdom

We look forward to celebrating with you!

In lieu of gifts, please donate to the Chariot Hills
Home for the Hopeless

"Oh my gosh," Brystal said.

"What is it?" Tangerina asked with bated breath.

"My brother's getting married!"

"Oh, thank God!" Skylene said. "I was afraid someone died!"

Brystal didn't know what was more shocking—the idea of *Barrie* being someone's husband or the fact that *she* was invited to the wedding.

"Congratulations," Pip said. "That should make you happy."

Brystal agreed, but despite the wonderful news, she felt just as melancholy as before.

"You're right," Brystal said. "It should make me happy.... It *should*...."

CHAPTER THREE

A RIGHTEOUS INTRODUCTION

When Brystal received the invitation to Barrie's wedding, the sixteenth of Champvember seemed like an eternity away, but because of the Fairy Council's demanding schedule, the days went by much faster than Brystal wanted them to. In the weeks leading up to the wedding, Brystal started to dread the date as she would an approaching storm. She had daily meetings with the world's most celebrated diplomats and dignitaries, and yet seeing her *family* again was a terrifying prospect.

The last time Brystal saw her brothers, Brooks and Barrie, she narrowly missed being executed on a courtroom floor. The last time she saw her father, Justice Evergreen, Brystal humiliated him in front of all the Justices in the Southern Kingdom. And the last time she saw her mother, Mrs. Evergreen, Brystal was told to leave home and find a better life.

Given how dramatic the farewells had been, Brystal had no idea what to expect or how to prepare. Without a doubt, Justice Evergreen would resent Brystal until the day he died, but *his* opinion wasn't what concerned her. Brystal worried about how her mother and brothers would react to seeing her again, and she wondered whether the last year had changed how they felt about her.

The invitation was probably a mistake....

Your family doesn't want to see you....

They probably *hate* how you've changed the world....

They're probably *ashamed* at the person you've become.

The situation was a breeding ground for the disturbing thoughts, and every day, Brystal was more and more tempted to skip the wedding altogether. However, she knew nothing would feel worse than missing such an important day in her brother's life. So despite all the fear and anxiety coursing through her, Brystal awoke on the morning of the sixteenth determined to go.

At three o'clock in the afternoon, Brystal departed the Fairy Territory and floated toward the Southern Kingdom in a large bubble. As she drifted through the sky, Brystal caused quite a scene in the villages and farms below her. Civilians ran out from their homes to wave at her, dogs barked and chased after her giant bubble, and even cows and sheep stopped grazing to watch her fly by.

Enjoy the affection while you can....

You won't receive the same welcome at home....

Strangers love you more than your family ever will.

At half past four, Chariot Hills appeared in the distance, and Brystal descended into the eastern countryside. Her first sight of the Evergreen house made her jolt, as if her nerves had grown legs and kicked her in the stomach. Brystal's modest childhood home looked exactly as it always had. The only difference was all the wedding preparations assembled on the front lawn.

A dozen rows of white chairs and a white gazebo were arranged under a long white tent. Carriages waited in a lengthy line down East Countryside Road, dropping off passengers one at a time. The wedding guests were an eclectic group of aristocrats and commoners, elderly and young people, and they mingled in an area with high tables and a refreshment stand. The setup was very classy and traditional, but it was much more elaborate than Brystal had predicted. If her father had had his way, Barrie would be getting married in a run-down barn.

Brystal landed in the center of the front lawn and popped the bubble with her crystal wand. The guests were thrilled to see Brystal and they surrounded her like a pack of hungry wolves.

"It's the Fairy Godmother!"

"I can't believe I'm seeing her in real life!"

"Do you think she'll talk to me?"

"I knew I should have dressed nicer!"

All the whispering made Brystal feel very awkward, not because of the attention, but because she recognized so many faces in the crowd. She spotted family friends and distant cousins, former schoolmates and teachers, and neighbors she had grown up with. Most of the guests had known Brystal since she was a small child, but now they were all gawking at her like she was from another planet.

"Fairy Godmother! May I have your autograph?"

"Fairy Godmother! Will you kiss my baby?"

"Fairy Godmother! Can I have a hug?"

"Fairy Godmother! Will you do some magic for us?"

The only people who weren't thrilled to see Brystal were a group of Southern Kingdom Justices huddled in the corner of the lawn. The men were dressed in their typical black robes and tall black hats, and they watched Brystal like a flock of vultures. Ironically, Brystal almost preferred the Justices' hateful scowls to the other guests' reactions.

"Fairy Godmother! Are you here to give gifts?"

"Fairy Godmother! Can you turn my dress into a gown?"

"Fairy Godmother! Can you make my hair grow back?"

"Fairy Godmother! Can you give me a good singing voice?"

As soon as her great-great-uncle knelt down to kiss her feet, Brystal started looking for a place to hide—but there was only *one* place to go. Without any other options, Brystal weaved through the excited crowd and hurried into the Evergreen house.

Once the front door shut behind her, Brystal sighed with relief, but the inside of the house was even more chaotic than the outside. Dozens of bridesmaids and groomsmen frantically raced around the house as if it were on fire.

"Has anyone seen my bow tie?"

"Hey! That's my shoe!"

"OH MY GOD! I've lost the rings!"

"How did I end up with two corsages?"
"False alarm! I have the rings!"

Luckily, the wedding party was so busy applying the final touches to their suits and dresses they didn't notice Brystal standing in the entrance hall. And at first, Brystal was so distracted by all the people running amok she didn't notice anything else. Once the bridesmaids and groomsmen cleared the front of the house, Brystal suddenly gasped. Unlike the outside, the *inside* of the Evergreen home had changed so much Brystal thought she was in the wrong place.

In the past, Justice Evergreen was so conservative he denied his family anything he considered *extravagant.* All the Evergreens' belongings, from their clothing to the wallpaper, were used or hand-me-downs. Servants were completely out of the question, forcing Brystal and Mrs. Evergreen to do all the cooking, cleaning, and gardening by themselves. However, as Brystal looked around the house with fresh eyes, she realized *that* was no longer the case.

All the rooms were furnished with brand-new furniture that matched. The plates and bowls in the china cabinet were the same color, and the silverware was from the same set. The drapes were made from the same fabric, and all the walls had recently been painted the same shade of pearl gray. But most surprising of all, Brystal found *maids* picking up after the wedding party and a *cook* preparing food in the kitchen.

It was so shocking Brystal felt like she had wandered into another dimension, and she wondered if *all the rooms* had been redecorated. Before she could stop herself, Brystal's curiosity took hold of her, and she climbed the stairs to her old bedroom at the very top of the house.

Brystal slowly opened the bedroom door and stepped inside. The bed was made with the same sheets, the nightstand held the same candle, the mirror and dresser stood in the same corner, even the loose floorboard hadn't been touched since she left. The bedroom looked exactly as she remembered it, but strangely, it *felt* completely different. Brystal couldn't believe how *small* and *cold* her old bedroom was, and yet the size and temperature had never stood out in her memory.

Perhaps the room seemed smaller because she had grown so much as a person, and perhaps the room felt colder because now she knew what the warmth of a *true home* felt like.

Tears welled in Brystal's eyes as she recalled what her life used to be like in the Evergreen house. She remembered all the nights she had cried herself to sleep, all the days she had lived in fear, and all the nightmares in between. She remembered the angst of wanting a better life, the pain of unanswered prayers, and the suffocation of feeling stuck. But Brystal didn't just remember the emotions, she *felt* them, too. All the fear and sadness surfaced from deep within her, stronger than ever before.

You'll never get rid of her....

No matter where you go, or what you do ...

Part of you will always be that scared, suppressed little girl....

She'll always be inside of you....

Always.

Brystal couldn't understand why she was feeling and thinking such things. Her life had changed so significantly she was practically a different person—so why was she carrying the same heartache from her past? She looked in the mirror for reassurance, but unfortunately, her reflection only made her feel worse. There was no difference between the sorrowful expression Brystal wore today and the sorrowful expression she had worn for most of her childhood.

Perhaps life hadn't changed as much as she thought.

"You're back!" said a voice behind her.

Brystal quickly wiped away her tears and glanced over her shoulder. A beautiful, middle-aged woman in a shiny teal dress was standing in the doorway. The woman was ecstatic to see Brystal and ran into the bedroom to embrace her.

"Mother?" Brystal gasped. "Is that you?"

Mrs. Evergreen looked so different Brystal didn't recognize her at first. Her hair was no longer styled in a constrictive bun on top of her head but flowed freely down to her waist. The dark circles under her eyes had vanished, and for the first time in Brystal's memory, Mrs. Evergreen looked *rested*. The teal dress also brought out the green in her mother's eyes, which Brystal had never noticed until now.

"Oh, my darling girl," Mrs. Evergreen said, and hugged Brystal a little tighter. "I've missed you so much! I can't tell you how happy I am to see you!"

"Mother, you look *amazing*!" Brystal said. "What happened?"

"I hope you're not *too* surprised," Mrs. Evergreen teased her.

"Of course not—I didn't mean it like that!" Brystal said. "Forgive me—everything is just so different. I wasn't expecting the house to look like this. I wasn't expecting *you* to look like this. There's new furniture, new china, new drapes—you even have *servants*! How is father allowing all of this?"

"I finally gave him an ultimatum," Mrs. Evergreen said. "I said if he didn't hire maids and a cook to help me around the house, I would leave him. And I reminded him that if I left, he'd have no choice but to hire maids and a cook anyway. You should have seen his face! The idea of losing me must have really scared him, because he hasn't denied me anything since."

Brystal was incredibly proud of her mother, but her thoughts quickly quashed the feeling and replaced it with shame.

You should have helped your mother....

If it weren't for her, you'd still be at the Bootstrap Correctional Facility....

But you *abandoned* her to help strangers....

You *failed* her and she had to do it all on her own.

"What's wrong, Brystal?" Mrs. Evergreen asked. "Why do you look so sad?"

"Oh, it's nothing," she said.

Mrs. Evergreen gave Brystal a stern look—it didn't matter how much time had passed, Mrs. Evergreen always knew when Brystal was lying to her.

"I just feel guilty," Brystal confessed. "After you signed my permission slip to attend Madame Weatherberry's school, I always told myself I would come back and save you from this place, but I never did. I've been helping strangers all over the world, but I never helped *you*."

Mrs. Evergreen seemed both heartbroken and amused by Brystal's confession. She lovingly placed a hand on her daughter's face and looked deep into her eyes.

"Brystal, you're not responsible for anyone's happiness but your own—including mine," Mrs. Evergreen said. "The last time we spoke, I told you to leave this horrible place and never return because *that's* what it was—*a horrible place*. I didn't think it was possible to change it. But then something amazing happened— someone came along and showed me nothing was impossible."

"Who?" Brystal asked.

"*You*, sweetheart," Mrs. Evergreen said. "I thought, *If my daughter can change the whole world, then I can make changes, too.* Without your example, I would never have had the courage to stand up to your father. So in many ways, you *did* save me. And not just me—you've inspired thousands of other people to improve their lives, too. I hope you know how special that is."

Brystal knew how significant her mother's words were, but her current state of mind wouldn't let the feeling sink in. She shrugged it off like Mrs. Evergreen was giving her a small compliment.

"It can be a little overwhelming at times," she said.

"I bet," Mrs. Evergreen said. "I've seen how those crowds react to you and your friends."

"You mean, you've been to one of our events?" Brystal asked in disbelief.

"Oh, I haven't missed a single event in the Southern Kingdom," Mrs. Evergreen said with a proud smile. "I was there when you rebuilt the orphanage that burned down, I was there when you gave a new roof to the hospital for wounded soldiers, and I was there just last week when King Champion presented you with a statue in the Chariot Hills town square—I actually brought a big poster with your name on it to that one. There were so many people there, I imagine it was hard to see me."

"I wish I knew you were there!" Brystal said. "I would have loved to see you!"

"All that matters is that you're here now," Mrs. Evergreen said. "It's a miracle you got the wedding invitation. I was afraid that big knight would lose it."

Brystal was certain she had misheard her. "Wait a second—*you* delivered the invitation yourself?"

"Of course. It was important," Mrs. Evergreen said. "I marched right up to the knight and I told him, *I don't care how scary you look, if this letter doesn't* get to my daughter, I'll *be the scariest thing you ever met*. He didn't seem very frightened but it must have worked."

Brystal was speechless—even her thoughts went silent. Clearly, Mrs. Evergreen had nothing but unconditional love and support for her daughter, and Brystal's mind couldn't spin it into anything negative.

"Mother! Where are you? I need your help!"

Mrs. Evergreen rolled her eyes. "I'm in your sister's room!" she called out.

"Was that Barrie?" Brystal asked. "He sounds more stressed than usual."

"Your brother's been such a nervous wreck ever since he proposed," Mrs. Evergreen said. "You'd think he was the first person in history to get married."

They heard frantic footsteps climb up the stairs and dash down the hall, and then Barrie burst into the bedroom at the speed of lightning. He was dressed in a sharp black suit and carried a handful of buttons that were supposed to be on his suit jacket. Barrie was in such a panic it took him a moment to notice his sister, standing beside his mother.

"Mother, it happened again! I didn't even realize I was playing with my buttons until I ripped them all

off! Oh, hello, Brystal. *I'm so sorry, Mother! Please don't be angry with me! I'm so nervous I feel like there are bats in my stomach! Do you think you can fix them before*—BRYSTAL?!"

Barrie's panicked rant quickly turned into a fit of joyous laughter. He gave Brystal an enormous hug and spun her around the room.

"Brystal! Brystal! Brystal!" Barrie cheered. "It's so wonderful to see you!"

"It's wonderful to see you, too, Barrie!"

"I can't believe you're here! Gosh, you've been busy! What you've been up to is *remarkable*! It means so much to me that you came!"

"I wouldn't have missed your wedding for the world," Brystal said.

"It's funny, of all the people to tell me that today, you're the first person who *actually* means it," Barrie said. "I've been following all your accomplishments in the newspapers. Penny helped me start a scrapbook with all the clippings I saved—oh, that's her name, *Penny*—but I suppose you already knew that from the invitation."

"I can't wait to meet her," Brystal said. "What's she like? Where did you guys meet?"

An enormous smile grew across Barrie's face as he thought about his future wife. Brystal had never seen him look so happy—actually, she had never seen *anyone* look so happy.

"She's—she's—she's the most incredible person I've ever met," Barrie said. "We met eleven months ago at the Chariot Hills Library—oh, thanks for changing the law by the way! We wouldn't have met if women were still banned! Anyway, we were in the same aisle and reached for *Locksmiths: A Turnkey Trade* at exactly the same time. Turns out she has a fascination with locks and keys like me! Naturally, I told her to take the book, but she insisted I check it out first. We kept going back and forth on who should take it, and finally, we agreed to *share* the book. And the rest is history!"

"Barrie, if you want a successful marriage, I suggest you learn how to sew," Mrs. Evergreen scolded. "It's going to take me an hour to put all of these buttons back on your suit! And the ceremony is about to start!"

"Actually, I can help with that," Brystal said.

With a flick of her wand, all the buttons flew out of Barrie's hand and reattached themselves to his jacket. Brystal also reached into the pocket of her pantsuit and pulled out a small gift topped with a golden bow.

"Here," Brystal said, and handed it to him. "I made you an enchanted sewing kit for a wedding present. Just put the thread through the eye of the needle and it'll do the rest. I was going to save it for later but you should take it now in case you need to fix your jacket again."

Barrie was touched by the gift. "You know me so well," he said. "Thank you."

The tender moment was cut short by another pair of footsteps stomping up the stairs, and this time, Brystal recognized them instantly—it was the sound she had feared the most when she was a child. Justice Evergreen charged into the bedroom with heavy breath and a tense brow.

"The ceremony is supposed to start in five minutes and not a single bridesmaid or groomsman is fully dressed!"

Brystal's father was already angry, but seeing *her* infuriated the Justice. His whole body went tense and his face turned bright red. The Justice refused to look at Brystal, and instead, he pointed at her and sent his furious scowl toward his wife.

"What is *it* doing here?" he asked.

"I invited her," Mrs. Evergreen said as if it were obvious.

Justice Evergreen closed his eyes and tried to suppress his anger. Brystal could tell it was a new exercise for her father, because the Justice wasn't very good at it.

"Lynn, we agreed we wouldn't—"

"We didn't agree to anything!" Mrs. Evergreen said, raising her voice to match his. "You told me you didn't want her here, and I listened, but I never gave you any impression that she wasn't invited. You can pretend she doesn't exist all you want, but Brystal is still *my* daughter and she has every right to be at her brother's wedding."

Brystal was pleasantly surprised at how effortlessly her mother stood up to her father. Mrs. Evergreen debated her husband like it was a fun new hobby. The Justice turned so red he was almost purple.

"I will allow it to stay for the wedding, but I will *not* allow it in my house!" he sneered.

Mrs. Evergreen raised a finger and stepped toward the Justice, but Brystal stopped her mother before the argument went any further. She didn't want anything to spoil Barrie's special day, especially a disagreement about *her*.

"Mother, it's all right," she said calmly. "I'm more than happy to wait outside until the wedding begins."

Brystal headed out of the bedroom but paused in the doorway.

"Besides," she whispered to her father, "from the look of things, this doesn't appear to be *your* house anymore."

· • ★ • ·

Brystal left the Evergreen house and joined the wedding guests outside. She was hoping to find a place to hide before anyone saw her return, but the guests were gathered around the front door waiting for her. The number of attendees had doubled since she had arrived, and clearly all the newcomers had been notified of Brystal's attendance.

"Fairy Godmother! Can you give me a bigger house?"

"Fairy Godmother! Can you cure my indigestion?"

"Fairy Godmother! Can you make my nose smaller?"

"Fairy Godmother! Can you teach my children some manners?"

The guests crept closer and closer, and Brystal dodged all the hands trying to touch her. She started to worry she'd be stuck on the Evergreens' front porch all day, but she was rescued by a belligerent voice coming from afar.

"OOOOOOH, PISS OFF! ALL OF YOU!"

Everyone on the front lawn turned toward a disheveled man at the refreshment stand. His shaggy hair was in desperate need of a barber, and his tight brown suit was in desperate need of a tailor. The man feverishly smoked a wooden pipe, and from the way he was leaning on the refreshment counter, it was obvious he had enjoyed one too many refreshments.

"FOR THE LOVE OF CHAMPION—IT'S JUST *BRYSTAL*! A FEW MAGIC TRICKS DOESN'T MAKE HER A SAINT!"

"Brooks?" Brystal gasped.

Unlike their mother, the last year hadn't been kind to her oldest brother. His muscular build had melted into a belly, his handsome face was puffy and covered in stubble, and his pompous attitude had been replaced with a noticeable chip on his shoulder. All the wedding guests slowly backed away from Brystal, and she zigzagged through the crowd to stand at her brother's side.

"Thanks for that," she told him. "Hi, Brooks. . . . You look so . . . It's so nice to . . . *Hi, Brooks.*"

"*Don't,*" he said.

"Don't what?" she asked.

"Don't bother wasting that fairy crap on me. I'm not like *those* idiots. A little kindness and a few sparkles aren't going to turn me into one of your deranged sycophants. I don't care who you are or what you've become, you'll always be my annoying, know-it-all little sister. So don't come over here expecting me to eat out of the palm of your hand—"

Brystal suddenly threw her arms around her brother and gave him a huge hug.

"You have no idea how nice it is to hear someone say that!" she said.

Brooks was surprised by her reaction. "Well . . . I mean it," he said. "Now get off me before your magic rubs off. I don't want those bootlickers asking *me* for favors."

Brystal released him from her embrace. Brooks ordered another drink from the bartender behind the counter. The bartender wasn't pouring as fast as Brooks liked, so Brooks yanked the bottle away from him and poured the drink himself. Brystal studied her brother with a long, pitying gaze. She tried to fix a strand of his messy hair, but Brooks slapped her hand away.

"So . . . *how are you?*" Brystal asked him, although the answer was pretty obvious.

"Oh, *juuuuuuuust* dandy!" Brooks said. "Things couldn't be better. Let's see, my little brother is getting married to one of the most eligible bachelorettes in the Southern Kingdom, my little sister is the most influential person to ever live, and *I'm* working in a cobbler's shop! So *noooooooooo* complaints here! Life is going great!"

"You're working in a shoe store?" Brystal asked, and quickly adjusted her tone. "I mean, *you're working in a shoe store!* How exciting! But why aren't you a Deputy Justice anymore?"

"Justice Oldragaid got me disbarred," Brooks said.

"What?! When?!"

"After your trial last year, he reported my *negligent*

behavior to the High Justices. They took away my title and my robes and banished me from the legal system for life."

"Brooks, I am so sorry to hear that," Brystal said. "If there's anything I can do to make it up to you, please don't hesitate to ask."

"Don't worry, it wasn't your fault," Brooks said. "Everyone knows Oldragaid had me sacked to get revenge on Father. Sometimes I think it was all worth it just to see the look on Oldragaid's disgusting face when Father burst into his courtroom and saved your life."

"I bet Father regrets it now," Brystal said. "Still, I'm sorry you had to pay the price for it."

Brooks took a long drag from his pipe and slowly let it out.

"It was probably for the best," he said. "Let's be honest, I was a lousy Deputy Justice anyway. I never cared about defending or prosecuting criminals; I only went to the University of Law to please Father. Now I'm finally free to follow my passion."

"And what's that?" Brystal asked.

She wasn't trying to be rude, she just genuinely

didn't know the answer. While they were growing up, the only subject Brooks was interested in was himself. He opened his mouth to respond, but he didn't know the answer either.

"Now I'm finally free to *find* a passion," he restated.

Brystal gave her brother a sympathetic pat on the shoulder.

"I know you'll land on your feet," she said. "You think too highly of yourself to stay in a funk forever."

"Yes, I do."

Brystal suddenly felt a strange sensation—it was like the feeling of being watched, but the exact opposite. For the first time since she had arrived, the wedding guests were no longer gawking at her. Their attention was drawn to something moving in the distance. A cavalcade of armed guards escorted an elegant carriage down the country road. The guards blew horns to announce their arrival and carried flags with the royal crest of King Champion XIV.

"Is the king coming to Barrie's wedding?" Brystal asked.

"I imagine," Brooks said with a hiccup. "Barrie's marrying his niece."

Brystal was stunned. "Really? I had no idea."

"As if my younger brother getting married before me wasn't humiliating enough, he also managed to bag himself a royal. From this day forward, Barrie will be known as *Lord Evergreen*, and I'll be expected to bow and call him *sir* whenever I'm in his presence."

The thought was too much for Brooks to bear. He reached behind the refreshment counter and started chugging the closest bottle.

The royal carriage parked on the front lawn and all the wedding guests surrounded it. The guards rolled out a red carpet for the royal passengers and then stood at attention while they emerged. A middle-aged man was the first passenger to step out of the carriage. He wore a red velvet cape with fur trim and a large feathered hat. The man had a black beard that was a little *too* dark to pass as a natural color and a cocky grin that never faded from his face. He scoffed at his first sight of the Evergreen residence, like he was far too important to be there.

"Who's that?" Brystal asked her brother.

"That's Prince Maximus Champion, the future King Champion XV," Brooks said.

"I wonder why I've never met him before," Brystal said.

"Probably because he hates your guts," Brooks said. "Prince Maximus is extremely old-fashioned and detests how you changed the constitution. I heard rumors that he begged his father to reinstate the old laws, but the king wouldn't hear a word of it. Apparently, ever since you defeated the Snow Queen, *you're* the only person King Champion takes advice from."

Prince Maximus was followed by five young men, all between the ages of twelve and twenty. The young men looked like younger versions of the prince and wore matching capes and feathered hats. They scanned the Evergreen property with a noticeable blankness behind their eyes, as if none of them had ever had a deep thought.

The wedding guests bowed as each of the royals climbed out of the carriage. Brystal was hoping King Champion XIV would emerge next, but the sovereign never appeared.

"I'm assuming those are Maximus's sons," Brystal said.

"Their names are Triumph, Conquer, Victory, Score, and Marvel," Brooks listed. "But don't ask me who's who. I doubt their father can even tell them apart."

"Why isn't the king with them?" Brystal asked.

"I've heard rumors his health is declining," Brooks said.

"How odd," Brystal said. "I just saw King Champion. He presented me with a statue in the Chariot Hills town square. He seemed perfectly healthy then."

"Well, you know the elderly—they reach a certain age and stop taking care of themselves," Brooks said, and then chugged a second bottle from behind the counter. "Maximus will probably be sitting on the throne sooner than we expect."

The idea of losing King Champion XIV plagued Brystal with an entirely new batch of worries. Last year, she had persuaded him and the other sovereigns to legalize magic in exchange for protection from the Snow Queen. But what if Prince Maximus wasn't as receptive as his father? How could Brystal protect magic, women, and the talking creatures from Maximus's old-fashioned values? And if she couldn't, would King Warworth, Queen Endustria, and King White follow his example?

**You better hope King Champion XIV sticks
around....**

**Once Prince Maximus is crowned, he'll
restore the old laws....**

He'll turn his people against you....

**He'll convince the other sovereigns to do
the same....**

Everything you've worked for will be lost.

For weeks, Brystal had worried about losing mankind's approval, and now her concerns felt more legiti-
mate than ever before.

The laws will change....

Women will lose their rights....

**The talking creatures will lose their
homes....**

Magic will be criminalized....

You and your friends will be hated once again.

The princes worked their way through the crowd of adoring guests. Prince Maximus eventually made it to the group of Justices and greeted them with friendly embraces. Brystal couldn't hear what they were discussing, but it was obvious the Justices were warning Prince Maximus of her attendance. All the men scowled at Brystal, but Prince Maximus's scowl was the nastiest of all.

He despises you...

Possibly more than the Justices do....

He'll *never* keep your amendments to the constitution....

He wants to eliminate you completely....

You've made yourself a powerful enemy.

Brystal had so many things to worry about already, adding Prince Maximus to the list gave her a headache. She searched the front lawn for something—*anything*—to take her mind off it. Luckily, Brystal found the perfect distraction.

While the princes greeted the wedding guests, a seventh passenger stepped out of the carriage. He was about sixteen years old and was much taller and better looking than the royals he traveled with. The young man had wavy brown hair, a chiseled jawline, and a scar on his left cheek that Brystal found very mysterious. Unlike the princes, he didn't wear a feathered hat, a cape, or even a tie, but a simple maroon suit with an open shirt.

"Who is he?" Brystal asked her brother.

"How do *you* not know any of this?" Brooks said. "That's Maximus's nephew—Prince *Gallivant*, I believe—or maybe it's *Galantine*? But he's so far down the line of succession, who cares?"

Brystal did. In fact, she couldn't take her eyes off the prince. Brystal thought he was so striking just the sight of him made her blush. The attraction was the first pleasant emotion she had had in weeks, so she welcomed it and savored it for all it was worth.

"Whatever his name is, he's very handsome," Brystal said.

"I used to look like him," Brooks said, and raised his bottle. "Enjoy it while it lasts, kid!"

Brystal could tell Prince Gallivant was overwhelmed by all the wedding guests competing for the royals' attention. He snuck around the crowd and headed straight under the tent. The prince sat in a chair in the back row and rested his feet on a seat in front of him. He removed a book from inside his jacket and read while he waited for the wedding to begin. Brystal didn't think he could be more attractive, but knowing he was a *reader* made her heart flutter.

A bell rang to announce the start of the ceremony and all the guests piled into the tent to find seats. Prince Maximus and his sons sat with the Justices, and the royal guards lined the perimeter of the tent to watch over them. Brooks sat in a section reserved for the Evergreen family at the very front. Brystal didn't want to sit anywhere near her father or Prince Maximus, but her options were limited.

"Pssst! Over here!"

Brystal turned toward the voice and saw Prince Gallivant was waving at her.

"Need a seat?" he asked, and nodded toward the empty chair beside him.

"Oh, no thank you," Brystal said. "It might be rude if I sit in the back at my brother's wedding."

"Suit yourself," Prince Gallivant said. "Although, I've learned from personal experience, sitting in the back row makes it harder for people to stare at you. Unless you *like* that sort of thing."

After he'd put it that way, Brystal couldn't refuse the offer, and she took the seat beside him. Being so close to the prince made Brystal blush even harder than before. She hoped her face didn't look as warm as it felt.

"You're that Fairy Godsmacker, aren't you?" he asked.

"It's Fairy Godmother," Brystal said. "But yes, that's what people call me these days."

"I've got a few titles myself," the prince said. "My official name is Prince Gallivant Victorious Heroic Courageous Champion of Chariot Hills, but I'm also called the Duke of Southwestington—although, I've never been there—the Lord of Southeasternshire—that's just a grassy field—and the Earl of Southnorthernburry—but I think they made that one up."

"I suddenly feel so much better about my title. Which of those names should I call you?"

"Everybody just calls me Seven."

"Seven?"

"Because I'm seventh in line for the throne," the prince explained. "What do people call you when you're not...um...*Fairy Godmothering*?"

It had been so long since someone asked for her real name Brystal had to think about it.

"Oh, I'm Brystal—Brystal Evergreen."

"It's nice to meet you, Brystal."

Seven shook Brystal's hand and smiled at her. She quickly pulled it away before he noticed how clammy he made her palm.

"You too, Seven," she said. "Very nice."

At half past five o'clock, the ceremony finally started. Barrie was the first to appear in the wedding procession and walked the mother of the bride down to her seat. Then he took his position under the gazebo, so nervous his entire body was shaking. Brystal noticed a few of his buttons were already loose again. She discreetly waved her wand and tightened the buttons before they fell off.

Barrie was followed down the aisle by his parents. Mrs. Evergreen was fighting back tears and gave her son a kiss on the cheek before taking her seat. The guests were touched by the sweet moment, but Brooks found it insufferable and groaned loudly.

"What's *his* deal?" Seven whispered.

"He's just being dramatic," Brystal whispered back. "Brooks has to be the best at everything—including failure."

The comment made Seven snort and the noise caught Prince Maximus's attention. He was furious to see that Seven was sitting next to Brystal and sent them both a scathing look.

"I'm pretty sure your uncle hates me," Brystal said.

"Don't take it personally—my uncle Max hates everyone," Seven said.

"When Maximus takes the throne, will I have to call you Six?" Brystal asked.

"That's assuming my grandfather doesn't outlive us all," Seven said.

"How's the king feeling? I heard he was ill."

"Nah, he's perfectly healthy," Seven said. "Uncle Max likes to spread those rumors, though. Every time my grandpa so much as clears his throat, Max starts planning his coronation. But I'm guessing Gramps will be around for another decade or so."

"Thank goodness," Brystal said.

The groomsmen and bridesmaids made their way down the aisle, then all the guests rose to welcome the bride. Lady Penny Charming was a short and skinny woman with bright red hair—but that was all Brystal could see. Penny's wedding dress and veil were so monstrous her face was hardly visible.

"Eeek," Seven said. "Is that Penny or has the Snow Queen returned?"

"HAAAA!"

The laugh erupted out of Brystal's mouth before she knew it was coming. The disruption made the whole wedding come to a screeching halt. Penny paused halfway down the aisle, and all the wedding guests turned in Brystal's direction.

"I'm so sorry," she said, and pretended she was crying. "Weddings make me emotional. Please, carry on."

Brystal couldn't believe she had just *laughed*. The feeling lasted only a moment, but it was a huge relief to know she was still *capable* of joy.

After an awkward silence, the ceremony resumed. Penny eventually reached the end of the aisle and the guests were seated. A monk appeared under the gazebo and took his place between the bride and groom. As the monk began his officiation, Seven opened his book and continued reading.

"Get comfortable," he whispered.

"Do you always bring a book to weddings?" Brystal asked.

"Only to *royal* weddings," he said. "They last forever. The Duke and Duchess of Northgate's wedding was so long, by the time it was over, they were already divorced."

Seven made Brystal laugh again, but this time, she kept it quiet.

"What are you reading anyway?" she asked.

Seven tilted the book to show her the title.

"*The Tales of Tidbit Twitch, Volume 4*," he said.

Brystal was shocked. "You're kidding! That's my favorite book series!"

"Seriously? I didn't think anyone else even *knew* about these books."

"I've read the first one a dozen times," she said. "I know they're meant for children, but nothing makes me happier than a story about a mouse defeating a monster."

Seven smiled at Brystal and looked so deeply into her eyes Brystal had to remind herself they had just met. She felt like she had known the prince her entire life—perhaps longer.

"Maybe we could read it together sometime," he said.

"I'd like that," she said.

Brystal's heart was beating so fast she thought it might pop out of her chest. Apparently, the prince could make her feel all kinds of things that no one else could.

The ceremony continued, and just like Seven had warned, it lasted much longer than any other wedding Brystal had been to. The monk gave lengthy thanks to each of the royals, Justices, and aristocrats in attendance, and once all the noblemen and noblewomen were singled out, the monk performed a long-winded monologue about the history of the Southern Kingdom, and he honored all the sovereigns from King Champion I to King Champion XIV with detailed tributes. Barrie and Penny drank from ceremonial cups, they cut ribbons and tied strings, they lit candles and crushed plates, and by the time they reached the vows, it was already night.

"Deputy Justice Barrie Evergreen, do you take this woman as your lawfully wedded wife, to help you serve Our Lord and obey the will of His Majesty, King Champion XIV?"

"I do," Barrie said.

"And do you, Lady Penny Charming, take this man as your lawfully wedded husband, to help you serve Our Lord and obey the will of His Majesty, King Champion XIV?"

"I do," Penny said—or at least, a voice under her veil did.

"Then with the power entrusted in me by the Southern Kingdom, I now pronounce you Lord and Lady Ever—"

BOOM! Suddenly, the roof was blasted clean off the tent! *BOOM!* The gazebo exploded! *BOOM!*

Justice Evergreen's hat was blown off his head! *BOOM!*
BOOM! Dirt flew into the air as the front lawn was covered in explosions! *BOOM! BOOM!* Mrs. Evergreen
screamed as huge chunks of the Evergreen house were
blown away! *BOOM! BOOM!*

"*What's happening?*" Seven shouted.

"*We're under attack!*" Brystal said.

In a matter of seconds, the wedding became a war
zone, and all the guests ran for their lives. The royal
guards pulled Seven away from Brystal and formed a
protective circle around the princes.

Brystal recognized the sound of cannons immediately, but there were so many people running amok
she couldn't see where the attack was coming from.

The firing stopped for a brief moment and the debris
cleared. Brystal spotted a row of smoking cannons on
the top of a nearby hill. At first, Brystal thought her
eyes were deceiving her, because it looked like the cannons were being reloaded by *ghosts*! Their attackers
wore silver robes with the images of white wolves on
their chests, and their faces were hidden under masks.
There were hundreds of them, and the ghostly men
reloaded the cannons with bright red cannonballs that
glowed in the dark.

"Don't worry!" she told the panicked guests. "I can protect us!"

Brystal waved her wand and covered the Evergreen property in a shield like a glass dome. The men lit the cannons again, and to Brystal's absolute horror, their cannonballs soared through the air and *pierced through her shield*!

BOOM! A cannonball whirled right past Brystal's head! *BOOM! BOOM!* The attackers were aiming at *her* now! *BOOM! BOOM!* The blasts struck the ground, getting closer and closer to where Brystal stood! *BOOM! BOOM!* Brystal was in a state of shock and couldn't move! *BOOM! BOOM!* She had never seen *anything* penetrate a magic shield before! *BOOM! BOOM!*

Right when Brystal was about to get hit, the attackers ran out of cannonballs—*but they weren't finished yet*! A man wearing a crown of metal spikes appeared through the smoky haze. He descended the hill with a sack of arrows in one hand and a crossbow in the other. Brystal knew she couldn't just stand there, but she didn't know what to do. If their weapons could penetrate her magic, how was she supposed to save herself?

"BRYSTAL!" Seven shouted.

The prince broke free from the royal guards and sprinted across the lawn. The man on the hill loaded his crossbow and fired his first shot. Seven jumped in front of Brystal, and the arrow hit the front of his leg. He fell on the ground screaming in agony.

"Don't just stand there!" Seven yelled at the guards. *"A prince has been shot! Go after them!"*

Half of the guards stayed with the princes, while the other half charged after the attackers on the hill. The archer had more than enough arrows to shoot the approaching guards, but instead, he gave the ghostly men a signal, and the attackers retreated into the countryside.

"Seven, hold still!" Brystal said. "This might hurt!"

She knelt beside him and pulled the arrow out of his leg. Seven screamed again, but Brystal waved her wand and healed his wound.

"Thanks," Seven said.

"No, thank *you*," Brystal said. "I don't know what came over me."

"Who are those men? Why are they attacking your brother's wedding?"

"I don't know," she said. "I've never seen anyone like— *AHHH!*"

Brystal suddenly screamed because the arrow was burning her hand. She dropped it on the ground and took a closer look at it. The arrowhead was made from the same material as the cannonballs that had penetrated her shield. It was as solid as rock and flickered as if there was fire trapped inside it.

"What's wrong?" Seven asked.

"The arrow—it burned me!" Brystal said.

Seven tapped the arrowhead with his finger but it didn't burn him.

"Are you allergic to it?" he asked.

"But what is it?" she said.

By the time the royal guards reached the top of the hill, all the attackers had disappeared with their weapons, but the ghostly men had left a message behind. A collection of tall wooden posts had been assembled and set ablaze to spell out three words:

DIE MAGIC SCUM

Brystal read the burning message, and her whole body went tense.

"I guess they weren't here for the wedding," Seven said.

"No," she said. "They were here for *me*."

CHAPTER FOUR

A BEWITCHING OFFER

The following morning, the Fairy Council was gathered around Brystal's glass desk, staring down at the glowing arrow as if it were a poisonous animal.

"They came out of nowhere and then disappeared without a trace," Brystal recalled. "There were hundreds of them. They all wore the same silver robes and masks that covered everything but their eyes. The image of a white wolf was stitched across their chests like a crest of some kind. They used wooden posts to spell out *Die Magic Scum* and set it on fire. It was the only thing they left behind."

"Creepy," Skylene said, and shivered at Brystal's account.

"Are you sure they didn't leave anything else?" Emerelda pressed. "There weren't any footprints or tracks? Any clues about who they are or where they came from?"

"I'm positive," Brystal said. "I searched the area for hours and found nothing."

Tangerina was vigorously flipping through the pages of a thick book. It contained illustrations of different armies, navies, and royal guards throughout history, and the official uniforms each division wore.

"Are there any other details you can give me?" Tangerina asked.

"The archer had a crown of sharp metal spikes," Brystal said. "That's all I could see."

Tangerina tossed the book aside. "None of these uniforms match your description," she said. "Whoever they are, they aren't from an official fleet in any of the kingdoms."

Brystal's eyes filled with fear. "Then maybe they *were* ghosts," she said.

The comment sent chills down the fairies' spines. Emerelda used a handkerchief to pick up the red arrow, and she inspected the glowing arrowhead with an emerald magnifying glass.

"And you said their cannonballs were made from the same material?" she asked.

Brystal nodded. "Their arrows and cannonballs went straight through my shield," she said. "Not only is the stone immune to magic, it also burns my skin whenever I touch it. Other people were in contact with it, too, but it didn't seem to hurt them. I suspect it's only harmful to people with magic in their blood."

Emerelda cautiously touched the arrowhead with her index finger and quickly pulled it away—it burned her skin, too. The fairies passed the red arrow around, and the glowing stone had the same effect on all of them, confirming Brystal's suspicion.

"How strange," Skylene said. "It burns but it doesn't leave a mark."

"It must be a new invention," Emerelda said. "I've spent my whole life around rare stones and gems, but I never saw anything like this in the mines."

"Actually, I think it's pretty old," Xanthous said.

Like Tangerina, Xanthous was also searching through a big book. The pages contained sketches of different weapons used throughout history. He opened the book to a section on archery and placed it on the desk beside the red arrow.

"Take a close look at the red arrow," Xanthous said. "Notice the *shape* of the arrowhead? See how it's been cut like a triangle? Now look at the shaft and the fletching. See how they've been painted black?"

The fairies studied the red arrow and nodded.

"Now compare the red arrow to the sketch of a *modern arrow* in the book," Xanthous went on. "See how modern arrowheads are shaped like diamonds? Notice how the shafts and fletching are colorless? There's a reason for that. Over time, archers learned that arrows fly better when the tips are narrow, and they travel farther without the weight of paint."

"So how old is it?" Skylene asked.

Xanthous gulped. "Well, if my theory is right, then it's not just old—it's *ancient.*"

He turned the page and showed them the sketches in the previous section. No one could deny it—the red arrow looked exactly like the arrows used in ancient times. Brystal paced behind her desk as she thought about the revelation.

"If the weapons are ancient, they must have a limited supply," Brystal said. "That explains why they used them so sparingly. They only used enough cannonballs to get my attention, and even though they had plenty, they only shot *one arrow* at me. They weren't there for a full-fledged battle—they were there to *hurt me*."

"I'm confused," Emerelda said. "Why haven't we heard of these weapons before? And where did those men find them?"

"Maybe they didn't *find* them, maybe they were saving them," Brystal said. "It's possible this group has been around since ancient times, too. There are a lot of secret societies that have been operating for centuries."

"Like what?" Skylene asked.

"Skylene, they wouldn't be *secret* if we knew about them," Tangerina said.

"Oh," Skylene said. "But then why wait until *now* to attack? Why only target *one* person? And at a *wedding* of all places?"

"Isn't it obvious?" Brystal asked. "For the first time

in six hundred years, magic is legal and accepted in all four kingdoms—whoever they are, they've never had a bigger reason to attack. And nothing starts a war faster than eliminating the leader of your adversary. So they waited for the perfect time to strike."

It was a very unsettling idea to process. The magical community had plenty of enemies, but none with such powerful resources.

"It's especially cruel to ruin such a special occasion," Skylene said. "As far as I'm concerned, hate is no excuse for rudeness."

"Poor Barrie," Tangerina said. "Are they going to have another wedding?"

"He and Penny decided to complete the ceremony in private," Brystal said. "I can't blame them. Everyone was pretty traumatized after the attack. My father was so shaken up he actually *asked* me to repair the damage with magic."

"We should postpone our events until these men are caught," Emerelda said. "It's a miracle no one was killed at the wedding, but imagine what might happen if thousands of innocent people were watching."

"I agree," Brystal said. "And I don't want the other

fairies hearing about this. The magical community has spent enough time living in fear."

"Are you two nuts?"

The Fairy Council turned around and saw Lucy had snuck into the office without their noticing. She was stretched out on the glass sofa, eavesdropping on their conversation.

"You're supposed to be suspended!" Tangerina reprimanded.

"You're supposed to be suspended," Lucy mimicked. "That's how dumb you sound."

Brystal sighed. "Lucy, I don't have the energy for this," she said. "You know you're not allowed at Fairy Council meetings."

Lucy hopped to her feet. "This is no time to be divided!" she declared. "There's a squad of ghostly terrorists using ancient weapons to enact hate crimes! We need all hands on deck!"

"We've got plenty of hands, thank you very much," Skylene said.

"But you're already making mistakes!" Lucy professed. "The last thing we should do is cancel events and keep quiet about this. We need as much public support as possible! The more awareness we spread, the more likely we'll find out who these creeps are. We should put up posters asking people to come forward with information. We can offer a reward in exchange for evidence—like a cash prize, a unicorn, or Tangerina!"

"Hey!" Tangerina yelled.

"As soon as word gets out that the beloved Fairy Godmother is in danger, people will be begging to help us!" Lucy continued. "In the meantime, we should hire a professional investigator to help us track down the men. I know a brilliant detective in the Eastern Kingdom—full disclosure, he's also a children's party clown, but no one can solve a mystery quicker than Juggles!"

Brystal rolled her eyes. "Thank you, Lucy," she said unenthusiastically. "The council will take your suggestions into consideration. Now, please, leave the office."

"Come on, Brystal, you've got to listen to me!" Lucy pleaded. "I've warned you what might happen if we don't keep people interested in magic! Getting the public involved in a manhunt is the perfect opportunity to keep them excited about us!"

"Lucy, please—"

"These ghost guys know *exactly* what they're doing," she went on. "They've got costumes, ancient weapons, sneak attacks, burning signs—they're putting on a great show! What happens if *destroying magic* becomes more entertaining than magic itself? What happens if they make it *trendy* to hate us again?"

Once again, Lucy was overwhelming Brystal with her unsolicited advice. Brystal waved her wand, and the office doors flew open.

"I've already asked you to leave," she said. "If I have to ask you again, consider yourself *banned* from the council."

It took all of Lucy's physical and mental restraint to bite her tongue. She sulked to the door, stomping her feet loudly as she went. As Lucy left the office, Mrs. Vee entered with her arms full of large scrolls. Lucy didn't even acknowledge the housekeeper as she passed her in the doorway.

"Well, Lucy seems quiet," Mrs. Vee said. "I guess there's a first time for everything. HA-HA!"

"What can I do for you, Mrs. Vee?" Brystal asked.

"I hope I'm not interrupting anything important," the housekeeper said. "I finally finished the blueprints for the kitchen expansion and I was too excited to keep them to myself. With your permission, I'm planning to knock down the south wall and add a modest ten thousand square feet. Yes, it's a little extravagant, and yes, it includes a day spa. But as the famous phrase goes, *Happy cook, happy outlook!* HA-HA!"

Mrs. Vee headed to Brystal's desk with a happy bounce in her step. Skylene gasped as an exciting idea popped into her head.

"We should show Mrs. Vee the arrow!" she told the others. "She's pretty ancient, too—maybe she knows the answers we're looking for?"

"Ancient?" The housekeeper was offended by the comment. "I may have more yesterdays than tomorrows, but I'm still a child in tortoise years! HA-HA!"

Skylene carefully raised the red arrow off the desk. "Mrs. Vee, have you seen something like this before?" she asked. "Brystal was attacked last night by men in silver robes! They had weapons made from this weird stone that defies magic!"

"Well, I'm no stranger to strange men, but that doesn't mean I know every Tom, Bob, and Joe in—"

As soon as Mrs. Vee laid eyes on the red arrow, she went silent and all the color drained from her face. The housekeeper dropped her blueprints, and her whole body started trembling. She fearfully backed into a wall and slid to the floor.

"*No!*" Mrs. Vee shrieked. "*It can't be!*"

Her reaction stunned the Fairy Council. They had never seen Mrs. Vee even *frown* before, but the arrow had sent the housekeeper into a nervous breakdown.

"Mrs. Vee, have you seen one of these arrows before?" Brystal asked.

"*N-n-never in person,*" she stuttered. "*B-b-but I know what it is.*"

"What about the men who attacked Brystal?" Emerelda asked. "Do you know who they are?"

Mrs. Vee nodded, and tears spilled down her face, like the question was painful to answer.

"*The Three Thirty-Three!*" she gasped.

"The Three Thirty-Three?" the fairies asked in unison.

"THE THREE THIRTY-THREE!"

Mrs. Vee became hysterical and wailed like she was being attacked herself. She jumped to her feet and ran out of the office without saying another word. The fairies could hear her screaming as she ran down the floating steps and headed to her chambers on the first floor.

"What the heck just happened?" Tangerina asked.

"Mrs. Vee just confirmed we have the right to be worried," Emerelda said.

"But what does the *Three Thirty-Three* mean?" Xanthous asked. "Is that just their name or are there specifically three hundred and thirty-three of them?"

"Either way, we need to find out," Brystal said. "I'll check on Mrs. Vee and see if I can get any more information from her. Emerelda will cancel all our upcoming appointments until further notice, and none of us will mention a word of this to anyone."

The Fairy Council nodded at her instructions. Brystal headed to the door, but before she could get out of the office, Lucy suddenly returned and blocked the doorway. Her round face was bright red and she was out of breath.

"Lucy, I told you to—"

"Sorry, I know I'm not supposed to be here!" Lucy panted. "But something is happening that you should know about!"

"Don't worry, we already know," Brystal said. "I'm on my way to check on her."

"Huh?" Lucy asked. "Oh, I'm not talking about Mrs. Vee—although, it's always unsettling to see an old woman running down a steep flight of stairs—I'm talking about the *border*! Something is trying to break into the Fairy Territory!"

The Fairy Council quickly dashed across the office and looked out the window. The grounds were filled with students practicing their magic, but they had all stopped to watch something moving in the distance. At the edge of the property, a section of the hedge barrier was shaking and swaying like a monstrous creature was trying to push through it.

"You think it's the Flirty Dirty-Three? Or whatever they're called?" Skylene asked.

"That's impossible!" Emerelda said. "No one can get through the barrier unless they have magic in their blood!"

"But their weapons broke through Brystal's shield!" Xanthous said. "They might have a way to break through the barrier, too!"

It was a horrifying possibility and Brystal wasn't

going to take any chances. She ran outside as fast as she could and her friends followed her. The Fairy Council hurried to the border and formed a line of defense between the hedge barrier and the students.

"Everyone inside the academy!" Brystal commanded. *"Now!"*

The students could sense the panic in her voice and quickly headed for the castle. Shortly after the Fairy Council arrived, Horence galloped across the property on his three-headed horse and joined the fairies. The knight leaped to the ground with his sword raised, ready to protect the academy at all costs, but Brystal worried it *still* wouldn't be enough to stop the 333.

The hedge shook and swayed harder and harder, and the branches snapped and crunched louder and louder. Suddenly, all the leaves in the area turned yellow and wilted to the ground. The hedge rotted away, forming a wide opening, and the trespasser appeared. It was a large carriage that was shaped like a human skull. The whole vehicle was painted black and its windows were designed like cobwebs. There were no drivers, horses, or wheels, and instead, the carriage crawled on eight wooden legs like a massive spider. It crept out of the hedge and stopped a few feet in front of the Fairy Council. The legs bent slowly as the carriage planted its belly to the ground. The door swung open with gusto and a passenger stepped outside.

The passenger was an attractive woman in a tight black gown that coiled around her body like a snake. Her skin was as pale as bone, her lips were as red as fresh blood, and she wore ashy makeup around her wide, dark eyes. The ends of her long black hair burned like thousands of dying matches, shrouding the woman in a smoky fog.

"Well, well, well," she said. "Look at all the *color*."

The woman spoke with an airy voice, and she gazed around the academy with a mischievous grin. Although Brystal was relieved the trespasser wasn't from the 333, there was still something menacing about the woman that Brystal didn't trust.

"Who are you?" she asked.

The woman's smile grew when her eyes landed on Brystal. As she walked toward Brystal, the grass turned brown and shriveled under the woman's feet.

Brystal raised her wand at the mysterious visitor, but the woman wasn't intimidated in the slightest.

"There's no need to point that thing at me, dear," she said. "We're on the same side."

"I'll be the judge of that," Brystal said. "Now, *who are you?*"

"My name is Mistress Mara," the woman said with a shallow bow. "And *you* must be the famous Fairy Godmother. I'd recognize your sparkling wardrobe and confident disposition from miles away. We are absolutely *thrilled* to make your acquaintance."

"We?" Brystal asked.

"Girls, come out and meet the Fairy Godmother!" the woman called to the carriage. *"And remember to use your manners!"*

At her request, four adolescent girls emerged from the carriage. They were all around the age of thirteen, and they wore identical black cloaks with pointed hoods, and striped stockings that matched the colors of their hair.

"Allow me to introduce Sprout, Hareiet, Beebee, and Stitches," Mistress Mara said. "Girls, this is the legendary Fairy Godmother, but she needs no introduction."

Sprout was the tallest of the group, and she had bushy green hair that barely fit under her hood. Hareiet was bucktoothed and had a twitchy nose and two purple braids, and one of her eyebrows was permanently raised in suspicion. Beebee was the smallest and roundest of the girls. She had short blue curls and very thick glasses, and she seemed to be buzzing with excitement. Stitches had wiry orange hair, an unusually wide mouth, and a blue eye that was slightly bigger than her red eye.

The girls bowed to Brystal, and she noticed that all the women—including Mistress Mara—wore a golden necklace with a white moonstone. Once they were introduced, the girls eyed the property with creepy smirks that made the Fairy Council uneasy.

"Are they your daughters?" Brystal asked.

"Oh, heavens no," Mistress Mara said with a laugh. "I'm merely a mentor to these four. Personally, I never understood the appeal of motherhood. Why create life when you could enjoy your own?"

The woman threw her head back and laughed at the remark. Brystal lowered her wand and the students at the castle figured it was safe to return. Slowly but surely, all the fairies throughout the territory gathered behind the Fairy Council and studied the curious visitors.

"Please forgive the mess we made on the way in," Mistress Mara said. "We got tired of looking for the entrance, so we created our own."

"What are you doing here?" Brystal asked.

"Why, we've come to pay our respects to the great Fairy Godmother, of course," the Mistress said. "What you've done for the magical community is nothing short of a miracle. I never thought I'd see a day when we could live as openly, as freely, and as safely as we do now. My girls and I are so grateful we were compelled to thank you face-to-face."

Her compliments were kind, but Brystal could tell they weren't sincere.

"I'm flattered," she said.

"As you should be," Mistress Mara said. "In fact, you've been such a source of inspiration, I decided to follow in your footsteps, and I recently opened a school of my own."

Brystal was surprised to hear it. "You opened a school of magic?"

"Not exactly," the Mistress said with a twinkle in

her eye. "There is so much more to the magical community than just *magic*. And while no one can deny the progress you've made, let's be honest, you don't represent the *entire* community, do you?"

"Excuse me?"

"I don't mean any offense, dear. I'm simply stating the obvious. *Half* of our community has been horribly neglected in all your endeavors. We've been shunned, shamed, and denied the same opportunities. So I've opened a school to fix that."

Skylene gasped. "They're *witches*!" she exclaimed.

"They can't be!" Tangerina said. "Witchcraft distorts people's appearance—and they're too pretty to be witches!"

Mistress Mara gave a patronizing laugh, like they were children in grown-up clothes.

"Witches have *evolved* in ways you couldn't imagine," she said.

Tangerina and Skylene were spooked by the comment. They pulled Lucy in front of them and used her as a shield.

"You're wrong about me," Brystal said. "I created the Fairy Territory so *everyone* in our community would have a home. It doesn't matter what your specialty is, or what your interests are, *everyone* is welcome. We don't discriminate here."

"You may *tolerate* witches, but you don't *encourage* them," Mistress Mara said. "If it were up to you, we'd all be converted into fairies by now. But witches aren't something you can just wish away. We've been in the world just as long as fairies have, and we're here to stay."

The witch moved through the Fairy Council, leaving a trail of dead grass behind her, and she addressed all the fairies watching her throughout the property.

"Without question, the Fairy Godmother has made magic more acceptable, respectable, and admirable than ever before. Dare I say it, she's made fairies *normal*. But some of us don't want to be normal, do we? Some of us were born with a strong desire to be different. Some of us prefer the strange and unusual to the safe and predictable. Deep down, you know you'll never be satisfied with granting wishes and rewarding good deeds. Deep down, you know you'll never thrive among flowers and unicorns. You and I are creatures of the night, children of the moon, and the only way to lead a fulfilling life is by embracing the darkness within us. And luckily, I can teach you how."

"So *that's* why you're here," Lucy said. "You're trying to poach our students!"

Mistress Mara turned to Lucy with her first genuine smile of the visit.

"My, my, my," she said. "Is that the notorious Lucy Goose I see?"

"Actually, it's pronounced GOO—oh wait, you said it right."

"I'm a big admirer of your work," Mistress Mara said. "Is it true you destroyed the Western Dam with just a touch of your hands?"

Lucy shrugged self-consciously. "It wasn't my finest moment," she said.

"I beg to differ," the witch said. "It's very rare to find someone with gifts like yours. We'd be honored to have you at our school."

"Seriously?" Lucy asked in disbelief. "Wow, it's been a long time since someone actually wanted me to—"

The Fairy Council shot her a dirty look.

"Um . . . I mean, *no thanks*," Lucy said. "I admit the

overall cheerfulness of this place can be obnoxious at times, but it's home."

"Pity," Mistress Mara said. "We could have done great things together."

The witch spun around and continued her pitch to the other fairies.

"As for the rest of you, the Ravencrest School of Witchcraft is officially open and ready for enrollment. If my words resonated with you today, if you're eager to connect to your true nature, to unlock limitless potential, and to expand your abilities beyond the Fairy Godmother's definition of magic, then perhaps you belong with us."

Mistress Mara extended an open hand toward her audience. Brystal nervously watched the fairies as they considered the witch's offer. She could tell some of them were intrigued by the invitation, but no one said a word or stepped forward.

"As you can see, we're all perfectly happy here," Brystal said. "I'm sorry you made the trip for nothing."

"Very well," Mistress Mara said. "Consider this an open invitation. Should any of you change your mind, the Ravencrest School of Witchcraft is in the North-western Woods between the Dwarf and Elf Territories. We hope to see you soon."

The witch returned to the black carriage and held the door open while Sprout, Hareiet, Beebee, and Stitches climbed inside. Just as Mistress Mara was about to shut the door behind herself, she was stopped by a voice across the grounds.

"Wait! Don't leave!"

Brystal recognized the voice immediately. She glanced over her shoulder, praying she was mistaken, but her ears weren't deceiving her. A young fairy pushed her way to the front of the crowd and presented herself to the witch.

"I'd like to join your school of witchcraft, Mistress Mara!" Pip announced.

The witch observed her like a cat observing a mouse.

"Excellent," she said. "Please come inside and take a seat."

Pip was excited to join the witches and sprinted toward the carriage. Before she could climb aboard, Brystal grabbed Pip's wrist and pulled her aside.

"Pip, what are you doing?"

"I'm joining the Ravencrest School of Witchcraft."

"No! I won't let them take you!" Brystal exclaimed.

"They aren't taking me; I want to go," Pip said.

"Everything Mistress Mara said about being different is exactly how I've been feeling—I've just never been able to explain why. Maybe the reason I feel so empty all the time is because I'm in the wrong place? Maybe I belong with the witches?"

"We *all* feel different from time to time, but that doesn't make someone a witch!"

"There's only one way to know for sure. If I don't go with them, I may regret it forever."

Brystal couldn't believe how determined she was to leave. Pip tried to get away from Brystal, but Brystal wouldn't let go of her wrist.

"Pip, you're like a sister to me! I can't let you do this!"

"It's not up to you! This is my choice!"

"But this isn't a choice—it's a mistake!"

"Then it's *my* mistake to make!"

As Pip pulled away from Brystal, her arm started to stretch like rubber. It expanded several feet as she headed toward the carriage, but Brystal reined her in like a long rope.

"Pip, trust me, you don't want to do this!" Brystal said.

"Don't tell me what I want!" Pip said.

"They're using your emotions to trick you! Witches earn people's trust so they can manipulate them later! They don't actually care about you!"

"Neither do you! You just want to keep me here so you can control me! This academy is no different from the Bootstrap Correctional Facility! But I won't be a prisoner anymore! I'm leaving whether you like it or not!"

Pip kept stretching and stretching, and eventually, her wrist slipped out of Brystal's hands. Her arm snapped back to normal and Brystal fell backward on the ground. By the time she got to her feet, Pip was already seated inside the carriage. Mistress Mara smiled and waved good-bye.

"Once again, thanks for all the inspiration," the witch said.

"Pip, wait!" Brystal pleaded. *"Please, come back!"*

Mistress Mara slammed the carriage door shut. The vehicle rose to its feet and crawled back into the hedge barrier. Brystal ran after the carriage, but there was nothing else she could do.

Pip was gone.

CHAPTER FIVE

WARMTH FROM A COLD HEART

After Pip's departure from the academy, Brystal spent the rest of the day inside her office.
She locked the double doors and applied a
spell to keep everyone out, but even with complete
isolation, Brystal never felt *alone*. Her disturbing
thoughts had become so persistent they developed a
presence of their own—like a shadow she couldn't
escape from.

You should have done more for Pip....

But you were too busy to help her....

You were too selfish to care....

You let her down, and she made the biggest mistake of her life....

The witches took her away, and she's never coming back.

The thoughts thrived in silence, as if a quiet room was their natural habitat. Although they didn't make a physical sound, Brystal could have sworn they echoed around her.

You can't handle all of this....

Mankind's approval...

Prince Maximus...

The Three Thirty-Three...

Witches...

You're going to drown.

Brystal had never felt more helpless in her life. She desperately needed advice on how to manage everything on her plate, but who in the world could help her? Who could answer all the questions tormenting her? Who could supply comfort and reassurance in a time like this?

Her weary eyes drifted toward the globe beside her desk. Thankfully, the northern lights were dancing above the Northern Mountains like always. Brystal was relieved to see the lights hadn't changed, but this time, they also gave her an idea.

Perhaps there *was* someone she could talk to—or at least, *half* of someone.

The idea quickly became a possibility, and the possibility quickly turned into a plan. Later that night, when the rest of the Fairy Territory was asleep, Brystal carefully wrapped the glowing red arrow in a handkerchief and dressed in a warm, sparkling coat. She quietly opened the windows of her office and floated outside in a large bubble.

Brystal flew as high as she could so no one on the ground would notice her. She steered her bubble over the academy grounds, across the Troll and Goblin Territories, and into the clouds above the Northern Kingdom. The night air became colder and colder as she flew farther north, and soon the snowy Northern Mountains appeared below her. Still, Brystal continued her northern excursion and drifted deeper into the mountains, far beyond the reaches of civilization.

In the distance, hovering above the sharp peaks of the mountain range, were the shimmering northern lights. Brystal landed on a snowy mountainside directly below the lights and popped the bubble with her wand. The howling wind was freezing, and Brystal pulled up the collar of her coat to shield her face. She had no clue *what* she should be looking for, but Brystal searched the frosted mountain for anything that might lead her in the right direction.

All Brystal could see was the snow whirling around her, but as her eyes adjusted, she eventually noticed the narrow opening of a small cave. She squeezed through the opening and was grateful to get out of the bitter wind. She waved her wand and illuminated the dark cave with hundreds of twinkling lights. The lights filled the darkness like a swarm of fireflies, and Brystal discovered it wasn't a cave after all, but a long tunnel.

She cautiously followed the tunnel as it snaked deeper and deeper into the mountainside. As she went, Brystal noticed the walls of the tunnel were covered in scratches, as if a frightening creature had been dragged through it. Strangely, the unnerving sight gave Brystal hope—a frightening creature was exactly what she wanted to see.

Brystal proceeded down the tunnel for miles. Just when she started to worry the passageway was endless, the tunnel opened into an icy cavern. The twinkling lights wrapped around the largest icicle on the ceiling and it illuminated the area like a chandelier. Brystal searched every corner and crevasse of the frigid cavern but found nothing out of the ordinary.

"What a waste of time," she mumbled to herself. "I was stupid for coming here—finding her is like finding a needle in a haystack."

Brystal knew the person of interest was somewhere in the Northern Mountains—otherwise the northern lights wouldn't be in the sky—but there were probably thousands of caverns she'd have to search before she found the person. Cold and defeated, Brystal sat on a boulder and rested her tired legs before heading home.

As she moped, Brystal spotted something strange out of the corner of her eye. A tall silhouette was watching her from the back of the cavern. Alarmed, Brystal leaped to her feet and pointed her wand at the strange figure.

"I see you!" she announced. "Don't come any closer!"

The figure obeyed Brystal's order and didn't move an inch.

"Who are you?" she asked.

They didn't respond. In fact, it was eerie how silent and still they were. Brystal slowly approached the back of the cavern and realized why she hadn't seen them before—*the figure was frozen in a wall of ice*! She wiped away a layer of condensation and immediately jumped back when she recognized the person trapped inside. It was a monstrous woman with an enormous snowflake crown and a white fur coat. Her skin was blackened and cracked from frostbite, her teeth were as jagged as broken glass, and a cloth was wrapped around her eyes. Without a doubt, Brystal had finally found the infamous Snow Queen.

"I knew you'd come eventually."

The voice came out of nowhere and startled Brystal—but this time, it wasn't just in her head. She spun around and pointed her wand in the direction of the voice. A beautiful woman with dark hair and bright eyes had appeared in the cavern behind her. The woman wore a plum gown and an elaborate fascinator and she beamed with a warm smile.

"*Madame Weatherberry?*" Brystal gasped.

The fairy looked younger and more vibrant than ever before. Brystal didn't know how it was possible for Madame Weatherberry and the Snow Queen to exist in two different places, but she didn't care. Without wasting another second, Brystal ran across the cavern to embrace her former mentor, but she passed through Madame Weatherberry like she was made of air.

"Are you a ghost?" Brystal asked.

"Something like that," Madame Weatherberry said.

"After we said our good-byes in the Tinzel Palace, I tried my best to keep the promises I made to you. I traveled as far away from civilization as my feet would carry me, but living in seclusion made the Snow Queen stronger. It was only a matter of time before she conquered me completely, so I searched the mountains for a place to imprison her and discovered this cavern. I froze myself in a wall of ice to trap her, and just in case it melted, I blinded myself so she would never find a way out. With my last bit of strength, I performed a detachment spell to separate us. As long as the Snow Queen lives, I'll exist like a phantom outside of her."

"Can you come back to the academy like this?" Brystal asked.

Madame Weatherberry's smile faded and she shook her head.

"We no longer share a body, but I'm still linked to her and can't stray beyond the walls of this cave," she explained. "Not that I deserve to anyway. I'm responsible for creating her, and therefore responsible for all the destruction she caused. I belong in this cavern just as much as the Snow Queen does."

"Then why perform a detachment spell at all?" Brystal asked.

"Well, for a couple of reasons," Madame Weatherberry said. "*First*, if anyone came here with the intention of freeing the Snow Queen, I wanted to talk them out of it. *Second*, I thought I might be useful to *you* one day. I left you with an impossibly heavy burden, Brystal. While I still have nothing but absolute faith in you, I figured you might need a little guidance at some point. Now that you're here, is it safe to assume my hunch was correct?"

Brystal nodded and her eyes filled with tears.

"Yes," she cried. "And you have no idea how much I need you."

Being in Madame Weatherberry's presence made Brystal feel safe. She put her guard down for the first time in months, and all her suppressed emotions surged forward. Brystal fell on her knees and sobbed in the middle of the cavern.

"You poor thing," Madame Weatherberry said. "This is all my fault. I shouldn't have placed so much responsibility on your shoulders."

"No, it's not that." Brystal sniffled. "We did it, Madame Weatherberry—we did *everything* we always dreamed about! Magic has been legalized in all four kingdoms! Mankind doesn't just *approve* of magic, they're *fascinated* by it. The academy is now home to thousands of fairies who are learning to develop their abilities. And not only have we made the world a safer place for the magical community, we've also done amazing things for women and the talking creatures, too!"

If Madame Weatherberry had had a physical form, she would have needed to sit down. The fairy placed a hand over her heart, and her eyes went wide with exhilaration. She let out such a deep breath, it was like she was sighing with relief for the entire magical community.

"Oh, Brystal," she said. "I've waited a long time to hear those words. You've brought so much warmth to such a cold place."

Brystal nodded and forced herself to smile.

"I know—it's amazing," she said. "I didn't think the world could change so much."

"Then why do you seem so sad?" Madame Weatherberry asked.

"I don't know," Brystal said with a shrug. "There's so much to be happy about, but lately, my mind only focuses on the bad stuff. There's a voice in my head that constantly reminds me of my failures and gives me reasons to fear the future. Every effort feels pointless, every accomplishment feels temporary, and every bump in the road feels like the end of the world. No matter what I do, I can't get it to stop. I'm worried I'm going to be miserable forever!"

Madame Weatherberry knelt beside Brystal and stroked her hair. Even though Brystal couldn't feel her apparitional hands, she could feel the fairy's empathy.

"The only thing in life that lasts forever is the fact that nothing lasts forever," Madame Weatherberry said. "Just like the weather, people have seasons, too—we all go through periods of rain and sunshine—but we can't let a particularly rough winter destroy our faith in the spring, otherwise we'll always be stuck in the snow."

"This doesn't feel like a winter, it feels like an ice age," Brystal said. "What if this isn't a season? What if it's more than just a phase?"

"Either way, it's up to *you* to change it," Madame Weatherberry said.

"But how?"

"Misery is like an animal, it needs food to survive—*so starve it*. Surround yourself with art and beauty that brightens your darkest days. Listen to music and poetry that always fill the cracks of your broken heart. Read quotes and passages that can soothe and motivate you when you feel the most discouraged. Spend time with people who make you laugh and distract you from your troubles. Nourish your soul and hopefully the mind will follow. However, if you find you can't help yourself, there's no shame in asking others for help. Sometimes asking for help is just as heroic as giving it. There are treatments and therapies and counselors that you could benefit from—but no one finds answers if they're too afraid to ask the questions. Don't let your pride tell you otherwise."

Brystal groaned. "It sounds easier said than done."

"Changing hearts and minds is never easy, especially our own," Madame Weatherberry said. "Sometimes, changing how we *think* and *feel* are the most difficult transformations a person can make. It takes time and effort like nothing else. You have to discipline your thoughts before they dictate your mood. You have to control your reactions before your reactions control you. And most important, you have to ask for help when you need it, despite how vulnerable it makes you feel. Take it from me, if I had learned to handle my emotions, and if I wasn't too embarrassed to ask for help, the Snow Queen wouldn't exist."

Brystal shuddered at the idea of another Snow Queen, growing inside her.

"That's why I'm here," she said. "I need help and you're the only person I can talk to."

"Well, no wonder you're so distraught," Madame Weatherberry said. "Every hurricane seems endless from the center of the storm. That's why it's so important to talk to people—getting a different perspective can be just as valuable as finding a solution. Now tell me about the things that are troubling you. I may not solve your problems, but I might change how you feel about them."

The cavern was so cold Brystal's tears were frozen to her cheeks. She wiped the ice off her face and got back to her feet.

"All right," she said. "The progress we've made is incredible, but I'm afraid we're going to lose mankind's approval. They changed their opinion about magic so quickly I worry they'll change their minds again. And magic may be legal now, but what if a king or queen amends the laws in the future? What will happen to us then?"

"It's all possible," Madame Weatherberry said. "But you've already accomplished the *impossible*, Brystal, so have faith that you'll handle the *possible* as it happens. If mankind changes their minds, then you *can* and *will* find a way to win them back. And if people love magic as much as you say they do, then a sovereign would be foolish to deny their people of something they love—that's how revolutions start. If the time comes, it wouldn't hurt to remind them of that."

Brystal went quiet as she thought about Madame Weatherberry's advice. Like the fairy said, talking about the issue didn't solve it, but hearing someone else's assessment made her feel *slightly* better.

"That's helpful, thank you."

"It feels wonderful to *be* helpful," Madame Weatherberry said. "What else is on your mind?"

"Well, there's also a witch who opened a school of witchcraft," Brystal said. "Her name is Mistress Mara and she came to the Fairy Territory to recruit students. She convinced my friend Pip to join her, and now I'm worried other fairies might leave the academy and become witches, too."

"I know it's difficult to hear, but this is a good thing," Madame Weatherberry said. "For the first time in hundreds of years, members of the magical community have *choices* over their own destiny. Thanks to you, witches and fairies get to be whoever they wish, whenever they wish, even if it's against *your* wishes."

"I think the witches are up to something," Brystal said. "Mistress Mara gave a big speech about wanting to help fairies embrace their inner darkness, but I don't trust her. Since when do witches care about anyone but themselves? What if she tricked Pip into something dangerous?'"

"If so, your friend will learn a valuable lesson, and the other fairies will have more reason to trust you in the future," Madame Weatherberry said with a shrug. "That's the most difficult part about being in your shoes—you have so much authority but are completely *powerless* over other people's choices. So don't blame yourself for your friend's mistakes—*that's* the biggest mistake you can make."

Brystal sighed. "I suppose you're right," she said. "Thanks."

"This is quite fun for me," Madame Weatherberry said. "What's next?"

"I'm afraid I've saved the worst for last," Brystal said.

She removed the handkerchief from inside her coat and unwrapped the red arrow. The glowing arrowhead filled the cavern with crimson light. Just like Mrs. Vee, Madame Weatherberry had a visceral reaction to the arrow. Her cheery disposition faded, her eyes grew large, and she slowly backed away from the weapon. Brystal didn't have to ask her—clearly, Madame Weatherberry knew exactly what the arrow was.

"Where did you get that?" she asked.

"I was attacked by the Three Thirty-Three," Brystal said.

Madame Weatherberry stared off into space and fearfully shook her head.

"So they're finally back after all this time," she whispered to herself.

"What do you know about them?" Brystal asked.

"I—I shouldn't say anything," Madame Weatherberry said. "You came to me for encouragement and it would only burden you with more—"

"Madame Weatherberry, you have to tell me!"

Brystal insisted. "They've already tried to kill me once and I suspect they'll do it again! Whoever they are, wherever they came from, I need to know everything I can so I can stop them!"

Madame Weatherberry closed her eyes and winced at the request. She quietly paced around the cavern as she found the words to explain.

"They call themselves the *Righteous Brotherhood*," she said. "They're a thousand-year-old clan that's obsessed with something known as the *Righteous Philosophy*. They believe mankind should dominate the world, and anything that poses a threat to that should be exterminated. Naturally, the Brotherhood's greatest threat has always been the magical community. For hundreds of years, they hunted witches and fairies like animals, and they spread vicious lies and rumors to validate their hatred of us.

"The Righteous Brotherhood is the reason magic was outlawed in the first place. Six centuries ago, they manipulated King Champion I and his High Justices into criminalizing magic in the Southern Kingdom, and soon the other kingdoms followed their example. Champion I gave the Brotherhood permission to enforce the law, and the clan carried out the biggest massacre in world history. The *Righteous Raid*, as it was called, almost annihilated the magical community completely, and the survivors went into hiding. After that, the Brotherhood faded into the shadows, but I imagine the legalization of magic has brought them out of retirement."

"Why did Mrs. Vee refer to them as the *Three Thirty-Three*?" Brystal asked.

"Because there's never more or less than three hundred and thirty-three of them. The duties have been passed down from father to eldest son in three hundred and thirty-three families in the Southern Kingdom. Traditionally, the clansmen swear allegiance to the Righteous Brotherhood on their father's deathbeds. They devote their entire existence—this life and whatever may come afterward—to upholding the Righteous Philosophy. The clan is so secretive the clansmen never reveal their identities to each other, making it nearly impossible to find them or predict what they'll do next."

"How did they create weapons like these? Where did they find a stone that defies magic?"

"It's called bloodstone and no one knows for sure," she said. "Of course, over the years there have been plenty of theories about its origins. Some say the stone fell from the stars, others say it was forged in the center of the earth by demons, and some claim it was a gift from Death himself."

"*Death himself?*" Brystal asked in disbelief. "You don't believe that, do you?"

Suddenly, a noise echoed through the cavern. Brystal and Madame Weatherberry turned toward the entrance and heard footsteps coming from down the tunnel.

"Someone must have followed you here," Madame Weatherberry said. "I have to go. If anyone finds out I'm part of the Snow Queen, it could ruin everything you've accomplished."

"Madame Weatherberry, wait!" Brystal said. "How do I stop the Righteous Brotherhood? Please, tell me what I'm supposed to do!"

Madame Weatherberry was the most optimistic person Brystal had ever known—she was always equipped with a promising plan or an empowering metaphor. However, Madame Weatherberry had no words of encouragement to give her. For the first time, the fairy looked down at Brystal with nothing but hopelessness in her eyes.

"Just keep everyone safe for as long as you can," she said.

Madame Weatherberry disappeared from the cavern like a fading rainbow. Brystal didn't know what to think of her mentor's parting words—it was almost like Madame Weatherberry was admitting defeat—but there wasn't time to analyze it. The footsteps echoed louder and louder as the stranger traveled closer and closer. Brystal wrapped the red arrow in the handkerchief and tucked it inside her coat. She hid in a corner of the cavern and pointed her wand at the tunnel, ready to defend herself from whoever or whatever was approaching.

"Freeze!" Brystal ordered.

"I'd say that's very likely given the temperature!"

"Lucy?"

Brystal was surprised to see Lucy stumble into the cavern. Her friend wore a thick coat of dark goose feathers but was still shivering from the cold air. She was breathing so heavily her warm breath looked like smoke venting from a chimney.

"Finally! I've been looking all over the Northern Mountains for you!" Lucy said.

"Were you *following* me?" Brystal asked.

Lucy nodded. "Call me crazy, but I was a little concerned after you snuck away in the middle of the night. I thought you were going to that Ravencrest joint to talk sense into Pip. I didn't want the witches to gang up on you, so I tagged along in case you needed backup. Had I known you were going to the *North freaking Pole* I would have stayed home. Gosh, I know you appreciate your alone time, but couldn't you find a quiet spot closer to the academy? What's so special about this cave?"

Lucy walked around the cavern, giving it a thorough inspection. Brystal moved with Lucy and tried to block the frozen Snow Queen from view.

"Nothing—*absolutely* nothing," Brystal said. "You're right, I came all the way up here for some time alone. I appreciate your concern, but as you can see, I'm perfectly fine. Now we should get back to the academy before anyone *else* tries to find us."

Brystal grabbed Lucy by the shoulders and directed her out of the cavern. As she pushed her into the tunnel, the red arrow slipped out of her coat and fell to the ground. Once again, the glowing arrowhead filled the cavern with flickering crimson light.

"What's the arrow doing here?" Lucy asked.

"Oh, look at that," Brystal said with a nervous laugh. "I must have forgotten it was in my coat. I should be more mindful when it comes to dangerous weapons."

Lucy crossed her arms and gave Brystal a suspicious gaze.

"Brystal, what the heck is going on?"

"Nothing! Why do you make such a big deal out of everything?"

"A *big deal*? I just found my best friend in a cave a thousand miles away from civilization with a lethal weapon! That is a big—" Lucy suddenly glanced over her shoulder. "Wait, are you alone? Or is someone else here?"

"What? No—of course not!"

"Then what's *that* over there?"

Lucy pointed toward the back of the cavern. Despite Brystal's efforts, she knew it was pointless to hide the Snow Queen from Lucy—her specialty always compelled her to wherever the most *trouble* was lurking.

"There's nothing over there," Brystal said.

"You mean *besides* that seriously creepy shadow in the back of the cavern?"

"You're just seeing things! I think you're dehydrated from the journey! It's getting late, anyway. We should really head home before—"

Brystal tried to stop her, but Lucy pushed her out of the way and headed for the back of the cavern. She wiped the condensation off the icy wall and then lunged backward when she saw the frightening face that was frozen inside.

"Holy icicle bicycle!" she gasped. "That's the *Snow Queen*, isn't it?"

Brystal panicked and didn't know what to do or how to explain it. Lucy looked back and forth between Brystal and the Snow Queen like a mystery was unraveling before her eyes.

"Ooooooh, it all makes sense now," she said. "This is why you haven't been acting like yourself lately! *You discovered where the Snow Queen was hiding!* You didn't want us to worry about it, so you kept it to yourself! And tonight, you snuck out of the academy and brought the red arrow here to *finish her off!*"

"Huh?"

"Brystal, this is fantastic! You became a hero just for sending the Snow Queen into seclusion! Imagine how the world is going to react when they hear you've finally *killed her*!"

"Lucy, I didn't come here to kill anyone!"

"Why not? The Snow Queen murdered thousands of innocent people and covered the entire planet in a blizzard! And she'll do it again if she gets the chance! Let's defrost this witch and stick the arrow through her heart while we can!"

"We can't—it's not that simple!"

"Ooooooh, I get it," Lucy said. "You're worried about protecting your image. People won't think the Fairy Godmother is very kind and compassionate when they find out you killed the Snow Queen in cold blood—no pun intended."

"Ummm...*yes*," Brystal said. "You see right through me, don't you?"

"Fine, you keep your hands clean. *I'll kill her!*"

Lucy grabbed the red arrow and charged toward the Snow Queen.

"*No!*" Brystal yelled. "*Don't do this!*"

Lucy was too determined to listen. She placed her

hand against the wall of ice, and just like the Western Dam, it started to crack and crumble.

"*Lucy, you have to stop!*" Brystal screamed.

"Don't worry, she won't feel a thing!" Lucy said.

"*I can't let you kill her!*"

"I have no problem doing your dirty work!"

"IT'S MADAME WEATHERBERRY!"

At first, Lucy had no idea what Brystal was talking about. She gazed up at the Snow Queen's hideous face, but then, slowly but surely, Lucy started to recognize Madame Weatherberry's features under the witch's frostbitten skin. She removed her hand from the icy wall and backed away before the damage exposed the Snow Queen.

"*No!*" Lucy gasped. "*This can't be real!*"

She was in complete shock and dropped the red arrow on the ground. Brystal let out a long, heavy sigh and tried to comfort her.

"I didn't want to believe it either, but it's the truth," she said.

"Is Madame Weatherberry still alive?" Lucy asked.

"Part of her is," Brystal said. "But she'll never be the same."

"How long have you known?"

"Since the Tinzel Palace. Madame Weatherberry thought the only way the fairies could get the world's acceptance was to create a problem that only the fairies could solve. She turned herself into a villain so *we* could be the heroes."

Lucy turned to Brystal with wide, heartbroken eyes.

"So you've been *lying* to us this entire time?" she asked.

Brystal was taken aback by the remark. "I—I promised her I wouldn't tell anyone," she said. "Madame Weatherberry was afraid you and the others would lose faith in the academy if you knew the truth."

"But I'm not just anyone—*I'm your best friend*!" Lucy declared. "What else have you been lying to me about? Is your real name Brystal Evergreen? Are you a natural brunette? Do you even like to *read*?"

"I haven't lied about anything else! I swear!"

"I don't know what to believe anymore!" Lucy said. "How could you do this to me, Brystal? You kicked me out of the Fairy Council for making a mistake, but meanwhile, *you've* been doing something way worse all along! Well, who's going to hold *you* responsible? Who's going to punish *you* for lying to everyone you know?"

Lucy stormed out of the cavern and raced down the tunnel. Brystal tried to follow her, but Lucy was moving so fast she could barely keep up.

"Lucy, wait! Where are you going?"

"As far away from you as possible!"

"I thought I was doing the right thing! Please, let's talk about this!"

"No! I'm done talking to you! I don't ever want to see you or speak to you again!"

Lucy placed her hand on the wall of the tunnel, and the Northern Mountains started to rumble. The tunnel caved in between Lucy and Brystal, separating them by a wall of fallen rocks. Brystal cleared the debris with her wand and then sprinted down the rest of the tunnel. By the time she was outside, Lucy had disappeared from sight.

There you go again...

Losing friends left and right....

You don't deserve their companionship....

You don't deserve their love....

You should be locked away, just like the Snow Queen.

The distressing thoughts seemed louder than the howling wind outside. Brystal wrapped her coat tightly around her body and searched the Northern Mountains for Lucy, but she didn't find a trace of her anywhere. As far as she could tell, Lucy had vanished into the cold, snowy air.

CHAPTER SIX

THE RAVENCREST SCHOOL OF WITCHCRAFT

Lucy flew as far away from the Northern Mountains as her geese would carry her. She had no idea which direction they were headed in, but Lucy couldn't care less—putting distance between her and Brystal was her only priority. Even though Lucy had said she never wanted to see or speak to Brystal again, she had imaginary arguments with Brystal for the entire journey.

The flock flew all night, and by sunrise the birds were too exhausted to take Lucy any farther. The geese unexpectedly dropped her off in the middle of a forest and Lucy landed with a *thump* on her behind.

"Pillow stuffers!" she yelled at the geese, and waved an angry fist.

Lucy got to her feet, brushed herself off, and continued on foot. She wandered aimlessly through the trees without a plan or a destination in mind. Although she was traveling alone, Lucy wasn't worried about crossing paths with anything dangerous—she was so angry she was convinced that *she* was the scariest thing in the forest.

She walked for miles and miles without seeing another living creature. Lucy was so distracted by her heated thoughts she barely noticed the land changing around her. When she finally looked up, Lucy discovered she had strolled into the middle of a creepy part of the woods. All the trees had black bark, their branches curled into the sky, and they were completely bare of leaves. A thick mist hung in the air, making it difficult to see more than a few yards in any direction.

Eventually, Lucy found a path that curved through the forest like an endless serpent. It was paved with black stones, and a sign was posted beside it that pointed in one direction:

Ravencrest Manor
7 Miles

Lucy couldn't believe her eyes and read the sign multiple times. It seemed too convenient to be a coincidence. Perhaps her journey hadn't been as aimless as she had thought—perhaps her knack for trouble had been guiding her the whole time. She assumed the Ravencrest Manor was the same location as the Ravencrest School of Witchcraft, but there was only one way to be certain. So Lucy followed the path deeper into the woods, and seven miles later, she had her answer.

The path led to an enormous house that sat on the top of a high hill. The home was constructed from a combination of black bricks, burned lumber, and dark stones—as if the property had been damaged and rebuilt several times over the years. Thirteen crooked towers sprouted from the roof at awkward angles that broke the laws of physics. The manor was surrounded by a graveyard of uneven tombstones and miniature crypts. The whole property was protected by a tall iron fence, and two grotesque gargoyles were perched on top of a gate that was chained shut.

The grounds were occupied by hundreds of lynxes with dark fur, wispy ears, and yellow eyes. The hefty felines prowled, played, and lounged among the tombstones, and judging by the size of their bellies, they were all well fed.

Without a doubt, Lucy knew she was looking at the Ravencrest School of Witchcraft—and not just because the words THE RAVENCREST SCHOOL OF WITCH CRAFT were arched over the gate. The property was so ominous it *had* to be the home of witches. It was the exact opposite of the Fairy Territory, and Lucy couldn't think of a better place to avoid Brystal. She cautiously walked toward the iron fence and peered through the bars for a better look.

"Hello?" Lucy called. "Is anybody home?"

Suddenly, a loud crunching noise came from behind her. Lucy turned around and screamed because two trees in the woods were moving on their own. The trees had pulled their roots out of the ground and were quickly shuffling toward her. They wrapped their curly branches around her arms and legs and raised her into the air.

"*Let me go!*" Lucy demanded. *"Don't make me turn you into toothpicks!"*

To make matters worse, the gargoyles on top of the gate suddenly came to life as well. The statues leaped to the ground and landed directly in front of Lucy with two heavy *thud*s.

"Looks like we've got our first visitor of the day," the first gargoyle said. "What do you think, Stone? Is this one a grave robber, a witch hunter, or a traveling salesman?"

"To be honest with you, Brick, I'm not sure what's worse," the second one joked.

The gargoyles shared a laugh. Their chuckles sounded like stone scraping against stone. Lucy groaned as she struggled to free herself from the trees' branches.

"Hey, Stoney-Dee and Stoney-Dumb! You better tell these overgrown weeds to put me down or you'll be sorry! I'm a member of the Fairy Council—well, I'm *usually* a member of the Fairy Council! You're going to be in big trouble if you don't release me!"

The gargoyles studied Lucy with their hollow eye sockets and smelled her with their stone snouts.

"That's funny, you don't *smell* like a fairy," Brick said.

"Nope, she smells like bird poop," Stone said.

"Look who's talking, mildew breath!"

"You don't *sound* like a fairy either," Brick said.

"Nope, she sounds like a sailor," Stone said.

Lucy rolled her eyes. "Is there a manager I can speak to?" she asked. "Where's that Mistress Mara lady? She invited me here *personally,* and I don't think she'd appreciate how you're treating me!"

"Hear that, Stone? The smelly fairy says she knows the Mistress," Brick said.

"Do you think she's telling the truth?" Stone asked.

"I hope not—I *love* watching what the Mistress does to intruders."

"Me too."

The gargoyles grinned and turned toward the gate. All the chains slithered away like snakes and the gate opened by itself. Brick and Stone headed up the hill to the manor, and the trees followed them, keeping Lucy suspended in the air as they went.

All the lynxes stopped what they were doing to

stare at Lucy. The felines were so interested in her that Lucy could have sworn there was something strangely *human* about the way they watched her.

The manor's enormous front door was made from stained glass depicting a terrifying owl preying on an innocent mouse. Brick pulled the lever for the doorbell, and instead of a traditional chime, Lucy heard a high-pitched scream echo through the house. A few moments later, the front door opened a crack and a butler peered outside. He wore a gold monocle, a three-piece suit, and white gloves—but besides his clothes, the butler was completely *invisible*.

"Tell the Mistress there's a rude teenager who wants to see her," Brick instructed.

The butler nodded—or at least his monocle bobbed up and down in the space above his collar. The invisible servant stepped back inside and shut the large door behind him. A few moments later, the servant returned and gestured for them to enter. The trees dropped Lucy on the doorstep, and the gargoyles pushed her inside the manor.

The interior of the Ravencrest School of Witchcraft was nothing like its mismatched exterior. In fact, Lucy was very impressed by its eerie yet elegant design.

The floor was covered in black and white tiles laid in spirals to resemble spiderwebs. The walls were completely blank and had the same color and texture as old parchment.

The entryway had an enormous chandelier of live hanging bats that fluttered through the air. An enormous taxidermy bear stood in the center of the entryway and had been turned into a grandfather clock. The bear clenched a ticking clockface in its mouth while a pendulum swung in its empty torso.

A grand staircase with railings made of bones curved around the bear. As Lucy's eyes followed the staircase up toward the high ceiling, she discovered it was connected to a labyrinth of bridges, landings, ladders, and other staircases that crisscrossed, zigzagged, and looped as they ascended to the upper floors. The layout was so complex Lucy became dizzy just from looking at it.

"What a pleasant surprise!"

At first, Lucy couldn't tell where the airy voice was coming from. Eventually, she saw Mistress Mara descending from one of the many levels above her.

"Thank you, boys," the witch said. "I can take it from here."

The gargoyles bowed to her and returned to their posts outside. Mistress Mara reached the ground floor, leaving a trail of smoke on the stairs behind her. The witch was so delighted to see Lucy her pale face was practically glowing. Lucy tried to greet the witch with a handshake, but Mistress Mara only stared at the gesture and wouldn't touch her.

"Welcome to Ravencrest, Miss Goose," Mistress Mara said. "I hope the trees and gargoyles didn't alarm you. They're just a few minor precautions I've put in place to keep the school safe. Witches can never have too much protection."

"If those were *minor precautions*, I'd hate to see your version of a fire drill," Lucy said.

Mistress Mara threw her head back and cackled at the remark. Lucy couldn't tell if the witch was genuinely amused or not, but it was nice to hear someone *laugh* at one of her jokes for a change.

"You just *kill* me," Mistress Mara said. "So, what brings you here?"

"Well, I was in the neighborhood and decided to check it out," Lucy said.

"Were you thinking about joining our school?" the witch asked.

Lucy shrugged. "Maybe," she said. "To be honest, I don't really have a game plan right now. I could use a break from the fairies, though. There's someone I'm trying to avoid and I didn't know where else to go."

"How delightfully vengeful," Mistress Mara said. "In that case, why don't you spend a few days with us?"

"Really? You wouldn't mind?"

"Oh, I insist," she said. "It'd be our treat to host you. Who knows, you might even like it here and decide to stay. Shall I give you a tour of the manor?"

"That'd be great," Lucy said. "Thanks, Double-Em."

"No nicknames, dear," the witch said. "Please, follow me."

Mistress Mara showed Lucy around the spooky yet sophisticated manor and, once again, made a point to not touch her.

The ground floor had a sitting room with furniture that was upholstered in reptile skin and porcupine needles. Next to the sitting room was a dining room with a long table and benches built from coffins. There was also a small library that seemed more like a zoo because all the books growled and hissed behind cages. The kitchen was in the basement—or at least, Lucy thought it was a kitchen. Instead of pots and pans, the room had a variety of cauldrons, and instead of a traditional pantry, it had shelves of colorful elixirs and grotesque ingredients.

"This place is so dreary it's almost charming," Lucy said.

"Thank you," Mistress Mara said. "I've put a lot of work into it."

"Have you always lived here?"

"I've lived so many places over the years I've lost count. When I decided to open a school of witchcraft, I looked for the perfect location, and Ravencrest Manor was exactly what we needed. It was originally the home of our benefactors, Lord and Lady Ravencrest. The couple didn't have any children to leave the property to, so they kindly donated it to us."

"Wow, that's one heck of a gift," Lucy said.

"It was so generous even *they* couldn't believe it," the witch said.

As they toured the different chambers, Lucy noticed each room had the same illustration drawn on the wall. It was of a black goat with long horns and a short beard, and the illustration had such an inquisitive expression Lucy was convinced there was a soul behind its eyes. She examined it closely and gasped—*the illustrated goat suddenly moved and roamed across the wall!* Apparently, the manor didn't have the same illustration in every room, but *one illustration* that moved *from* room to room.

"What the heck is that?" Lucy asked.

"Oh, that's just Old Billie," Mistress Mara said. "She's an illustration that lives in the walls. She's also a mischievous little creature, so try to stay away from her."

Like the lynxes outside, the goat watched Lucy with a level of curiosity that seemed strangely human.

"Why is she looking at me like that?" Lucy asked.

"Knowing her, she's probably hungry."

The witch snapped her fingers, and a quill appeared in her hand. She drew a patch of grass on the wall, and Old Billie gobbled it up. Lucy could have watched the living illustration all day, but Mistress Mara escorted her back to the entryway.

"How big is this place?" Lucy asked.

"The last time we counted, the manor had thirteen floors and seventy-seven rooms," the witch said. "Only one room is off-limits and that's my personal study on the seventh and a half floor."

"That's assuming I can find it," Lucy said.

Once again, Mistress Mara threw her head back and cackled at Lucy's joke. This time Lucy knew the witch was only pretending, but she appreciated it nonetheless.

"The girls are going to love your sense of humor," Mistress Mara said. "Now come with me and I'll show you to the bedroom. You'll be sharing a room with the other girls in the East Tower on the eleventh floor. Pay very close attention to how we get there—it's easy to get lost in a house like this. The maid went missing two months ago and we still haven't found her."

Lucy let out a nervous laugh. "Good help is hard to find," she said.

After six flights of stairs, four walkways, and three windy hallways, Mistress Mara and Lucy finally arrived at the East Tower on the eleventh floor. The witches' bedroom door was shaped like a star and there was a sign pinned to it that said WITCHES ONLY—NO WARLOCKS ALLOWED.

"Girls, are you decent?" Mistress Mara asked as she knocked on the door.

She and Lucy squeezed through the doorway and stepped inside the bedroom. To Lucy's surprise, instead of regular beds, the witches were lounging in large nests like a family of giant birds. The girls were dressed in striped pajamas and were in the middle of different activities when Lucy entered. Sprout was brushing her bushy green hair, Stitches was sewing limbs onto a knitted doll, Beebee was shaking a container of bugs, and Hareiet was braiding her long purple hair. Pip, on the other hand, seemed sad and was silently gazing out the window. Pip hadn't been at Ravencrest for a whole day yet, and Lucy could tell she was already homesick.

"Ladies, we have a special visitor," Mistress Mara announced.

"*Lucy!*" Pip was thrilled to see a familiar face. "What are you doing here? Are you joining Ravencrest?"

"To be determined," Lucy said. "I thought I'd stick my toe in the witch pond before I jumped in."

"Miss Goose will be spending a few days with us," Mistress Mara told them. "Let's all make sure she has a very enjoyable visit."

The witches had different reactions to the news. Stitches stared at Lucy like she was a new toy to play with. Beebee was so excited about another roommate she was practically vibrating. Sprout seemed completely indifferent about Lucy; in fact, she was more interested in a piece of lint floating through the air. Hareiet wasn't happy about the situation at all—she crossed her arms, and her nose twitched with suspicion.

"Mistress Mara, are you sure this is a good idea?" Hareiet asked. "She's part of the Fairy Council—the Fairy Godmother probably sent her to spy on us!"

"Then I'm certain she'll have nothing but *good things* to report back," Mistress Mara said.

"Actually, I was recently suspended from the Fairy Council," Lucy said. "I'm not sure if I'll ever go back to the Fairy Territory. There's some bad blood at the moment."

"*Blood is never bad,*" Stitches whispered.

"I hope you decide to stay with us," Pip said. "We were just getting ready for bed. Here, you can sleep in the nest next to mine."

"You're *getting ready* for bed?" Lucy asked. "But it's morning."

The girls cackled at Lucy's obliviousness.

"You don't know much about witches, do you?" Hareiet asked.

"We sleep during the *day* and stay awake *all night*!" Stitches said.

"B-b-because we're c-c-creatures of the moon!" Beebee stuttered.

"Actually, witches are just naturally nocturnal," Sprout noted. "You know, like bats, owls, moths, foxes, badgers, raccoons, mice, the northwestern hedgehog, certain breeds of tree frogs—"

"I think she gets the point, Sprout," Mistress Mara interjected. "Now, Lucy, why don't we get you something more comfortable to wear for bed? And maybe something more *appropriate* to wear around the manor?"

Mistress Mara guided Lucy to the back of the bedroom and she stood in front of a wardrobe with a mirrored door. They stared into the mirror for a few moments, and just when Lucy was about to ask what they were waiting for, the wardrobe popped open on its own. Hanging inside were a pair of pajamas, a black cloak with a pointed hood, and striped stockings in Lucy's size.

"Well, unless you have any other questions, I think I'll head to bed myself," Mistress Mara said "Everyone try to get some rest—we've got a *long* night ahead of us. Good day."

"Good day, Mistress Mara," the witches said in unison.

After Mistress Mara left the bedroom, Lucy changed into her pajamas and sat on the edge of her nest. The witches watched her in complete silence and Lucy suddenly felt like a lamb in a lion's den.

"Sooooooo," she said to break the tension. "Tell me about yourselves. How did you guys end up at the Ravencrest School of Witchcraft?"

"I don't see how my life is any of your business," Hareiet said.

"I was abandoned at b-b-birth," Beebee sputtered. "I b-b-bounced from orphanage to orphanage until Mistress Mara f-f-found me."

"My parents are just extremely open-minded," Sprout said. "They had no problem with me joining a school of witchcraft. They were happy I had a reason to get out of the house."

"My family was *mauled to death by bears*!" Stitches was excited to share. "Then the bears were *shot by hunters!* And then the hunters were *attacked by wolves*! I had to hide in a hollow log for *nineteen hours* before it was safe to come out! And the whole thing happened on *my birthday*!"

"Gosh, that sounds traumatic," Lucy said. "I'm so sorry."

"Don't be," Stitches said with a creepy grin. *"It was the best day of my life."*

Lucy could tell Stitches was proud of how uncomfortable she was making her. Her abnormally wide mouth curved into a creepy grin and she winked at Lucy with her small eye.

"Hey, you want to know *why* they call me Stitches?" she asked.

"Absolutely not," Lucy said.

After the first round of questions, the bedroom went silent again. Lucy looked around the room, desperate to find something to talk about. She noticed each of the witches had a unique collection on the shelves above their nests. Hareiet was growing a small vegetable garden in pots, Beebee kept a variety of insects in small containers, Stitches had an assortment of knitted dolls, and Sprout collected jars of what Lucy *hoped* was dirt.

"It looks like you guys have hobbies," Lucy said. "Hareiet, do you enjoy gardening?"

"*Obviously*," Hareiet snapped.

"And Beebee, you like to collect bugs?"

"It m-m-makes me feel p-p-powerful," she said.

"Sprout, are those containers of *soil* I see?"

"Oh no—it's fertilizer."

"Excuse me?"

"I grew up on a farm," Sprout said. "The smell reminds me of home. You know what they say, you can take the girl away from the fertilizer, but you can't take the fertilizer away from the girl."

"And *Stitches*," Lucy said to change the subject. "Tell me about your dolls! Are they significant to you?"

Instead of answering, Stitches lunged toward Lucy and plucked a strand of her hair. The witch carefully sewed the hair into the head of her doll, then closed her eyes, and whispered an incantation. When it was finished, Stitches began poking the doll with her sewing needle.

"Can you feel that?" she asked.

"Feel what?"

"How about *this*?"

"Um . . . no?"

"What about *that*?"

"I feel *annoyed*, does that count?"

Stitches sighed and tossed the doll aside. "Then to answer your question, *no*, my dolls aren't as significant as I wish they were," she said.

Lucy noticed the witches were still wearing the

golden necklaces with white moonstones that they wore yesterday in the Fairy Territory.

"What's up with your necklaces?" Lucy said.

"What's up with all your questions?" Hareiet asked. "Are you writing a book?"

"They just seem fancy, that's all," Lucy said. "I see everyone has a necklace except for Pip."

"That's b-b-because you have to earn it," Beebee said.

"Before someone is officially enrolled at Ravencrest, they have to pass four entrance exams," Stitches explained. "Mistress Mara tests their skills in jinxes, hexes, potions, and curses. Once you pass all the tests, she presents you with a golden necklace at your Enrollment Ceremony!"

Lucy was confused. "If you guys have done *that* much witchcraft already, why do you look so normal? Why hasn't witchcraft distorted your appearance like other witches?"

"Ooooooh, we have our secrets," Sprout teased.

"S-s-stick around and you'll s-s-see," Beebee said.

The witches exchanged a sly smile. Lucy knew they were eager to tell her, but the girls didn't spill any other details.

"Tell me more about Mistress Mara," Lucy said. "Where is she from? What was she up to before she opened Ravencrest?"

"We don't know much about her," Sprout said. "None of us knew her before the school opened—and that was only a couple of months ago."

"But we have *theories* about her," Stitches said, raising her eyebrows suggestively.

"Theories?" Lucy asked.

Stitches hurried to the bedroom door and peeked through the keyhole to make sure Mistress Mara wasn't standing in the hall. When the coast was clear, she took a seat beside Lucy.

"I'm sure you've noticed Mistress Mara has a unique specialty," Stitches said.

"You mean, her frightening but fashionable taste?" Lucy asked.

"No," Sprout said. "Everything she touches *dies!*"

"At first, we thought Mistress Mara was a witch with a *specialty for death*," Stitches said. "But now we're convinced she might be something *more* than a witch! Have you heard the legend about *the Daughter of Death*?"

"The Daughter of Death?" Lucy asked as she thought about the name. "Is that the undertaker in the Eastern Kingdom who runs the cadaver puppet show?"

"Not even c-c-close," Beebee said.

"Then I'm thinking of someone else," Lucy said. "Who's the Daughter of Death?"

"Oh, I know that story," Pip said. "When I lived at the Bootstrap Correctional Facility, the wardens used to talk about her to give us nightmares!"

"Would you care to fill me in?" Lucy asked.

Pip sat up straight and cleared her throat.

"According to legend, in the beginning of time, Death was very different than he is today. They say that he dressed like an angel, that he loved to sing and dance, and that he treated life with kindness. They say Death allowed every creature to live for one hundred years before escorting them to the other side. However, all this changed when *humanity* was created. Unlike the other species, humans always *grieved* the people they lost, despite all the years they had together. Death found this behavior extremely curious and he became desperate to understand it. So Death created a *daughter* and sent her into the world of the living. The separation made Death miss his daughter terribly and he finally understood what it was like to *grieve*. He looked forward to reuniting with his daughter once her hundred years of life were over.

"Unfortunately for Death, his daughter *liked* the world of the living. Over time, she learned how to avoid her father and *live forever*. On the day of her one-hundredth birthday, Death searched for his daughter everywhere, but he couldn't find her. Panicked, Death invented *disease* and *injury* to help him look, but his daughter was clever and knew how to avoid his inventions, too. Death was so distraught, he traded his angel wings for the black cloak he's infamous for. Although it's been thousands of years since he's seen his daughter, Death still hasn't given up hope, and he continues to invent new ways of finding her. Today, they say whenever Death takes someone before their one hundred years are up, it isn't because he's cruel—he's just searching for his daughter, and he takes people randomly in case she's wearing a disguise."

Even though the witches knew the story by heart, Pip's version was the most chilling they had ever heard.

"That was some s-s-seriously scary s-s-stuff," Beebee said.

"I'm going to have daymares now!" Sprout cried.

"Are you guys yanking my tail feathers?" Lucy chuckled. "I mean, you don't actually think Mistress Mara is the *Daughter of Death*, do you?"

"Of course, we do!" Stitches said.

"Have any of you just *asked* her?" Lucy asked.

The witches looked at Lucy like she was crazy.

"Why are fairies always trying to *solve* everything?" Hareiet grumbled. "Can't you people just enjoy a perfectly good mystery?"

Stitches let out a big yawn and stretched out her arms. "The Daughter of Death story always puts me right to sleep. We should go to bed before it gets too early."

The girls shut the curtains and lay down in their nests. Within a few minutes, the witches were fast asleep, but Lucy couldn't sleep after hearing about the Daughter of Death. She didn't know if the witches were serious or if they were just trying to scare her, but either way, they had given Lucy a lot more questions about Mistress Mara than she already had.

"Pssst, Lucy," Pip whispered. "How do you like Ravencrest so far?"

"It's hard to say," Lucy said. "I've only been here a couple of hours, and so far, I've been manhandled by possessed trees, insulted by talking gargoyles, stalked by a living illustration, and spooked by ghost stories about Death."

"I know, I know," Pip said. "It's not for everybody."

Lucy smiled. "Actually, I could learn to love this place."

CHAPTER SEVEN

A MISCHIEVOUS LITTLE CREATURE

E ven though Lucy hadn't slept a wink the night before, she was having a terrible time adapting to the witches' nocturnal schedule. She tossed and turned for hours in her nest but couldn't get comfortable—apparently nests had to be broken in like a new pair of shoes. Even worse, all her roommates snored like wild animals, and their constant belches and flatulence sounded like an orchestra of wind instruments that never stopped.

When it was around three o'clock in the afternoon, Lucy decided to search for a softer bed. She quietly snuck out of the witches' bedroom and tiptoed down the windy hall of the eleventh floor. The hall eventually split into three directions, and Lucy didn't know whether to take the spiral stairs going down, the crooked ladder going up, or the bridge that zigzagged ahead. As she weighed her options, Lucy had the unsettling feeling of being watched. She turned to the parchment wall beside her and jumped when she made eye contact with a dark figure that was glaring at her.

"Oh, hey, Old Billie," Lucy said. "You scared me."

The goat didn't move, but Lucy knew it was her from the liveliness in her illustrated eyes.

"Do you know where I could find a normal bed?" Lucy asked. "I mean, there's got to be a mattress in *one* of these seventy-seven rooms, right?"

The illustration stared at Lucy as if it was looking into her soul and then slowly nodded.

"Would you mind showing me where it is?" Lucy asked. "I'll sketch you a big, juicy patch of grass as a thank-you."

Old Billie suddenly sank through the floor and descended to the tenth story below. Lucy hurried down the spiral staircase to catch up with her. She followed the goat through the manor like she was being led through a giant maze. Old Billie took her down foyers that were slanted like slides, over walkways that were humped like camels' backs, and through corridors that were built completely upside down. They eventually came to a tall hallway with dozens of black doors that covered the walls like a checkerboard. Old Billie moved through the wall and brushed her horns against the door in the center of the farthest wall.

"So I'm assuming there's a bed behind the door?" Lucy asked.

The goat nodded eagerly. Lucy found a scaly armchair in the corner of the hallway and used it to climb into the open doorway. Once she was through the door, Lucy discovered a frightening office behind it. All the furniture and fixtures, from the desk to the chandelier, were made from human skulls. The walls were decorated from floor to ceiling with black masks, and each one was uniquely terrifying, as if they were all screaming with different expressions of pain and fear.

"Nope," Lucy muttered to herself. "No mattress is worth *this* nightmare."

As she climbed back out the door, Lucy saw something moving out of the corner of her eye. She looked up and saw that a door behind the skull desk had opened on its own. It was only open a crack but filled the office with an orange glow. The light was alluring, and before Lucy could talk herself out of it, she crept across the office and peered inside.

The door led to a long closet lined with shelves made from charred wood. Hundreds of glowing jack-o'-lanterns were displayed on the shelves, and every single pumpkin was carved with a different lifelike face. Lucy thought it was a strange collection to keep in a closet, so she stepped inside for a closer look. She peeked inside a few of the jack-o'-lanterns and saw that a black candle was burning inside each of them and that the wicks were burning at different heights and different speeds.

At the very end of the closet, set on a shelf of its own,

was a pumpkin carved with the face of a young woman. As soon as Lucy laid eyes on it, the jack-o'-lantern gave her chills. The young woman was eerily familiar—it was a face Lucy had seen many times before—but she couldn't recognize who she was off the top of her head. Lucy knew the young woman's name would come to her if she concentrated, so she leaned down and studied the carving.

"Aha! Gotcha!"

Lucy whipped around and saw that Hareiet was standing in the office behind her. The young witch's eyebrow was raised with so much suspicion it was practically floating above her forehead, and her nose twitched so wildly Lucy thought it might fly off her face.

"Hareiet, what are you doing in here?"

"The real question is, what are *you* doing in here, Lucy?"

Lucy shrugged. "I was looking for a mattress."

"Save your lies!" Hareiet exclaimed, and dramatically pointed at her. "As soon as I saw you were missing from the bedroom, I knew you were up to no good! And now I have proof! The Fairy Godmother sent you to Ravencrest to *spy* on us!"

"*What?!* I'm not a spy!"

"You expect me to believe that you stumbled into Mistress Mara's private study by *accident*?"

Lucy's eyes grew large and she nervously glanced around the chamber.

"Wait, *this* is Mistress Mara's private study?" she asked in disbelief. "Dang, I should have known that from the creepy masks! She decorates like an actor going through a breakup!"

"Don't act innocent, Lucy! I'm not as dumb as you think I am!"

"Hareiet, if you were *half* as dumb as I think you are, you wouldn't be able to stand and talk at the same time—but that's beside the point! I promise you this is a big misunderstanding! Honestly, I didn't even know I was on the seventh and a half floor!"

"*Mistress Mara! Mistress Mara!*" Hareiet shouted into the manor.

"*No, wait!*" Lucy pleaded. "*I'm telling you the truth!*"

"*MISTRESS MARA! MISTRESS MARA!*"

Suddenly, the study's windows were burst open by a powerful wind. The sound startled the girls and they both dropped to the floor. A cloud of smoke seeped inside and floated to the center of the room. The smoke began to swirl, growing thicker and thicker, and soon Mistress Mara appeared in the midst of the smoky vortex.

"*What are you two doing in my study?*" the witch roared.

"I was right, Mistress Mara!" Hareiet said as she got to her feet. "The Fairy Godmother sent Lucy to Ravencrest to spy on us! I caught her peeping around your private chambers!"

"*Lucy, how dare you!*" Mistress Mara hollered. "I give you a place to stay and this is how you thank me?"

Lucy knew she was in serious trouble. She wanted to tell Mistress Mara that Old Billie had brought her there, but the witch had specifically warned Lucy to stay away from the goat.

"I didn't know this was your study—I swear!" she said, and quickly thought of a different excuse. "It's my *specialty for trouble*—it's always sending me to places I shouldn't be!"

"She lies even worse than she spies!" Hareiet declared. "Don't believe a word she says, Mistress Mara! She broke the rules and deserves to be punished! *Punish her! Punish her! Punish her!*"

Hareiet was rabid with excitement, and an evil smile grew under her twitchy nose. Lucy curled into a fetal position on the floor while she waited for Mistress Mara's punishment. To the girls' surprise, the witch's anger faded and was replaced with curiosity.

"Did you say you have a *specialty for trouble*?" she asked.

Lucy nodded vigorously. "I've been causing strange and unfortunate things to happen for as long as I can remember," she said. "Actually, since *before* I can remember."

"Really?" Mistress Mara asked. "Do tell."

"Oh gosh, where do I begin?" Lucy asked herself. "For starters, when my mother was pregnant with me, a flock of ravens gathered outside my family's home and didn't leave until the night I was born. Then, when I was a baby, I caused all kinds of weird things to happen around the house. I made frogs appear in the bathtub every time my mother tried to bathe me, I used to levitate out of my crib whenever I took naps, and I even turned my stuffed animals' button eyes into *real eyes* that blinked and stared at people. And it only got worse when my family went into show business—I'm sure you've heard of the world-famous Goose Troupe."

"No," Mistress Mara said.

"Not once," Hareiet said.

Lucy frowned. "Well, you weren't our target demographic," she scoffed. "Anyway, my specialty would really show itself whenever we performed for tough crowds. This one time, we were in a pub in the Western Kingdom, and when the audience started booing us, I accidentally turned all their drinks into dog urine. Another time, we were doing our act for aristocrats in the Northern Kingdom, and when a lady yawned during my tambourine solo, I turned her hair into snakes! And then one night, we were doing a gig in the Southern Kingdom, and at the end of our performance, the theater manager refused to pay us. So I made the whole theater collapse!"

"My, my, my," Mistress Mara said. "How delightfully ghastly."

"My parents were worried something bad might happen to me if I stayed on the road, so they sent me to live with the fairies. And the rest is history."

"And all these incidences happened *unintentionally* without any magical training whatsoever?" Mistress Mara asked.

"Yeah," Lucy said with a sigh. "But even when I'm

not causing trouble, trouble has a way of finding me! My specialty is what guided me through the woods to your school, and now it's guided me directly into your study! Please don't be angry with me!"

Mistress Mara didn't seem angry at all; in fact, she was fascinated by everything Lucy had told her. The witch quietly rubbed her pale chin, like she was deep in thought about several things at once.

"We mustn't punish people for what they can't control; otherwise, we'd be no better than mankind," Mistress Mara said. "You're forgiven, Lucy, but just this once."

"Ah, gee, thanks!" Lucy said. "I promise it'll never happen again!"

Mistress Mara turned to Hareiet, scowling with disappointment.

"Unfortunately, the same can't be said about *you*, Hareiet," she said.

"Me?" Hareiet gasped. "What did I do wrong?"

"Lucy may have *accidentally* broken the rules, but you *intentionally* disobeyed me by following her inside my study," she said. "I'm sorry, my dear, but it's *you* who deserves punishment."

Mistress Mara crept toward her, and Hareiet fearfully backed away.

"But...But...But I was only trying to protect the school!" Hareiet proclaimed.

"I warned you about sticking your twitchy little nose in other people's business, Hareiet," the witch said. "If my words aren't enough to teach you a lesson, then perhaps *a curse* will."

Mistress Mara pointed at Hareiet, and the young witch was surrounded by a whirlwind of black smoke. As the smoke spun around her, Hareiet's appearance started to change. Her purple braids shrank into wispy ears, her skin was covered in dark fur, and her twitchy nose turned into a snout. Hareiet tried to run away, but she tripped as her hands and feet turned into paws. She tried to scream but a *growl* came out of her mouth instead. In just a few moments, Hareiet had completely transformed into a *lynx*!

"Now get out of my house and join the other animals outside!" Mistress Mara ordered.

Horrified, Hareiet jumped out the window and climbed down the side of the manor to the graveyard below. A jack-o'-lantern appeared on the floor where

Hareiet had been standing, and it was carved with a lifelike depiction of Hareiet's face. Mistress Mara hummed a pleasant tune as she scooped the pumpkin off the floor and put it with the others in her closet.

Lucy was mortified by the whole ordeal and was too frightened to speak.

"Don't be scared, Lucy," Mistress Mara said. "Hareiet made a grave mistake, and I wouldn't be a good teacher if I didn't enforce consequences. As long as you follow the rules of this house, you'll have nothing to fear. Besides, Hareiet's pompous attitude was starting to get on my nerves. It'll be nice to have a break from her."

"How long will Hareiet be a lynx?" Lucy asked.

"One hundred years," Mistress Mara said.

"*One hundred years?*" Lucy gasped.

"Lessons are like stones; the harder and heavier they are, the more they'll sink in."

"So are *all* the lynxes outside other people you've cursed?"

"My techniques may seem cruel, but I'm doing them a favor," the witch said. "Now they have a century to reflect on their poor decisions, and when they transform back into people, they'll be *better people* than they were before."

"And the pumpkins? Are they some sort of curse record?"

Mistress Mara smiled. "We'll save that for another time," she said. "*Trouble* may have guided you to my study, Lucy, but I believe you were guided to my school by something much greater. I'm confident Ravencrest can offer you more than the fairies ever could—that is, if you're willing to be *adventurous*."

Lucy was too afraid to turn the witch down.

"Sure," she said with a nervous quiver. "It'll give me something to do while I'm here."

"Splendid," Mistress Mara said. "Now you should go back to the eleventh floor and try to get some sleep while you can. Your and Pip's introduction to witchcraft begins tonight. I'll meet you and the other girls in the graveyard after dusk."

Lucy nodded and hurried out of the study, but Mistress Mara stopped her when she was halfway through the door.

"Oh, and, Lucy? Just one more thing before you leave," the witch said. "Don't take the mercy I showed you today for granted. If I catch you anywhere near this study again, you'll be spending the next hundred years hunting mice with Hareiet. Is that understood?"

Lucy gulped. "Yes, Mistress," she peeped.

Once she was out of the study, Lucy ran through the manor until she found her way back to the eleventh floor. She was panting so hard Lucy was afraid she might wake her roommates, so she leaned against the bedroom door and slid to the floor while she caught her breath. As she rested, Lucy spotted something moving out of the corner of her eye and saw Old Billie standing in the wall beside her.

"What the heck is your problem?" Lucy whispered. "I asked you for a bed and you almost got me cursed!"

The illustration beamed with confidence, as if the goat knew *exactly* what she had done.

"Well?" Lucy asked her. "Did I do something to offend you? Or do you just put people in danger for fun?"

Old Billie stared at Lucy for a few moments of silence, like she was trying to communicate something telepathically. Lucy could tell the goat had a *reason* for sending her to Mistress Mara's study, but she couldn't figure out what it was.

"You're trying to send me a message, aren't you?" Lucy asked. "There's something in that room you wanted me to see, isn't there?"

The goat walked down the hallway and disappeared from sight, but her confident gaze remained on Lucy as she went. Mistress Mara had warned Lucy that Old Billie was *a mischievous little creature*, but there was obviously much more than *mischief* on her mind....

CHAPTER EIGHT

JINXES AND HEXES

At six o'clock in the evening, the taxidermy clock in the entrance hall erupted with a bloodcurdling roar to wake everyone in Ravencrest Manor. Lucy was already wide awake and anxiously pacing across the witches' bedroom floor. The events in Mistress Mara's private study played over and over again in her mind, and each time she watched the scene unfold, the more questions and fears she developed.

Why had Old Billie sent Lucy to Mistress Mara's study? Was the goat trying to show her the closet of jack-o'-lanterns or was there something *else* Lucy had missed? Did Lucy actually *recognize* one of the carvings or was her exhausted mind playing tricks on her? And now that she saw how Mistress Mara punished her students, was Lucy foolish for staying at Ravencrest? Or was it more dangerous to leave and risk disappointing the witch?

As her concerns rose, Stitches, Beebee, Sprout, and Pip rose, too. The witches began to yawn and stretch in their nests as they slowly stirred to life.

"Good evening, everybody," Pip said. "How did you sleep?"

"B-b-blissfully," Beebee said.

"Like a log," Sprout said.

"Well, *I* had terrible *daymares* all day!" Stitches declared. "First, I dreamed I was swimming in an ocean full of man-eating *sharks*! And then I was chased up a tree by a pack of *lions*! And then I was plucked out of the tree by an enormous *hawk*! And then the hawk *dangled me* over the open mouths of her hungry babies!"

"I'm sorry, Stitches," Pip said. "That doesn't sound very restful."

"What do you mean?" Stitches asked with a wide grin. *"It was the best sleep I've had in months."*

Lucy's tired eyes darted back and forth between her roommates and Hareiet's empty nest. She didn't know how she was going to explain what had happened to Hareiet, and she worried the witches might blame *her* for it. Lucy felt like she might explode if she kept the news to herself for a moment longer and decided to just get it over with.

"Guys, something horrible has happened!" she blurted out.

Stitches, Beebee, and Sprout seemed rather *excited* by the announcement and scooted to the edges of their nests.

"Did we g-g-get termites?"

"Did my dolls move while I was asleep?"

"Did you make your own fertilizer?"

"No—and *gross*, Sprout!" Lucy said. "It's about *Hareiet*! Last night, I couldn't sleep in my nest so I went looking for another bed. I accidentally wandered into Mistress Mara's private study and Hareiet followed me inside! She thought I was spying for the fairies and tattled on me! Mistress Mara let me off the hook with a warning but *she turned Hareiet into a lynx for breaking the rules*!"

Pip shrieked but the witches were disappointed by the news.

"Well?" Lucy pressed. "One of your friends is going to spend the next century as a big cat! Doesn't that concern you?"

The witches exchanged smiles and giggled at Lucy.

"N-n-not really," Beebee said.

"Mistress Mara turns students into lynxes all the time," Stitches said.

"It happened to Deerdra, Collie, Wizabeth, and Jorilla," Sprout listed. "And Fincher, Dogatha, Hogbert, Smuggles, Camella, Pandy, Hylena, Rat Mary—"

"She g-g-gets the point, Sprout."

"I'm just bummed I didn't get to see Hareiet transform in person," Stitches said with a frown. "It always makes me warm and fuzzy on the inside when someone becomes warm and fuzzy on the outside."

"Who put her down on the lynx pool?" Sprout asked.

Stitches pulled out a large board from behind her nest, and the witches inspected a colorful chart drawn on it.

"Aw, man!" Sprout moaned. "Beebee wins again!"

"She *always* wins!" Stitches groaned. "How does she do it?"

"It's a g-g-gift," Beebee gloated. "Now p-p-pay up, witches!"

Sprout and Stitches begrudgingly handed Beebee a few gold coins each. Lucy and Pip couldn't believe what they were seeing.

"You guys make *bets* on who you think is going to be cursed next?" Pip asked.

"Yeah," Stitches said with a shrug. "Witches never miss the fortune in a misfortune."

Once they finished placing bets for the next lynx pool, all the girls changed into their black cloaks and striped stockings and went downstairs for breakfast. In the dining room, the invisible butler served them tarantula-leg stew and squid-ink smoothies. Lucy hadn't eaten since the day before, but after watching the hairy legs floating in her bowl, she didn't think she'd ever be hungry again.

"I know what you're thinking," Stitches said. "It needs more salt."

Lucy felt sick to her stomach and pushed her spoon aside.

"Are all the meals this *decadent*?" she asked.

"Oh yeah, the butler is a wonderful cook!" Sprout said. "He also makes great feetloaf, chicken-and-lice soup, stench fries, yak-and-bony cheese, beaver salad, ferret cake—"

"B-b-breathe, Sprout! B-b-breathe!"

"Sorry, I like making lists," Sprout said, and then tapped on her head. "It fills the space."

When the girls were through with breakfast, they gathered in the graveyard outside and waited for Mistress Mara to join them. The sunlight was fading fast, and the darker it got, the creepier and colder the graveyard became. The lynxes roamed through the grounds around them, and now that Lucy knew they were all *cursed people*, their prying eyes seemed even more eerie than before.

"Which lynx do you think is Hareiet?" Pip asked.

"Mhmmm," Lucy said as she glanced around. "Oh, definitely *that* one."

She pointed to a lynx that was lounging on a tombstone nearby.

"How can you tell?" Pip asked.

"Because a cat's never given me such a dirty look before."

Sure enough, the lynx was glaring at Lucy with human-level hatred. Lucy felt horrible about what had happened to Hareiet, and clearly, Hareiet blamed Lucy as much as Lucy blamed herself.

"It's ironic," Pip said. "They say curiosity killed the cat, but curiosity *turned* Hareiet into one."

Hareiet didn't appreciate the comment. She hissed at the girls and then dashed to the other side of the graveyard.

"At least she's not pussyfooting around her feelings," Lucy said.

Once the light had completely faded from the sky, a cloud of smoke blew out of an open window at the manor and floated to the center of the graveyard. The smoke swirled into a tall vortex, and Mistress Mara appeared inside it. The witches applauded their teacher's entrance, but Lucy took a timid step back.

"Welcome to witchcraft!" Mistress Mara declared with open arms. "Tonight, Pip and Lucy will discover talents they never knew they possessed, and they'll begin the first day of their authentic lives! However, before becoming a student at the Ravencrest School of Witchcraft, your abilities will be put to the test. Lucy and Pip must pass four entrance exams that represent the fundamentals of witchcraft—jinxes, hexes, potions, and curses. Once you complete the exams, you'll be officiated in our sacred Ravencrest Enrollment Ceremony under the next full moon. And then you'll continue your education with the others. Any questions?"

Pip raised her hand. "Why does the Enrollment Ceremony take place during a full moon?" she asked.

"Purely for *tradition*," Mistress Mara said, but the twinkle in her eye told another story. "You're both in luck because the next full moon is only two days away. Some girls have to wait weeks for it."

"I had to wait *two months* because it was cloudy!" Stitches said.

Lucy raised her hand next. "And what happens if we *don't* pass the exams?" she asked.

"Then I'm afraid Ravencrest is not for you and you'll be asked to leave," Mistress Mara said. "But neither of you should worry about that. The exams are merely a precaution to make sure my students are *capable* and *serious* about witchcraft. We don't want any impostors roaming through Ravencrest—at least, not on *two legs*."

Mistress Mara threw her head back and cackled at the remark. Lucy and Pip exchanged an anxious glance and laughed along with her.

"Now before we begin our first exam, I want you to forget everything you've been told about witchcraft," Mistress Mara said in a somber tone. "It's commonly believed that witchcraft is a vile, cruel, and demonic alternative to magic—but that is utter nonsense you must unchain yourself from. In truth, magic isn't any kinder, more pleasant, or more natural than witchcraft—it's simply *different*. Like darkness to light, cold to heat, and death to life, witchcraft and magic have their own unique purposes and importance, and they cannot exist without the other. So when someone says magic is better or worse, right or wrong, moral or immoral compared with witchcraft, they are *not* stating a fact but giving an opinion. And just because more people enjoy the daytime doesn't mean the night shouldn't exist. No, no, no—the planet needs the sun *and* the moon to work properly. So therefore, the world *needs witchcraft*, whether they like it or not."

Mistress Mara motioned toward the manor, and the invisible butler emerged through the front door. He carried a hefty wooden chest into the graveyard and placed it on the ground in front of Lucy and Pip. The butler opened the chest, and the girls saw it was full of pots and pans, combs and toothbrushes, tools and gears, pens and pencils, among several other household objects.

"Since fairies like to make *improvements* with magic, to keep a harmonious balance, it's a witch's job to make *impoverishments* with witchcraft," Mistress Mara said. "One of the ways we accomplish this is by performing *jinxes*. A jinx is an enchantment that temporarily alters an appearance, behavior, or function in a negative way. It usually lasts a couple of days and can easily be reversed with a little magic. For your first examination, you will each select an object from the chest and *jinx* it to appear, behave, or function abnormally. Pip, let's start with you."

Pip was a little nervous but mostly excited to do witchcraft for the first time. She dug through the chest and searched for the perfect object to bewitch. Eventually, Pip settled on a small hand mirror with a brass frame. She held it close to her chest, closed her eyes, and concentrated on how she wanted to jinx it. The hand mirror started to rust in her grip, and when Pip looked into it, instead of seeing her normal reflection, she saw the face of a wild boar.

"I did it!" Pip cheered. "I jinxed the mirror to show a hideous reflection!"

The witches gave Pip a polite round of applause.

"Holy scratch-and-sniff!" Lucy exclaimed. "Pip, look at your hands!"

The celebration was cut short when Pip glanced down. After performing the jinx, Pip's fingernails had grown three inches long and were as thick as animal claws. She screamed and dropped the mirror on the ground.

"*What's happening to me?*" Pip shrieked.

"Don't be alarmed, dear," Mistress Mara said. "It's just a little side effect of the witchcraft. But fret not, once you pass your entrance exams, your appearance will return to normal."

Pip was very embarrassed of her new nails and hid her hands in her pockets.

"Lucy, you're up next," Mistress Mara said.

Lucy was afraid to follow the witch's instructions. She wasn't a stranger to causing damage, but she had never before caused harm *intentionally* or without *good intentions*. What would happen when she mixed her specialty with witchcraft? How horribly would it affect *her* appearance? Lucy wondered if she could pass the exam *without* performing a jinx. She found a watch at the bottom of the chest and came up with an idea.

"*What's that over there?*" Lucy shouted.

She theatrically pointed toward the gate at the edge of the property. All the witches turned around to see what Lucy was referring to. While they were distracted, Lucy used her teeth to rip the dial off the side of the watch, and the gears stopped ticking.

"I don't see anything," Sprout said.

"What are you p-p-pointing at?" Beebee asked.

"Sorry, it was probably one of those moving trees," Lucy said. "Anyway, I finished my jinx. *Behold!* A watch that is frozen in time!"

Lucy presented the broken watch to the witches, but they weren't impressed. Stitches took the watch from Lucy and examined it with her bigger eye.

"Are you sure you used *witchcraft* to jinx this?" she asked.

"Of course I did," Lucy lied.

"Then why d-d-didn't the witchcraft affect you like P-p-pip?" Beebee asked.

"Yeah, you don't seem any uglier than you were before," Sprout noted.

Lucy groaned and adjusted her striped tights. "Actually, I think a nasty wart just popped up, but believe me, you *do not* want to know where it is," she said.

The witches weren't buying it. Mistress Mara wasn't convinced either, but surprisingly, she looked past Lucy's blatant dishonesty.

"Congratulations, ladies, you've both passed the first examination," Mistress Mara said. "Your next exam will test your *hexing* abilities, but hexes are more challenging than jinxes. They require *special participation*."

Mistress Mara whistled and the girls heard a loud *bang*. They turned toward the noise and saw Brick and Stone burst through the doors of a nearby mausoleum. The gargoyles dragged a man and a woman behind them whose hands and feet were wrapped in chains. Brick and Stone placed the prisoners on the ground in front of Mistress Mara. They trembled in her presence.

"*Please, don't hurt us!*" the man pleaded.

"*We have children!*" the woman cried.

Mistress Mara rolled her eyes. "Children, children, children," she said. "Why do people always bring up their children when they're caught doing something wrong? If you *really* loved your children, you wouldn't have tried stealing from me in the first place!"

She snapped her fingers, and the couple were silenced by two black cloths. Lucy had a horrible feeling in the pit of her stomach about whatever was going to happen next.

"This man and woman are grave robbers and were recently caught raiding the tombs on my property," Mistress Mara said. "For your next examination, you will alter their appearance, behavior, or functionality with a hex. Now, a hex is just like a jinx but it's applied to a living thing. Hexes can range in severity, but there's really no point if it's subtle or easily remedied. Remember, *if it can be cured by a doctor, then don't even bother.* Pip, would you like to go first?"

Lucy could tell Pip didn't want to hurt the couple but still wanted to prove herself to Mistress Mara. The grave robbers shook their heads and mumbled frantically, begging her to stop, but Pip stepped toward the couple anyway and waved a hand over their frightened faces. The witches heard two pairs of *pops* but couldn't tell what had changed.

"Am I missing something?" Stitches asked. "How did you hex them?"

"I gave them each two left feet," Pip said.

Sprout and Beebee removed the grave robbers' shoes to be certain. The grave robbers let out muffled screams when they saw Pip's enchantment.

"That's not so b-b-bad," Beebee said.

"Are you kidding?" Pip asked. "They won't be able to dance or walk in a straight line! And if there's an emergency, they'll be running in circles for—"

Pip went quiet because she felt something itchy under her nose. Unfortunately, the hex had caused long whiskers to grow on her upper lip. Pip was mortified and covered her whiskers with her hands.

"Never be ashamed of your accomplishments, dear," the witch said. "Congratulations, Pip, you've passed your second examination. Lucy, it's your turn."

"But I don't want to hex them!" Lucy said. "Look, I know they tried to rob you, but they didn't do anything to me personally!"

"You're very mistaken," Mistress Mara said. "A crime against one witch is a crime against every witch.

And it's important we stand together and demand the world's respect! Without hexes, people would have no reason to fear us. Now go on."

Lucy didn't know how she was going to get out of this one—the witches were watching her like hawks. She reluctantly stepped toward the grave robbers, raised her hand, and summoned the most harmful—yet *painless*—hex she could muster. As if the grave robbers were being marked by invisible pens, the couple were suddenly covered in hundreds of awkward tattoos. Their skin was full of disproportionate animals, unflattering symbols, and motivational phrases that were misworded like *Live everyday like it's your past*, *The glass is always half bull*, and *Knowledge is powder*.

The witches didn't know what to make of Lucy's strange hex—even the grave robbers seemed more confused than scared.

Lucy shrugged. "What? It was the worst thing I could think of."

While she defended herself, Lucy felt a strange tingle at the top of her forehead. She ran her fingers through her hair and felt something unusually soft in her bangs. The witches pointed and cackled at Lucy when they noticed it, too.

"*What's going on?*" Lucy gasped. "*What's wrong with my hair?*"

"The witchcraft gave you *feathers*!" Stitches said.

"White feathers!" Sprout said.

"And they're f-f-fluffy, too!"

Lucy plucked a feather from her head and stared at it in utter horror. She retrieved Pip's mirror from the ground and saw that a patch of fluffy white feathers had appeared at the front of her hairline.

"Oh my God!" Lucy cried. "I look like a woodpecker!"

"It could be worse," Pip said, and pointed to her whiskers.

"Congratulations, Lucy, you've also passed the second exam," Mistress Mara said. "Give me a moment to clear our supplies and we'll move on to the next exam."

The witch twirled her fingers, and the grave robbers were suddenly surrounded in black smoke. As the smoke swirled around them, the couple were slowly transformed into lynxes. Once the transformation was complete, the chains slipped off their bodies, and the grave robbers dashed into the graveyard to join the other cursed felines. Two jack-o'-lanterns with lifelike carvings of their faces appeared on the ground behind the couple.

"Put them with the others," Mistress Mara instructed the butler.

The invisible servant scooped the pumpkins off the ground and headed inside the manor.

"Moving on," Mistress Mara said. "The next examination will test your potion-brewing abilities. Unlike jinxes and hexes, the potions examination doesn't require *witchcraft*, but instead will test your aptitude for following instructions and making measurements for—"

The witch was interrupted by the sound of galloping. In the distance, the witches saw someone approaching the manor on a black horse. Whoever it was, Lucy assumed they weren't a stranger to Ravencrest because neither the trees nor the gargoyles tried to stop them. When the visitor reached the iron fence, the gate automatically swung open and the horse entered the graveyard.

As the visitor rode closer, Lucy got her first good glimpse. It was a man, wearing a red suit that shimmered in the dark, but his identity was hidden behind a mask shaped like a ram's skull. The man dismounted his horse, tied its reins to a gravestone, and then approached Mistress Mara. The witch was anything but happy to see the visitor—in fact, his presence had made her tense. It was the first time Lucy had seen Mistress Mara look uncomfortable. Without saying a word to him, Mistress Mara nodded toward the manor, and the man headed for the front door.

"Forgive me, ladies," the witch told the girls. "We'll have to finish your entrance exams at another time. I'll see you again tomorrow after dusk."

Mistress Mara followed the man inside the manor without saying another word.

"Who was that?" Pip asked the witches.

"We're not sure," Sprout said. "We just call him the *Horned One*. He visits Mistress Mara every so often but she's never told us anything about him."

"He g-g-gives me the c-c-creeps," Beebee said.

"Me too," Stitches said, and her eyes fluttered. "It's so attractive!"

"What are we supposed to do now that Mistress Mara is busy?" Pip asked.

"If I were you, I'd search the grounds for some spotted fungi and purple-leaved shrubbery," Sprout suggested. "They might be helpful for your examination tomorrow—they always give potions a little extra kick."

"Thanks for the tip," Lucy said. "But first I'm going to go inside and try to do something about these feathers."

Lucy returned to the manor on her own and headed to the witches' bedroom. She was fairly familiar with the layout by now, but still, the labyrinth of staircases, bridges, and hallways was tricky to navigate by herself.

She was halfway across a corridor on the fourth floor when, out of nowhere, the corridor started spinning. It spun so fast Lucy became dizzy and had to hug the wall to stay on her feet. When the corridor finally came to a stop, it led to a completely different part of the manor than it normally did.

"What the heck was that all about?" Lucy asked, but no one was there to answer her.

Once she regained her bearings, Lucy found a circular chamber at the end of the corridor that she had never seen before. The chamber had thirteen doors that were all different shapes and sizes. As soon as Lucy took her first step inside the chamber, a door slammed shut behind her, locking her inside. She tried to go back but the door wouldn't budge.

"Hello?" Lucy called. "Is someone there?"

She pounded on the door but there was no response.

"Okay, this isn't funny anymore! Who's doing this? Is that *you*, Stitches?"

Still, no one replied—in fact, Lucy didn't hear a single sound come from another soul. It was as if the manor *itself* was playing a practical joke on her.

Lucy checked all the doors in the chamber, but all of them were locked. Just when she thought she would be trapped in the chamber forever, one of the doors suddenly opened on its own. Without anywhere else to go, Lucy cautiously peeked through the open doorway and found a very familiar hallway on the other side— *it was the hall outside Mistress Mara's study*! Before Lucy could turn around, the door slammed shut and pushed her into the hallway.

"No, I can't be here!" Lucy whispered. *"Whoever is doing this, you've got to let me back in! If I get caught anywhere near the seventh floor, Mistress Mara is going to—"*

Suddenly, Lucy heard footsteps coming from the study. She quickly dashed to a corner of the hallway and hid behind the scaled armchair. The Horned One stormed out of the study, and Mistress Mara chased after him.

"Wait! Don't leave!" she pleaded.

"I've given you months, and you've given me *nothing*."

"But we're so close! We can't stop now!"

"There is no *we*. Our alliance is over."

The Horned One spoke in a soft yet commanding whisper, but the horns of his mask amplified his voice to the volume of a scream.

"I understand your frustration, but I'm telling you, the curse is going to work this time!" Mistress Mara said. "This one is different—she was *born* to be the host! And the next full moon is a *blood moon*! When it reaches the center of the night sky, for a few brief moments, all of witchcraft will be heightened!"

"I can't waste any more time," he said. "The clan is growing restless. If they lose their faith in me, I'll lose *everything*."

"But you'll gain *nothing* if we don't work together," Mistress Mara said. "You do your part, I'll do mine, and by this time next week, you and I will be *unstoppable*. King Champion XIV will be gone, the Fairy

Godmother will be dead, and mankind will finally be held accountable for what they've done to us."

Lucy covered her mouth to silence a gasp. Mistress Mara had got the Horned One's attention now, and he stopped in his tracks.

"How much longer for the curse?" he asked.

"Three days," she said.

"And you're certain it'll take?"

"Positive."

The Horned One seethed and clenched his fists as he considered his options.

"Very well," he said. "But if you're wrong about the curse, I'll send the clan after you and your students. The Brotherhood will need *something* to occupy their time while I find another partner."

After the warning was issued, the Horned One proceeded down the hallway and disappeared from sight. Once he was gone, Mistress Mara's face filled with fear and she let out a desperate sigh. The witch returned to her study and locked the door behind her.

Lucy was so overwhelmed by what she had just witnessed, she felt like she was in the spinning corridor all over again. She had no idea how or why she had ended up in the hallway outside Mistress Mara's study again, but she was glad she had. Hearing that Brystal's life was in danger made all of Lucy's bitterness toward her fade away. The hard feelings were replaced with an urgency to return to the Fairy Territory and inform the Fairy Council about everything she had just learned. However, as Lucy planned her departure, she had a sudden change of heart.

"Wait a second, I don't need the Fairy Council's help with this—*I'm* going to save the day this time!" she whispered to herself. "I'll stay at Ravencrest, figure out exactly what Mistress Mara is up to, and then *I'm* going to stop her! And once I do, Brystal and the fairies will *beg* me to come back!"

Lucy nodded confidently—this was *her* moment to shine.

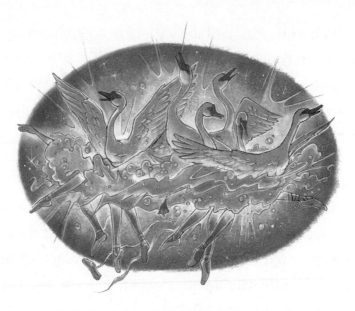

CHAPTER NINE

POTIONS AND CURSES

It was a good thing their closest neighbors were miles away, because the fumes wafting out of the Ravencrest chimney were anything but pleasant. The witches were in the kitchen brewing potions and wore clothespins on their noses to ward off the smell. For their third entrance exam, Lucy and Pip had each selected a recipe from an old book of potions and did their best to follow the complicated instructions. As they mixed the bizarre ingredients into their cauldrons, the potions bubbled and gleamed with bright colors.

"Remember to always stir counterclockwise," Mistress Mara said as she paced between them. "And make sure your measurements are precise. One lizard scale more, or one crow feather less, and your potion could end in disaster."

Lucy was trying to brew an Ease Elixir—a concoction someone could drink to make all of life's challenges seem easy—but ironically, the potion was incredibly complicated to create. Pip seemed much more confident with her potion and whistled while she chopped up a scorpion tail and sprinkled it into her potion. Lucy read her recipe over and over again, but it might as well have been written in a different language.

"'Four goblets of platypus broth, six chalices of donkey dandruff, three pickled peacock feet, one liberal leech, and an elfspoon of emu gizzard,'" she read. "What the heck is an elfspoon?"

"It's a quarter of a teaspoon," Stitches whispered.

"Don't forget to add eye of newt," Sprout suggested.

"It's like b-b-butter for witches," Beebee said.

"Girls, stop helping Lucy," Mistress Mara said.

"She's supposed to do this on her own. Stay focused on your own assignment."

While Lucy and Pip made potions for their exams, Stitches, Sprout, and Beebee were brewing something in a cauldron the size of a bathtub.

"What are you guys making?" Lucy asked.

"It's for the Enrollment Ceremony tomorrow night," Sprout said.

"Don't worry, you'll find out soon enough," Stitches said.

"Assuming you p-p-pass the exams," Beebee said.

At this point, Lucy wasn't sure she would. It was incredibly difficult to concentrate on the potion with all the questions she had about what she'd seen and heard the night before. What exactly were Mistress Mara and the Horned One planning? What kind of curse was the witch trying to produce? Why hadn't it worked before and why did it require a *host*? And most concerning of all, if Mistress Mara was successful, how would it put King Champion XIV, Brystal, and mankind in danger?

The questions were daunting and worrisome, but if Lucy failed the entrance exams and got kicked out of Ravencrest, she would never find the answers she needed to stop the witch. So she tried to quiet her troubled mind and put all her energy into finishing her potion.

Lucy went to the supply shelves for her missing liberal leech and elfspoon of emu gizzard. Finding the right ingredients was the hardest part of making potions. Lucy searched a pot of leeches for a *liberal* one, but she couldn't tell what their political views were. So she picked one at random. She didn't know which jar contained *emu* gizzard, because the majority of the ingredients were labeled GIZZARD. Lucy selected the gizzard that looked the most birdlike and hoped it was the correct one.

She added the leech and the gizzard to her potion and then double-checked the recipe's final instructions.

"'Yee whoth wish for completion, may doeth by bestowal of childhood remembrance,'" she read aloud. "Oh, I understand—to finish my potion, I have to give it a childhood memory. Well, I suppose I wouldn't miss remembering the time I—"

Suddenly, Lucy couldn't recall what memory she was talking about, but her potion bubbled with more intensity than before.

"I think I'm done," she announced.

"I just need one more second," Pip said.

She reached into her pocket and dropped in the spotted fungi and the purple-leaved shrubbery Sprout had recommended the night before. Pip's potion churned and turned bright blue.

"Finished!" she said.

"Fantastic," Mistress Mara said. "Pip, you had such wonderful beginner's luck yesterday, let's start with you. Tell us which potion you selected and give us a demonstration."

"I chose the Tooth Tonic," Pip said. "It's supposed to grow teeth on everything it touches."

Pip held up the wooden spoon she was using to stir the potion, and it was covered in dozens of human teeth.

"I guess it demonstrates itself," she said.

"Terrific work, Pip," Mistress Mara said. "Lucy? Which potion did you choose?"

Lucy lost confidence after seeing how successful Pip's potion was. Her final product looked nothing like the illustration in the book of potions. Instead of a smooth green liquid, the potion was brown and chunky. Lucy felt sick just from looking at it, so she improvised.

"Actually, I created my own potion," she said. "I call it an Indigestion Draft! It's guaranteed to give you the worst stomachache of your life! Would anyone like to try it?"

The witches glanced inside her cauldron and almost puked.

"No, thanks," Stitches said.

"We believe you," Sprout said.

"Good j-j-job, Lucy," Beebee said.

Mistress Mara eyed the potion with a doubtful gaze.

"Congratulations, girls, you've both passed your third exam," she said.

Lucy knew she wasn't fooling Mistress Mara, but once again, the witch had let her shortcoming slide. She didn't understand why Mistress Mara was turning such a blind eye to her failures—unless Mistress Mara had a *reason* for keeping her around. Whatever the reasoning was, Lucy was grateful for it—she had her *own* reasons for sticking around Ravencrest.

· • ★ • ·

Once the potions exam was complete, Mistress Mara took Pip and Lucy into the graveyard by themselves. Stitches, Beebee, and Sprout stayed behind to work on the potion for the Enrollment Ceremony. The invisible butler was waiting for them outside and held a black ceramic vase decorated with the face of a ferocious lion.

"For your fourth and final entrance exam, we'll be covering the most important part of witchcraft, and my personal favorite—curses," Mistress Mara told the girls.

Lucy and Pip looked to each other with anxious eyes, already fearing what the next examination might entail.

"Although the word itself has a negative connotation, a curse can be very positive depending on your point of view," Mistress Mara said. "Fairies pride themselves on rewarding good deeds, healing the sick, and giving to the needy—but not everyone deserves to be *helped*. On the contrary, some people deserve to be *punished* for their wicked ways. Too often, the same people get away with the same sins over and over again. When their cruelty goes unchecked, when the law fails to avenge the mistreated, and when the saying *What goes around comes around* isn't enough, then it's up to *us* to provide retribution. Sometimes a *curse* is the only source of justice.

"Curses are similar to jinxes and hexes, but much

more complex. They can be applied to the living or the inanimate, and occasionally, an entire environment. Curses can last for as long as you wish, and they are extremely difficult—if not *impossible*—to remedy with magic. They're fueled by anger, and the more pain and fury within us, the more powerful our curses can be. While plenty of *advanced curses* require very specific conditions to activate, the kind we'll be focusing on today only requires a bit of imagination."

Mistress Mara took the black vase from the invisible butler.

"For the next exam, we'll be taking a little *field trip*," the witch said. "This vase may seem small and unassuming, but it's a very powerful tool we call a Vex Vessel. With one drop of blood, the vase will bring you face-to-face with the person—or persons—who caused you the most physical or emotional pain. To complete the exam, you must vindicate your suffering by *cursing* the offenders from your past. It may be surprising to see *who* and *where* the Vex Vessel takes you to, and although the three of us will be traveling together, only *you* will be visible. Confronting the people who've hurt us is never easy, but I promise, nothing is more exhilarating than the empowerment you'll feel afterward. I find it's rather *addicting* to hold the corrupt responsible."

Mistress Mara raised the vase toward Pip, and the invisible butler handed Pip a pin. Pip cautiously peered into the vase like it contained a poisonous spider.

"Don't be scared, dear," the witch said. "Wherever it takes you, I'll be right by your side."

"Actually, I know *exactly* where it's going to take me," she said.

Pip took a deep breath, pricked her finger with the pin, and let her blood drip into the vase. The Vex Vessel suddenly became so heavy Mistress Mara had to set it on the ground. As if the vase had turned Pip's drop into a fountain, a geyser of blood shot out of it with the power of a volcano. The blood swirled through the air, completely surrounding them. Once the graveyard disappeared from sight, the blood returned to the vase, and the girls discovered they had been transported to a different part of the world.

Mistress Mara, Lucy, and Pip were standing on a hill in the middle of a dry and desolate plain. There was nothing but parched earth for miles around them except for one building that sat on top of the hill. It was a large, five-story structure with crumbling walls, broken windows, and a crooked chimney. The building was surrounded by a tall stone wall with spikes at the top.

"What is this place? A prison?" Lucy asked.

"Worse," Pip said. "It's the Bootstrap Correctional Facility."

Even though it was late, they found a man and woman doing chores in the yard. The man was shaped like an upside-down pear; he wore an unraveled bow tie and was hard at work patching a hole in the side of the building. The woman was taller than the man and shaped like a cucumber. She wore a lacy dress with a high collar and used a hoe to plow the dirt of a wilted vegetable garden.

The couple looked utterly exhausted—as if they hadn't had a good night's rest in years. The man took a break to wipe his sweaty brow and noticed Pip standing nearby. Just like Mistress Mara had said, Pip was the only one the couple could see.

Mr. Edgar scowled at Pip. "Where did *she* come from?" he grumbled.

His wife looked up and a matching scowl appeared on her face.

"The facility is closed," Mrs. Edgar said. "We don't take delinquents anymore. Go back to wherever you came from!"

The sound of their voices made Pip tense, like she was in the presence of two dangerous predators. She tried to run away, but Mistress Mara stopped her.

"You can do this," the witch said. "Make them *pay* for the anguish they caused you."

Pip closed her eyes and gathered up the courage to face them.

"Mr. and Mrs. Edgar?" she said. "It's Pip—Pip Squeak."

"*Who?*" the man scoffed.

"You don't remember me?" Pip asked.

Mrs. Edgar folded her arms. "Why should we?" she asked.

"Because—because I lived here for most of my life," Pip said. "I was the girl who kept sneaking out at night. . . . I used to squeeze through the bars on my door and wander the halls. . . . I used to borrow blankets from your closet—"

"Oh, she's one of *them*," Mr. Edgar told his wife.

The woman angrily tossed her hoe aside.

"How dare you show your face again!" she yelled.

"We were kind enough to give you a home! We tried to cure you of a demonic disease! And then you heathens ran off with the Fairy Godmother! You put good people out of work and put an honorable establishment out of business!"

"Honorable?" Pip asked in disbelief. "You abused hundreds of innocent girls! You starved us and forced us to work like slaves! You filled our heads with lies and made us ashamed of who we were! You're horrible, horrible people!"

"You *should* be ashamed!" Mr. Edgar said. "We lost everything because of you! And now we have to work day and night just to survive! *Get off our property at once*—um—*Skip Sheet!*"

"It's *Pip*!" she repeated. *"Pip Squeak!"*

All of Pip's trepidation quickly turned into rage. She'd thought about the Edgars every day since she left the facility and seen their faces in her nightmares every night. Pip would never forget the horrible things they had done to her, and yet, *they* didn't even remember her name. She clenched her jaw and stared daggers at the Edgars, and then all of a sudden, the ground started to rumble under their feet.

"That's right, Pip . . . ," Mistress Mara said. "Relive

all the painful memories.... Think about all the terrible things that happened here.... Feel all the sadness it caused you.... Let your anger rise to the surface.... And now, *unleash it*!"

The ground started shaking so hard the Bootstrap Correctional Facility began to sway. The Edgars grabbed hold of each other and could barely stay on their feet.

"She's bewitching us!" Mr. Edgar shouted.

"Lord help us—she's been sent straight from the devil!" Mrs. Edgar cried.

Pip let out an angry roar and reached toward the facility. Brick by brick, the building started to break apart, but the structure didn't collapse to the ground. Instead, the wreckage floated into an enormous pile, and as the pile rose higher and higher, it formed the silhouette of a giant monster. The wreckage came to life and growled at the Edgars. The couple screamed and ran away as fast as they could, but the monster stomped after them, chasing the Edgars into the horizon.

"Absolutely outstanding!" Mistress Mara said. "Equally victorious and vindictive! Congratulations, Pip, you've passed your final exam!"

Casting the curse had knocked the wind out of Pip, but she was thrilled to hear it.

"Wow," she panted. "You were right, Mistress Mara, *that felt great*!"

"How long will that thing be chasing them?" Lucy asked.

"One day for every girl they hurt," Pip said. "But who knows how long that'll take."

"As a matter of fact, you'll know *precisely* how long it takes," Mistress Mara said.

The witch gestured to two jack-o'-lanterns that had appeared on the lawn. The pumpkins had lifelike carvings of Mr. and Mrs. Edgar's faces. Mistress Mara collected the jack-o'-lanterns and handed them to Pip.

"These are called Curse Counters," the witch said. "One will appear after every curse you cast. If you're ever curious about the progress of your curse, just inspect the black candle inside. The candles burn as long as the curse is still active. The higher the wick, the more time the curse has left."

"What should I do with— *AAAHHH!*"

Pip suddenly dropped the pumpkins and fell on her hands and knees. She screamed in agony as a large bump appeared at the base of her spine. It grew bigger and bigger by the second until something hairy ripped through the back of Pip's cloak. She glanced over her shoulder and was horrified to see she had grown a bushy black-and-white tail.

"*The curse turned me into a skunk!*" she exclaimed.

"Don't let the side effect ruin the moment, dear," Mistress Mara said. "That was one of the finest entry-level curses I have ever seen. You should be nothing but proud of yourself. And I guarantee the Edgars won't forget the name *Pip Squeak* after tonight."

"More like *Pip Stink*," Lucy said under her breath.

Mistress Mara turned toward her. "That brings us to you, Lucy. Are you ready to prove yourself with the final exam?"

"I suppose so, but that was a tough act to follow," she said.

Unlike Pip, Lucy didn't know *who* or *where* the Vex Vessel was about to take them to. She pricked her finger with the pin, and her blood dripped into the vase. Once again, a geyser erupted from the vase and wrapped around them. When the parched landscape was completely covered, the blood rapidly returned to the Vex Vessel, and they found themselves in a new location.

Mistress Mara, Lucy, and Pip had been transported to the backstage of a theater. They were standing between a row of cardboard trees and a backdrop of a scenic lake. Ahead of them, two enormous red curtains had been drawn shut, and the girls saw the shadows of seven people dancing on the other side. They could hear the rustle of a large audience beyond the dancers, and somewhere close by, a live orchestra was playing classical music.

Lucy recognized the venue immediately. "Oh no," she gasped. "We're in the Old Spinster Theater in the Eastern Kingdom! They must be in the middle of a show!"

"Who?" Pip asked.

Lucy gulped. *"The Binkelle Sisters!"*

The music momentarily stopped playing, the dancers struck a pose, and the audience gave the performers a round of applause. As the praise died down, seven tall and lean ballerinas slipped through the curtains. They were all very beautiful and wore elegant white tutus.

"Okay, girls, we have two minutes to change for act three!" said the tallest one.

The Binkelle Sisters headed for a rack of black tutus

but came to a halt when they noticed Lucy standing backstage.

"Hey! No fans allowed backstage until after the show!" said the smallest one.

Lucy gave the ballerinas an awkward wave. "Hi there, Gina, Lina, Mina, Nina, Tina, Vina, and Zina," she said. "It's *bina* long time. Remember me?"

"Wait a second—is *that* who I think it is?"

"Oh my gosh, it *is* her! It's *Fat Lucy*!"

"She's still living?"

"We haven't seen you in years! Or should I say *meals*!"

"We've missed you, Fat Lucy! Where have you been?"

"Besides lunch!"

The Binkelle Sisters burst into a fit of giggles. Lucy blushed at their mean comments, and her bottom lip quivered. Being near the ballerinas made Lucy feel like she was eight years old all over again. For the first time in years, Lucy's trademark wit and sarcasm abandoned her, and she didn't know how to defend herself.

"No, I don't perform as much as I used to," Lucy

said. "I was living in the Fairy Territory for a while, but recently I've been looking for a change."

"Of what? *Pants?*"

"So what brings you here, Fat Lucy?"

"Are you getting back into show business? Or did someone mention dessert?"

"Unfortunately, we don't have any openings—*that you could fit through*!"

"You could always be a wrecking ball!"

Lucy's eyes filled with tears and she looked to the floor. "Actually, I've lost a little weight since the last time I saw you," she said.

"Don't worry, I'm sure you'll find it!"

"Have you looked under that double chin?"

The Binkelle Sisters laughed hysterically and couldn't stop themselves. Unbeknownst to the ballerinas, Mistress Mara strolled to Lucy's side and whispered in her ear.

"They may still be predators, but you aren't their prey anymore...," the witch said. "You're not the little girl they remember.... You've grown in ways they never will.... You've crossed bridges they wouldn't dream of stepping on.... Now, *prove it*."

Lucy had gone into this exam with deep reservations, but now she found herself agreeing with Mistress Mara—some people *deserved* to be cursed.

The orchestra played the opening notes of the third act, and as the music swelled into its crescendo, Lucy swelled into hers, too. She bit her lip and groaned at the chuckling ballerinas. Suddenly, the curtains flew open, the cardboard trees caught on fire, and the backdrop started to melt. The Binkelle Sisters stopped laughing and looked around in terror. The audience thought it was part of the show and sat on the edge of their seats.

Lucy pointed at the ballerinas one at a time and they started to spin out of control. As they spun, their necks stretched, their legs shrank, and their tutus began to molt. By the time the orchestra finished the climactic song, Lucy had transformed the Binkelle Sisters into *seven squawking swans*!

The audience was amazed and gave Lucy a standing ovation. It had been a long time since Lucy felt the warmth of applause, so she took a grand bow and basked in the affection. The audience threw roses at her feet, they cheered until their voices became hoarse, and they clapped until their hands were sore.

As seven Curse Counters appeared onstage, Lucy felt a tingling sensation on the top of her head. She dashed to a mirror in the wings and let out a horrified gasp. The curse had turned the rest of her hair—and even her eyebrows—into fluffy white feathers!

"What have I done?!" she shrieked. *"Now I look like a daffodil!"*

Mistress Mara appeared in the mirror behind Lucy and beamed with a sinister smile.

"Well done, Lucy," the witch said. "Not only have you passed your fourth and final exam, but you also gave the performance of your life. You're an inspiration to witches everywhere."

Lucy was mortified as she ran her fingers over her fully feathered head. She was still determined to stay at Ravencrest and stop Mistress Mara's secret plot, but until now, Lucy had never realized what *saving the world* might cost her. . . .

CHAPTER TEN

TEA WITH THE PRINCE

After their argument in the cavern, Brystal spent hours searching for Lucy in the Northern Mountains but didn't even find a footprint. So she raced back to her office at the academy and looked for Lucy's star on the Map of Magic. Eventually, she found it in the northwest corner on the border of the Dwarf and Elf Territories, and she immediately knew where her friend was. The discovery left Brystal so heartbroken she had to sit down.

Lucy joined the *witches*....

And it's all your fault....

Had you kept her in the council...

Had you just told her the truth...

She would still be here.

The next two days were some of the worst of Brystal's life. Even though she had been purposely keeping her distance from Lucy, not having her best friend close by made Brystal feel like she had lost part of her armor. She didn't want the other fairies to learn the details of their falling-out, so Brystal told them Lucy had gone to visit her parents, but lying only made Brystal feel lonelier than she already was.

Not having anyone to talk to about Lucy sent

Brystal down a spiral of guilt and self-doubt, and she wondered if she was even equipped to be the Fairy Godmother anymore.

You can't please your friends....

You can't protect them from the witches....

You can't stop the Righteous Brotherhood....

You can't prevent the laws from changing....

You can't even *think* positively....

You're going to ruin everything.

By now, Brystal was so used to the negative thoughts she hardly noticed the melancholy they caused—in fact, she barely felt anything at all. Brystal didn't eat or sleep, she didn't make plans or try to solve her problems, and she didn't even have the energy to brush her hair or change her clothes. She was depleted of all motivation, so Brystal just sat in her office hour after hour and watched the world go by without her.

Adding Lucy to her ongoing list of grievances had finally pushed Brystal over the edge. She wasn't just distraught anymore—Brystal was *horribly depressed*.

That morning, her office doors swung open and Tangerina, Skylene, and Xanthous walked in. Their faces were covered in flour, and they wore aprons doused in egg yolks and baking grease. It had been three days since Mrs. Vee retreated into her chambers and the housekeeper was still too frightened to come out. Without any other cooks on hand, Tangerina, Skylene, and Xanthous had had no choice but to take on Mrs. Vee's cooking responsibilities. After making breakfast for the whole Fairy Territory, the fairies looked as if they had been to war and back. They collapsed on Brystal's sofa and kicked their feet up onto her tea table.

"Well, breakfast was served," Xanthous said. "Or should I say, it served us."

"What a day," Tangerina said. "And it's not even noon yet."

"I'm never going to take Mrs. Vee for granted again," Skylene said. "When she comes out of her room, I'm going to compliment every meal she makes and laugh at every one of her terrible jokes."

"*If* she ever comes out," Tangerina said. "She locked her door and doesn't even respond when I knock!"

"Brystal, have you spoken with Mrs. Vee?" Xanthous asked.

Brystal was staring out the window, lost in a train of somber thoughts, and didn't hear his question. Xanthous cleared his throat and tried again.

"Brystal? Have you spoken with Mrs. Vee?"

"No," she mumbled softly.

"Have you found any new information about the Three Thirty-Three?" Tangerina asked.

"No."

"What can we do to help you?" Skylene asked.

"No."

Xanthous, Tangerina, and Skylene eyed one another with concern—clearly, something was wrong with Brystal. Before they had a chance to question her further, Emerelda entered the office. She held an envelope with a royal seal and carried it to Brystal with an urgency in her step.

"Brystal, a messenger just delivered this for you," she said.

Emerelda tried to give her the envelope, but Brystal wasn't responsive.

"Brystal, did you hear me?"

Still, Brystal didn't move a muscle or make a sound. Impatient, Emerelda pointed to the high ceiling and sent dozens of bright, screeching, emerald fireworks through the office. The sound made everyone jump, and Brystal snapped out of her trance.

"I'm sorry, did you say something?" Brystal asked.

"I said *this* just arrived for you," Emerelda said. "It's from the Champion Castle."

"Oh," Brystal said. "Just write back and tell them we aren't doing any public appearances right now."

"It's more of a *personal* request," Emerelda said. "Trust me, you'll want to read it."

Curious, Brystal took the envelope and read the letter inside.

Dear Brystal,

It was wonderful meeting you at Barrie and Penny's wedding. Aside from being attacked by a fleet of mysterious men and getting shot in the leg, I thought it was a lovely ceremony! How about you?

I'd like to invite you for tea at the Champion Castle so we can continue our conversation about *The Tales of Tidbit Twitch*. I'm free tomorrow at noon, but since I'm seventh in line for the throne and have nothing important do, anytime is also a good time for me.

If you're available, please send my messenger back with a date and time that work for you, but if not, you can just keep him.

Of course, I'm kidding—his wife would kill me.

Hope to see you very soon,

Sincerely,
His Royal Highness, Prince Gallivant
Victorious Heroic Courageous
Champion of Chariot Hills,

Duke of Southwestington, Lord
of Southeasternshire, Earl of
Southnorthernburry, and a bunch of
other things I can't remember at the
moment.
(AKA Seven)

Without realizing it, Brystal smiled and chuckled as she read Seven's letter. Her friends stared at her like they were witnessing a miracle—they couldn't remember the last time they had seen *anything* make Brystal happy.

"Who's the letter from?" Tangerina asked.

"A prince I met at my brother's wedding," Brystal said. "He invited me for tea."

The fairies became giddy, as if it was a much bigger deal than Brystal was letting on.

"Interesting," Xanthous said. "How old is he?"

"Close to my age," she said.

"Is he cute?" Tangerina asked.

"*Extremely*. But why would that matter?"

"Oh my gosh!" Skylene exclaimed. "Brystal got asked on a *date*!"

Her friends were thrilled to have something positive to talk about. Brystal waved their excitement off, like she was fanning the flames of a fire.

"It's not a *date*," she assured them. "We just really enjoyed talking to each other and have a lot of things in common and—" Brystal paused and thought about what she was saying. "Actually, it might be a date."

"Well, are you going to go?" Xanthous asked.

"Of course not," Brystal said. "There's too much going on and I haven't been feeling—"

Emerelda raised a hand to silence her. "Brystal, *you're going*," she said.

"What? But I can't!"

"Yes, you can," Emerelda insisted. "You've been moping around the academy since Pip ran off with the witches. I know we have a lot to worry about right now, but taking one afternoon off isn't going to make anything worse. All our problems will be waiting for you when you get back."

"Besides, if you don't have tea with the handsome prince, *I will*," Tangerina warned her.

Brystal groaned at the peer pressure. The twinkling northern lights on the globe caught her eye and she remembered her conversation with Madame

Weatherberry in the cavern. The fairy had told Brystal to surround herself with people who made her laugh and distracted her from her troubles. And at the moment, Seven seemed to be the only person in the world who made her feel anything but sorrow. The idea of seeing him again made Brystal excited, and she had forgotten what it was like to *look forward* to something.

"I suppose it wouldn't *hurt*," Brystal said.

Her friends were even more excited than she was and jumped up and down.

"What are you going to wear?" Xanthous asked.

Brystal shrugged. "Probably one of my pantsuits," she said.

"How are you going to get there?" Skylene asked.

"Probably by bubble. Why do you ask?"

The fairies seemed disappointed in her choices.

"Pantsuits and bubbles are just a little *basic*," Tangerina said. "I mean, *you're having tea with a prince*! You should wear a ball gown and take Madame Weatherberry's golden carriage!"

"I'll help you pick out an outfit!" Xanthous said.

"And I'll do your makeup!" Skylene said.

"Guys, the prince asked Brystal to tea because he

likes *Brystal*," Emerelda said. "She doesn't have to change anything about herself to please him."

Brystal was touched. "Thanks, Em," she said.

"You're welcome," Emerelda said. "But before you go, and I say this with love, you *definitely* need to take a bath and do something with that hair. When's the last time you brushed it?"

· • ★ • ·

The following morning at eleven o'clock, after bathing and *thoroughly* brushing her hair, Brystal departed the Fairy Territory for the Southern Kingdom. She drifted through the sky in a large bubble and landed on the front steps of Champion Castle at five minutes to noon. Brystal had tried to be discreet as she descended through the Chariot Hills town square, but as soon as the citizens noticed her bubble, they charged toward the castle. Brystal hurried up the steps to the entrance but a soldier stopped her before she could get inside.

"Name?" the soldier asked.

"Seriously?" Brystal asked.

The approaching crowd was screaming her name at the top of their lungs, but the soldier didn't seem to notice.

"No one gets in the castle unless they're on the list," he said.

"I'm the Fairy Godmother," she said. "I'm here to see Prince Gallivant."

The soldier checked his scroll. "Sorry, but I don't see your name," the soldier said.

"What about Brystal Evergreen?"

"No, that's not here either."

"There must be some sort of mistake. The prince invited me here personally."

"Sorry. No name, no entry."

Brystal nervously glanced over her shoulder at the crowd behind her and didn't know what to do. What other name could Seven have given him?

"What about the *Fairy Godsmacker*?" she asked.

"Welcome, Ms. Godsmacker, please come inside."

The soldier stepped out of Brystal's way, and she dashed into Champion Castle just as the excited citizens reached the front steps.

The entrance hall was decorated with red carpets and crystal chandeliers, the walls were covered in portraits of royalty from the past and present, and the hall was lined with soldiers in silver armor. Brystal found Seven waiting for her just beyond the front door. He was grinning from ear to ear, trying his best not to laugh.

"Trouble getting in?" he asked innocently.

"That wasn't funny," Brystal said.

"Then why are you smiling?"

"Okay, it was a *little* funny," she admitted. "You're lucky I'm not a vengeful person. I could easily turn you into a pig for that."

"But an *adorable* pig, I'm sure," he said with a wink.

Seven offered Brystal his arm and escorted her down the hall.

"I'm so glad you could join me," he said. "Have you been to the castle before?"

"A few times, but always for official business with your grandfather."

"Great, then I'll give you the *social* tour," he said. "As you can see by all the painted faces surrounding us, *this* is the Royal Portrait Gallery. Every member of the Champion dynasty gets an official portrait on their eighteenth birthday, on their wedding day, and on their coronation day if they're in line for the throne. And as you can tell by all the stoic expressions, the Champions don't like to smile."

Brystal was in awe of how many portraits there were.

"Your family is huge," she said. "Holiday shopping must be a nightmare."

"I have a lot of *relatives* but I wouldn't say I have a big *family*," he said. "The Champions are in constant competition with each other and they treat the line of succession like a food chain. They may exchange pleasantries here and there, but deep down, everyone secretly hopes someone will fall down a flight of stairs and move them closer to the crown."

"And I thought *my* family had issues," Brystal said. "If it's helpful, I don't think it matters what group you're born into. Sometimes family are the people we *choose* to be around. I learned that when I moved to the academy."

Seven smiled at the notion. "I think I'm making good choices so far," he said.

The remark filled Brystal's stomach with butter-flies, and her face flushed. As they walked down the gallery, Seven stopped to show Brystal the portrait of a teenage boy. He wore a crown that was too big for his head and a fur cape that barely fit him, and his eyes were wide with angst.

"This is my grandfather's coronation portrait," Seven said.

"He was so young," Brystal said. "Look how terrified he is."

"He was only sixteen when he became king. Can you imagine having that kind of responsibility at such a young age?"

Brystal laughed. "As a matter of fact, I can."

Seven cringed like he had accidentally offended her.

"Sorry, I keep forgetting who I'm with," he said. "I think that's what I like the most about you, Brystal. You're essentially the most powerful person in the world, and yet you don't carry yourself that way. Lesser people would let it go straight to their head, but you're surprisingly *normal*. I hope it's all right for me to say that."

"Don't apologize; it's refreshing to hear," she said. "I think that's what I like the most about *you*, Seven— you make me *feel* normal."

They continued down the gallery and passed the wedding portrait of a young couple.

"These are my parents on their wedding day," Seven said. "May they rest in peace."

"How did they die?"

Seven looked to the floor and sighed with a heavy heart.

"When I was three, we were traveling to the countryside when our carriage was attacked by an angry mob," he said. "I don't remember much besides all the screaming. My parents shielded me, otherwise I wouldn't have survived. They died trying to protect me, though. Maybe that's why I threw myself in front of the arrow at your brother's wedding—maybe protecting people just runs in my blood."

"I'm so sorry—I had no idea," Brystal said. "Is that how you got the scar on your face?"

The prince nodded. "It's a constant reminder," he said. "It could have been so much worse, though. Thankfully my grandfather took me under his wing and raised me like a son. Honestly, I don't know what I would have done without my grandpa Champs."

"Still, I imagine it was lonely growing up without your parents," Brystal said.

"I came up with different ways to keep myself entertained," he said. "Have you ever played the game And Now We Run?"

"No."

"Oh, it's simple."

Seven suddenly snatched the helmet off the soldier beside them.

"*And now we run!*" he exclaimed.

Before she understood what was happening, Seven had pulled Brystal down the hall, and the soldier chased after them. They charged down corridors, sprinted through sitting rooms, and bolted across ballrooms—dodging servants, leaping over furniture, and narrowly knocking over statues along the way. Brystal didn't understand the point of the game, and she felt sorry for the soldier running after them, but she couldn't deny how much fun she was having. She and Seven laughed the entire time and their adrenaline rose more and more as the soldier got closer and closer. They eventually became too tired to run any farther and they collapsed on lounge chairs in a drawing room. Seven surrendered the helmet, and the soldier returned to his post, swearing under his breath as he left.

"Those poor soldiers must hate you!" Brystal giggled.

"Without a doubt! But that game never gets old!" Seven laughed.

"I have to admit, I haven't had that much fun in months!"

"In that case, should we celebrate with some tea?"

The prince escorted her into a beautiful royal garden where a table had been set for two. While they enjoyed their tea, Brystal and Seven talked about every subject under the sun. They discussed politics and philosophy, history and the future, family and friendships, and of course, their love for the Tales of Tidbit Twitch series. Their tea turned into lunch, the lunch turned into dinner, and before they knew it, Brystal and Seven were being served a midnight snack.

Brystal was so grateful her friends had persuaded her to go. For reasons she couldn't explain, being near Seven made all her despair fade away. She wasn't plagued with fear or negative thoughts—on the contrary, she felt protected and happy in his presence. The world didn't seem as overwhelming or as difficult as it had before.

"I think we have an audience," Seven said.

He pointed to a window above the garden, and Brystal saw Prince Maximus glaring down at them. She couldn't tell how long the prince had been watching them but Maximus was clearly furious to see his nephew and his enemy getting along so well. Once he was spotted, Prince Maximus angrily shut the drapes and retreated from sight.

"I'll take that as my cue to leave," Brystal said. "I can't thank you enough for inviting me. Yesterday, I was convinced this was the worst week of my life, but now, I think it might be one of the best."

"I can relate," Seven said. "I've been feeling so negative lately—like my mind has been stuck in a rut I can't get out of—but being with you makes everything seem so much *brighter*. Does that make any sense or do I sound crazy?"

Brystal couldn't believe her ears—it was like Seven was reading her mind.

"I know *exactly* what you mean," she said.

In that moment, Brystal knew she and Seven had developed something much more than a friendship. It was unlike anything Brystal had experienced before, and she couldn't put her feelings into words, but she suddenly understood why poets and songwriters talked about *love* so much.

The prince escorted Brystal to the front steps of the

castle. It was so late, Brystal and Seven had the whole town square to themselves.

"It's a beautiful night," Brystal said.

"It is," Seven said. "Oh, and look—there's a blood moon tonight! They say those are supposed to bring luck."

"I think it already has," Brystal said with a smirk. "Well, I should say good night."

"Me too," Seven said.

The two stood for a few moments in awkward silence. Clearly, they both wanted the same thing to happen, but each was too afraid to initiate it. Slowly but surely, Brystal and Seven leaned toward each other. Brystal's mind went blank and her heart began to race as Seven's lips moved closer and closer to hers.

Unfortunately, they were interrupted by something moving in the distance. They turned toward the motion and spotted a man in a silver robe. The man crossed a corner of the town square, walking so softly his boots didn't make a sound against the cobblestones. Brystal and Seven hid behind a lamppost before the man noticed them. After a closer look, they saw that an image of a white wolf was stitched to the chest of the man's robe and that a silver mask was draped over his face.

"It's a member of the Righteous Brotherhood!" Brystal whispered.

"The what?" Seven asked.

"The men who attacked us at my brother's wedding—that's what they call themselves," she said.

"Where do you think he's going? Should I call the guards?"

Brystal went quiet as she thought about what to do. She knew the encounter presented them with a wonderful opportunity—but an opportunity to do what? How could she use the moment to her advantage?

"Don't call the guards," Brystal decided. "Even if we captured him, he couldn't give us the information we want. The Brotherhood is so secretive even *they* don't know who their fellow clansmen are."

"Then what should we do? We can't just let him get away!"

Suddenly, Brystal was struck with a dangerous idea.

"We should *follow* him," she said.

CHAPTER ELEVEN

THE ENROLLMENT CEREMONY

After a long night of cursing, Lucy and Pip returned to Ravencrest in the early morning and went straight to bed. It didn't matter how uncomfortable her nest was, Lucy was so sleep-deprived she passed out the moment her body became horizontal. That evening, the taxidermy clock didn't go off at six o'clock per usual, and Lucy slept into the night. When her eyes eventually fluttered open, she saw Stitches, Beebee, and Sprout standing at the foot of her nest, waiting for her to rise. The witches watched her with huge smiles and Lucy instantly felt uneasy.

"Can I help you?" she asked.

"Wakey, wakey, sleepy daisies," Sprout said.

Pip yawned and stretched in her nest. "What time is it?" she grumbled.

"Almost m-m-midnight," Beebee said. "Mistress Mara told us to let you two s-s-sleep in."

"Why?" Lucy asked.

"Because you're going to need all your strength tonight," Stitches said. "Now get up and get dressed. *It's time for your Enrollment Ceremony!*"

Lucy and Pip climbed out of their nests and changed into their cloaks and tights. They followed the witches through the manor, and when they reached the ground floor, the invisible butler was waiting by the door with five broomsticks.

"What are those for?" Lucy asked.

"We're meeting Mistress Mara in the forest," Stitches said. "She left early to set up the ceremony."

"And we're going to *sweep* our way there?" Lucy asked.

"No, s-s-silly, we're going to f-f-fly there," Beebee said.

"Witches fly on broomsticks made from the wood of *floating trees*," Sprout informed them. "The trees are extremely hard to find because they float away when their branches outgrow their roots."

"But why do witches make *brooms* of all things?" Pip asked.

Stitches shrugged. "They're multifunctional," she said. "And mops would just be obnoxious."

The girls each took a broomstick from the butler and then headed into the graveyard. As soon as they stepped outside, the girls were awestruck by the massive blood moon shining in the night sky. It was four times the size of a regular full moon and illuminated the land with a scarlet glow. Stitches, Beebee, and Sprout mounted their broomsticks, and one by one, the witches leaped into the air. The broomsticks carried them high above the manor, and they hovered in the sky while they waited for Pip and Lucy to join them.

"Come on!" Stitches called down to them.

"Don't be scared," Sprout said. "It's like riding a bike!"

"B-b-but hundreds of f-f-feet in the air," Beebee said.

Lucy and Pip straddled their broomsticks and nervously gripped the handles. They jumped as high as they could and the broomsticks pulled them into the sky toward the others. Once their feet left the ground, the magic broomsticks made their bodies feel as light as feathers, and they bobbed in the air above the manor's tallest tower.

"What a rush!" Pip exclaimed. "We can see the whole forest from here!"

"I feel like I just drank a barrel of Fabubblous Fizz!" Lucy said.

"Now hold on tight and try to keep up!" Stitches said. "We might hit turbulence."

The witches leaned forward on their broomsticks and zipped across the sky. Lucy and Pip copied the movement and zoomed after them. They soared over the Northwestern Woods at the speed of rockets, and the wind rushed past Lucy's face so quickly she could barely see or breathe. As they flew, the witches howled and cackled at the moon, their voices echoing through the forest below them.

Eventually, they saw a trail of steam drifting up from the woods ahead, and the witches descended toward the ground.

"How do you land this thing?" Lucy asked.

"Think heavy thoughts!" Sprout said.

Lucy thought of boulders, dumbbells, anchors, and how she packed her suitcase when she traveled, and sure enough, her broomstick glided toward the earth below. Once all the girls landed, they followed the steam through the woods and entered a small clearing. They found Mistress Mara in the clearing, hovering over a massive, steaming cauldron. The witch stirred a bright purple potion that was bubbling with energy.

A collection of drums, horns, and chimes drifted through the air around the clearing, as if the instruments were caught in a slow-moving cyclone. As soon as the girls arrived, the drums began to beat on their own, playing at the pace of a soft heartbeat.

"Welcome, ladies," Mistress Mara greeted them. "For thousands of years, witches and warlocks have embraced new brothers and sisters into their covens by performing a sacred induction ceremony. We will honor that age-old tradition tonight as we officially welcome you to the Ravencrest School of Witchcraft. The ritual once required animal sacrifices, contracts signed in blood, and the tears of enemies—but luckily, we've been able to *simplify* it over the years. Tonight, all we need is a little potion, a little music, and a little moonlight."

The witches cheered and the floating chimes shimmered. Mistress Mara gazed into the sky and saw the blood moon was directly above the clearing.

"The time has come," the witch announced. "Lucy and Pip, to finalize your enrollment, each of you will take the Oath of Witchcraft and then solidify the oath by drinking from the potion. I must warn you, once you take the oath, there is no going back. You will be fully committed to a life of witchcraft and must obey the oath until your last breath."

Lucy and Pip went stiff after learning about the oath. Trying to stop Mistress Mara and the Horned One had already cost Lucy her hair and eyebrows— what was she going to lose next?

"Pip, we'll begin with you," Mistress Mara said.

The floating drums started beating faster and louder, which only increased the girls' anxiety. Mistress Mara filled a goblet with the purple potion and raised it into the air to soak in the beams of moonlight.

"Pip, do you *vow* to always live authentically, do you *promise* to never compromise your potential, and do you *swear* to never suppress your true feelings, no matter what approval, popularity, or affection you may receive in return? That is the sacred Oath of Witchcraft, and to become a witch, you must pledge it here and now."

"In other words, *just be yourself*!" Stitches whispered.

Lucy and Pip were relieved the oath wasn't as menacing as they had feared.

"Well, that doesn't sound so bad," Pip said. "Yes, Mistress Mara, I pledge my allegiance to the Oath of Witchcraft."

The witch handed Pip the goblet and she drank the potion. According to her foul expression, the potion had a horrible taste, but Pip managed to down the whole thing.

"Nicely done," Mistress Mara said. "Lucy, please step forward."

The witch refilled the goblet and raised the potion toward the moon.

"Lucy, do you *vow* to always live authentically, do you *promise* to never compromise your potential, and do you *swear* to never suppress your true feelings, no matter what approval, popularity, or affection you may receive in return?"

"I mean, why stop now?" Lucy laughed. "Yes, Mistress Mara, I also pledge my allegiance to the Oath of Witchcraft."

The witch handed Lucy the goblet with an extra twinkle in her eye. Lucy drank the whole potion and nearly gagged from the bitter taste. Once the potion was finished, all the floating instruments erupted in a festive melody.

"The ceremony is complete!" Mistress Mara announced. "Congratulations, Lucy and Pip, you are hereby *enrolled* in the Ravencrest School of Witchcraft! To celebrate, the girls and I shall lead you in a traditional *midnight dance*! Ladies, remove your necklaces and reveal your true selves to the moon!"

At her command, Stitches, Beebee, and Sprout pulled their golden necklaces over their heads. As they removed the jewelry, the witches transformed into creatures that Lucy and Pip had never seen before. Stitches's skin turned into patches of burlap that were stitched together, her eyes became red and blue buttons, and her orange hair changed into orange yarn. Two antennae grew out of Beebee's forehead, a pair of wings popped out of her back, and a stinger stuck out of her backside. Sprout's bushy green hair became an actual bush, her fingers and nose grew into long vines, and her skin filled with chlorophyll and turned green.

Mistress Mara removed her golden necklace next. The witch's pale face became paler and paler, her arms and legs shrunk thinner and thinner, and her torso became hollow. After a lifetime of witchcraft, Mistress Mara's authentic appearance was a *skeletal figure*!

Lucy and Pip were shocked and terrified as they watched their roommates and teacher morph into the giant doll, the large insect, the overgrown plant, and the skeleton before them. Apparently, the witches *had* been affected by witchcraft after all—*their golden necklaces had just been disguising it*!

The witches danced around the cauldron as the floating instruments played on. As the potion coursed through Lucy's body, she started to feel funny. She became dizzy and unstable, as if the ground were moving under her feet. Her vision went blurry and distorted, and the witches looked like *monsters* as they twirled, hopped, and skipped around her. She glanced to her side and could tell Pip was feeling the same way.

Both of the girls suddenly collapsed to the ground.... They tried to get up, but they were too weak to stand on their feet.... Lucy and Pip reached for help, but the witches kept dancing, as if nothing were wrong.... Mistress Mara leaned over them, lowering her bony face close to theirs.... The witch waved her skeletal hands over their bodies and muttered an incantation, but Lucy couldn't make out what she was saying....

All she could hear were the blaring instruments swirling through the air.... All she could see was the blood moon shining above them.... All she could feel was the potion rushing through her veins....

And then everything faded to black.

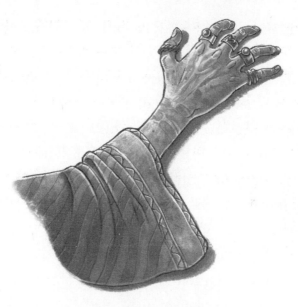

CHAPTER TWELVE

THE MEETING

Brystal and Seven followed the clansman through the empty streets of Chariot Hills. They darted from streetlamp to streetlamp and statue to statue as they went. Occasionally, the clansman would stop and glance over his shoulder, but he never noticed the teenagers trailing behind him. The pursuit continued into the countryside, and then, with only a few trees and fences to hide behind,

Brystal and Seven had to keep their distance so they weren't seen.

Once the clansman was a few miles outside the city, he lit a torch and journeyed off the cobblestone roads. Brystal and Seven crossed over hills, muddy fields, and shallow streams as they stalked him. The uncharted land was dark and difficult to trek, but thankfully, the blood moon illuminated the earth enough for Brystal and Seven to see where they were going.

A few hours later the smell of salt filled the air, and Brystal and Seven found themselves approaching the South Sea. The clansman headed for an enormous stone fortress on the beach at the base of a mountain, and just the sight of it put Brystal's stomach in knots. It was ancient and built out of crumbling stone. Five towers stretched into the sky like the fingers of a decaying hand, and sharp rocks hung over the drawbridge, making the entrance seem like the mouth of an enormous creature.

The beach was swarming with other clansmen gradually trickling in from different directions. Brystal pulled Seven behind a tall sand dune to stay hidden.

"That fortress must be the Righteous Brotherhood's headquarters!" Brystal whispered.

"We need to get inside and find out what they're up to," Seven whispered back. "Can you change our clothes into robes like theirs?"

"Yes, but it's too dangerous for us both to go," she said. "I'll sneak inside and see what I can learn. You stay here, and if anything happens to me, hurry back to the castle and tell your grandfather."

"Excuse me? I'm pretty sure *I* saved *you* from these guys last time," he said. "Dangerous or not, I won't let you go in there alone. The world can spare a prince, but it only has *one* of you."

Even in the current situation, Seven's remark made Brystal blush.

"All right, we'll go together," she said. "But changing our clothes won't be enough. There are exactly three hundred and thirty-three members of the Brotherhood. I'm sure they'll notice if two extra clansmen show up."

"So we've got to take out two clansmen before we go inside?" he asked.

"Right."

Brystal waved her wand and transformed their clothes into the Brotherhood's silver robes. Although she knew it was Seven under the robe and mask

293

beside her, just being near someone in that uniform was unsettling. They peeked over the sand dune and waited for an unsuspecting clansman to walk by. When one finally crossed the beach in front of them, Brystal pointed her wand at him, and the clansman was suddenly knocked unconscious. He fell face-first onto the sand, and Brystal and Seven dragged him behind the dune. Once they had their first victim, they peered over the dune and waited for the second.

"This is kind of fun," Seven whispered. "It's almost like we're hunting them."

Brystal grinned under her mask. "It's nice to be the hunter for a change," she said.

Soon another clansman had the misfortune of crossing the beach nearby. Brystal put him to sleep and they heaved him beside the other.

"They'll be out for a couple of hours," Brystal said.

"Great, now let's go to the fortress," Seven said.

He headed toward the structure but Brystal lingered at the sand dune. She couldn't stop staring at the unconscious clansmen. Dragging them had pushed up their masks and exposed the bottoms of their chins. It was the ultimate tease and Brystal couldn't fight the desire to see the *rest* of their faces.

"Are you coming?" Seven asked.

"One second," she said. "I want to know who they are."

Brystal pulled off the clansmen's masks and gasped when their identities were revealed.

"What is it?" Seven asked. "Do you know them?"

"No," Brystal said. "I've never seen them before in my life."

"Then why are you so shaken?"

"Because *not knowing* them makes it worse," she said. "I've never said or done anything to these men, and yet they've devoted their whole lives to harming people like me. They have no reason to hate us, but they *choose* to hate us anyway. Of all the things in life to feel, why would anyone choose *hatred*?"

"I have no idea," Seven said. "But most people choose love. And that's why we're here—to make sure hate doesn't win."

Brystal nodded and put the masks back on the clansmen's faces.

"You're right," she said. "Let's go to the fortress and find a way to stop these creeps. If we get separated, we'll meet back here."

Determinedly, Brystal and Seven headed to the

fortress and joined a line of clansmen at the entrance. One by one, each clansman recited a password before being allowed to enter. When it was Brystal's turn, she gripped her wand under the sleeve of her robe and discreetly pointed it at the clansman guarding the entrance.

"You don't need a password from me or the man behind me," she said.

The enchantment made the guard's eyes grow wide and his pupils dilated.

"I don't need a password from you or the man behind you," he said.

"Good," she said. "Now tell me I look pretty and wish me a good night."

"You look pretty and I wish you a good night," he said.

The guard let Brystal and Seven through the entrance and they met up on the other side of the drawbridge.

"Great work," he whispered. "Did he genuinely think I looked pretty or was that your doing?"

"I thought it'd be a nice touch," she whispered back.

Brystal and Seven followed the clansmen through the structure and entered a vast courtyard in the center of the fortress. The majority of the Righteous Brotherhood had already arrived, and as they filed in with the others, Brystal lost track of which silver uniform belonged to Seven.

At around five o'clock in the morning, a flag bearing the image of a white wolf was hoisted from the tallest tower. A clansman with a crown of sharp metal spikes appeared and climbed to the top of a platform. Brystal instantly recognized him as the archer from her brother's wedding. The Brotherhood bowed to the man in the crown, and Brystal copied the movement— apparently, he was a superior.

"Welcome, my brothers," the archer said. "Time is only a luxury for the young, so I'll get straight to the point. Ever since we attacked the Evergreen wedding, there have been concerns growing among us. Many of you believe the Brotherhood is not doing enough, some say it is foolish to delay our next attack, and a few have lost faith in our Righteous King. While I've assured you his plan is still on track for success, my words have not been enough to convince you. So we have called this meeting tonight to finally put your qualms to rest."

"With all due respect, High Commander, the Evergreen attack was a failure!" a clansman shouted.

"*We could have killed the Fairy Godmother! Why did we retreat?*" said another.

"*Now the fairies know the Brotherhood is back!*"

"*We need to strike again before they strike us!*"

"*Why does the Righteous King make us wait like dogs?*"

The High Commander raised a hand to quiet the clansmen.

"All of your questions will be answered in due time, but *I* will not be answering them," the High Commander said. "For the first time, our gathering will be led by our commander in chief himself. He has decided to pay us a visit to address your concerns personally. So, without further ado, please welcome the *Righteous King.*"

Suddenly, the courtyard filled with a crimson glow as the Righteous King appeared on the platform. He wore a shimmering red suit and a matching mask that was shaped like a ram's skull. Brystal let out a quiet gasp when she realized why the Righteous King's clothing was glowing—*it was made from the same bloodstone as the Righteous Brotherhood's weapons*!

The clansmen greeted their Righteous King with

a generous bow, but Brystal could detect a sense of resentment in the air.

"Hello, my brothers," their leader said. "It's an honor to finally meet you face-to-face."

The Righteous King spoke in an authoritative whisper, but the sound was amplified through the horns of his mask and echoed through the fortress.

"*Why is your plan taking so long?*" a clansman asked.

"*You said you would be sitting on the throne by now!*" said another.

"*You promised to restore the Righteous Philosophy to the constitution!*"

"*You swore to destroy the magical community!*"

"*None of your promises have come to fruition! Why should we trust you anymore?*"

The Righteous King stood calmly and listened to the clansmen until all their complaints were voiced.

"I sympathize with your frustrations," he said. "You've all waited a long time—some of you have waited your entire lives—but do not confuse *patience* with *failure*, my brothers. I *will* sit on the throne of the Southern Kingdom, I *will* restore the Righteous

Philosophy, and together, we *will* destroy the magical community. But such conquests don't happen overnight and they cannot be achieved by force alone. If we want to succeed, we must strategize."

"*The Fairy Godmother should be dead!*" a clansman shouted.

"*Why did you order the High Commander to keep her alive?!*" asked another.

"*What sort of strategy is that?!*"

"Eliminating the Fairy Godmother is the key to our victory—but eliminating her *now* will lead to our downfall," the Righteous King said. "You forget she is just as *beloved* as she is powerful. If we want to destroy her, we must destroy her *popularity* first. If we don't give the world a reason to hate the Fairy Godmother before we kill her, they'll turn her into a saint, and her influence will live forever. That is why I ordered the High Commander to keep her alive at the wedding. The attack was never meant to be an assassination—it was only meant to *instill fear*. Fear leads to mistrust, mistrust leads to mistakes, mistakes lead to disapproval, and disapproval leads to demise. And I'm proud to say my plan is working beautifully. Soon, the Fairy Godmother will make the biggest mistake of her life, and she'll become the most despised person on earth. And once the world loathes her, we can annihilate her without consequence."

"What mistake?"

"What could make the world hate her so much?"

"My friends, this Brotherhood's greatest attribute is its *secrecy*," the Righteous King said. "The less I tell you, the less our enemies can interfere. All you need to know is that the Fairy Godmother is about to commit the *unthinkable*. In fact, she'll be so distraught over her own actions, the Fairy Godmother will *willingly* surrender herself to us! And once she does, the rest of my plan will fall perfectly into place. Have faith, and I promise, your patience will pay off."

The Righteous King's scheme was so far-fetched Brystal almost laughed at it. She could tell the clan wasn't convinced either.

"More false promises!"

"We should have never pledged loyalty to you!"

"If you're so confident, tell us when it will happen! Give us a time frame!"

"Didn't I mention it?" the Righteous King asked in a playful tone. "Oh, forgive me for burying the lead—it's all happening *tonight*."

A distrusting murmur swept through the courtyard. They wanted to believe him, but it all seemed too good to be true.

"That's right, my brothers, you heard me correctly," the Righteous King said. "Mark my words, by the end of this coming night, I will deliver *everything* I've promised you! The Fairy Godmother will be eliminated, King Champion XIV will be dead, I'll be seated on the throne, and the Righteous Philosophy will be *permanently* restored to the Southern Kingdom! Without the Fairy Godmother to guide them, and without the laws to protect them, nothing will stop us from obliterating the magical community once and for all!"

Despite his enthusiasm, the Brotherhood remained skeptical. The High Commander stepped forward to reassure the doubtful clan.

"The Righteous King is telling you the truth," the High Commander said. "This is not the time to be cynical, my brothers, because the moment we've all been waiting for is here at last. This gathering isn't just a meeting of the minds—*it's the dawn before battle*! This coming afternoon, we will march to the Fairy Territory and accept the Fairy

Godmother's surrender. And once we put an end to her vile regime, *the war on magic will begin!*"

The Brotherhood erupted with pure exhilaration. They roared so loudly the fortress rattled around them. The High Commander and the Righteous King climbed to the ground and hoisted the platform upward like a hatch. The courtyard filled with an even brighter crimson glow as the Righteous Brotherhood's arsenal of weapons was exposed. The High Commander distributed the weapons, handing out crossbows, arrows, swords, chains, and spears to the excited clan.

As the clansmen prepared for battle, Brystal slowly backed toward the exit. The men were so occupied with the weapons they didn't notice her slip away. She hurried through the fortress, and once she passed the drawbridge, Brystal broke into a run. She returned to the designated sand dune and kept a watchful eye on the fortress, hoping Seven would make it out in one piece. A few minutes later, a clansman raced out of the structure and joined her. Before he got too close, Brystal cautiously pointed her wand at the clansman, and he put his hands in the air.

"Brystal, it's me—it's *Seven*," he whispered, and removed his mask to prove it.

"Thank goodness," she said, and lowered her wand.

"What the heck did we just witness back there?" Seven asked. "Why would the Righteous King promise so many ridiculous things? Was there *any* truth to what he said?"

"There can't be," Brystal said. "Even if I did *commit the unthinkable*, as he said, I would never surrender to them!"

"I can't believe the Brotherhood would fall for such nonsense!"

Brystal went quiet as she replayed the Righteous King's words in her head.

"I'm not sure *all* of it was nonsense," she thought aloud. "We're forgetting there *is* someone who could easily take the throne and restore the Righteous Philosophy by the end of tonight. And they're just as hateful and old-fashioned as the Brotherhood."

Seven's eyes went wide as he came to the same conclusion.

"That was my uncle Max," he said. "I mean, who else could be the Righteous King? Maximus has hated magic his entire life, he doesn't think women should have rights, and he doesn't think the talking creatures should have territories! He's practically a walking Righteous Philosophy!"

"There's only one contradiction," Brystal said. "Maximus was at my brother's wedding when the Brotherhood attacked. Why would he go if he knew it would be dangerous?"

"That'd be obvious if you knew him like I do," Seven said. "Max is the most conniving person I've ever met—he thinks everything through a million times and always has a backup plan. Being at your brother's wedding makes him look innocent. It's the perfect alibi in case he was ever caught!"

Brystal nodded as all the pieces came together. "We've got to get back to Champion Castle," she said. "I think your grandfather is in danger!"

Brystal and Seven sprinted across the beach away from the fortress. When they were completely out of sight, Brystal transformed their uniforms back into their regular clothes. She surrounded herself and the prince in a large bubble and they flew over the Southern Kingdom. By the time they reached Chariot Hills, the sun had just started to rise. Brystal and Seven figured the king would still be asleep, so they headed straight to his chambers. As they descended toward Champion Castle, Seven pointed out the windows of his grandfather's bedroom, and Brystal landed her bubble on the king's balcony. They rushed inside and found the elderly king snuggled in his four-poster bed, sleeping facedown in his pillow.

"Gramps, you've got to wake up!" Seven said. "Something terrible is happening!"

The prince nudged his grandfather but the sovereign didn't move.

"Gramps, this is no time to be lazy!" Seven said. "We just uncovered a plot to kill you! We've got to get you someplace safe!"

Still, the king didn't move or make a sound. Seven pushed the sovereign onto his back and let out a horrified gasp. His grandfather's skin was as cold and pale as snow, and his body was as stiff and still as stone. The king's eyes were wide open, but there was no life behind his tranquil gaze. Seven was in shock and didn't want to believe what he was seeing, but Brystal knew exactly what had happened.

"*We're too late,*" she said.

"This can't be happening!" Seven shrieked. "I

just saw him yesterday! He was in good spirits—he seemed perfectly healthy! He couldn't have died on his own!"

"This isn't a coincidence," Brystal said. "Someone must be working with your uncle—they must have done something to him while we were at the fortress!"

"But what? There isn't a single scratch on him!"

Seven and Brystal searched the king's body but they didn't find an obvious cause of death. The only peculiar marks they found were ashy fingerprints on his right wrist—but the king couldn't have died from someone's touch alone . . . or could he?

"Brystal, you have to bring him back!" Seven cried.

"I can't bring someone back from the dead," Brystal said. "Even if I knew how, he would come back as something dark and unnatural—he wouldn't be the grandfather you remember."

"Then maybe there's still time to save him!" the prince said. "Try to restart his heart! Make him take a deep breath! Anything! *Please!*"

Brystal knew there was nothing she could do, but she appeased the prince anyway. She took a step back and raised her wand over the king's body. Just as she was about to perform a spell, the chamber doors flew open. Prince Maximus burst into the room with a dozen armed soldiers.

"WHAT THE DEVIL IS GOING ON IN HERE?" he shouted.

Seven glared at his uncle with the hatred of a hundred angry men.

"How did you get here so fast?!" he asked.

Maximus acted confused. "I was asleep next door until I heard shouting," he said. "What on earth are you two doing—"

"Liar!" Seven yelled. "We just saw you at the fortress! We know who you really are!"

"Seven, are you ill?" his uncle asked.

"Don't play dumb!" Seven shouted. "You did this to him! *You killed your own father!*"

"I beg your pardon?"

Maximus glanced at the deceased king and pretended to be shocked. Brystal could tell he had been practicing the performance—his tearful eyes looked genuinely devastated.

"They've murdered the king!" Maximus declared.

"We didn't murder anyone!" Brystal said. "Seven and I just got here!"

"Lies!" Maximus screeched. "I saw you both in the

courtyard just a few hours ago! And now I find you hovering over my father's body with your wand in the air! Any idiot could see what's going on! *Guards, seize them immediately!*"

The soldiers charged across the room and tackled Seven to the floor. Brystal defensively raised her wand, and the approaching soldiers backed away from her.

"Don't waste your energy—she'll never let you take her alive!" Maximus said, and then pulled one of the soldiers aside. "I want you to leave this room and inform everyone in the castle of what you've just seen! Send messengers and notify the papers! I want the whole kingdom to know *the Fairy Godmother was caught in the act of killing the king!*"

"*No! She didn't do anything!*" Seven yelled as he struggled to free himself from the soldiers' grip. "*My uncle did this! He's been plotting to kill him for months! Arrest him!*"

"And clearly, she bewitched my nephew in the process!" Maximus told the soldier he'd pulled aside. "Now go! Quick, before the Fairy Godmother enchants us all!"

The soldier hurried out of the bedroom. Brystal wanted to stop him, but she knew it would only make her seem more guilty. Maximus glared at her with a look of triumph in his eyes.

"I told my father to stay away from you, but he wouldn't listen," he said. "I've always known you people shouldn't be trusted! And now I have proof! When the rest of the world finds out what happened here tonight, they'll finally see you and the magical community for what you truly are—*a group of abominable, unnatural, power-hungry barbarians*!"

Suddenly, the Righteous King's outlandish plan didn't seem so outlandish anymore. Everything he had promised the Brotherhood was happening right before Brystal's eyes. Without a doubt, Maximus was going to claim the throne and restore the Righteous Philosophy as soon as the Southern Kingdom awoke. He was going to *destroy her popularity* by framing Brystal for the murder of King Champion XIV! And the *biggest mistake of her life* had been walking right into his trap!

"Brystal, you've got to get out of here!" Seven said. "The Southern Kingdom isn't safe for you anymore! You need to go back to the Fairy Territory!"

"No—I won't leave you!" Brystal said.

"Don't worry about me! You're the only person who can stop the Brotherhood!"

"Seven, I can't—"

"*Go!*"

There wasn't time to think of a better option. Brystal dashed to the balcony outside and flew away in a large bubble. She drifted back to the Fairy Territory without a plan and without a clue of what was going to happen next. The Righteous King had successfully outsmarted her, and the damage was so significant Brystal didn't know how she would ever recover.

CHAPTER THIRTEEN

THE MORNING AFTER

L ucy awoke with a jolt. She had been in such a deep sleep it took a couple of minutes for her senses to kick in. She found herself safe and sound in her nest at Ravencrest Manor, but she had no recollection of how she had got there.

The last thing she remembered was being at the Enrollment Ceremony.... She and Pip had drunk the potion and become dizzy.... They had lain on the ground as the witches danced around the clearing. . . . Mistress Mara had hovered over them, conducting a spell of some kind. . . . And then everything had gone dark.

She sat up and looked around the bedroom. It was light outside and the sun was peeking through the curtains. Stitches, Beebee, Sprout, and Pip were still asleep in their nests. The witches were wearing their golden necklaces again and all traces of witchcraft had been erased from their appearances. Lucy noticed Pip was wearing a necklace, too, and her whiskers, claws, and skunk tail had disappeared.

"Good morning, Lucy."

The unexpected voice made her jump. Lucy looked up and saw Mistress Mara standing in a shadowy corner of the bedroom. The witch stared at Lucy with a devious grin, and Lucy had a hunch Mistress Mara had been watching her sleep all night.

"Um . . . good morning," Lucy said. "What are you doing?"

"Just checking on you, dear," the witch said. "How are you feeling?"

Lucy had to think about it, and the answer surprised her.

"Actually, I feel great," she said. "Better than I've felt in a long time."

"Excellent," Mistress Mara said. "I'm happy to report the Enrollment Ceremony was a complete success last night. In fact, you *responded* to the ceremony better than any student I've ever had."

"Well, that's the first time I've been top of my class," Lucy said with a laugh. "What happened exactly? I don't even remember how I got back here."

"Don't be worried, the ceremony is always an *exhausting* process to new participants," Mistress Mara said. "You and Pip lost consciousness shortly after taking the Oath of Witchcraft. Once the ceremony was over, the girls and I brought you back and tucked you into your nest."

"I'm a little embarrassed—usually I can party with the best of them," Lucy said. "Did you cast a spell on us last night? I vaguely remember you standing over us and muttering an incantation of some kind."

Mistress Mara's smile faded—clearly, she wasn't expecting Lucy to remember *that* part.

"Just a minor spell of *protection*, my dear," the witch said. "Nothing to fret over."

Lucy rubbed the back of her head and discovered

something around her neck. She glanced down and saw *she* was wearing a golden necklace with a bright moonstone, too. Lucy hopped out of her nest and hurried to the wardrobe to see her reflection in the mirror. Not only had her hair and eyebrows returned to normal, but the necklace also made Lucy much *prettier* and *taller* than she had ever been.

"Holy makeover!" Lucy said in disbelief. "I look fantastic!"

"From now on, your necklace will conceal all traces of witchcraft and correct whatever you don't like about your appearance," Mistress Mara said.

"Gosh, I wish I hadn't cursed the Binkelle Sisters," Lucy said. "Their pointed jaws would have hit the floor after seeing me like this!"

"That reminds me," Mistress Mara said. "Brick and Stone asked if you could keep the swans somewhere besides the graveyard. Apparently, the lynxes have been trying to hunt them."

Lucy was so fixated on her new appearance she barely heard a word Mistress Mara said. She wanted to compare her new reflection with her old reflection and started pulling the necklace over her head. Mistress Mara lunged forward and stopped her before the necklace was removed.

"*Don't take it off just yet,*" the witch said in a panic.

"Why not?" Lucy asked.

"The enchantment needs a chance to *cook* first," Mistress Mara explained. "Give your new appearance a couple of days to settle in, then you can remove the necklace as you wish."

"In that case, I promise to keep it on," Lucy said.

Mistress Mara's devious smile returned to her face.

"Wonderful," she said. "Well, I'll excuse myself so you can admire your new appearance in peace. You've certainly earned it."

Mistress Mara strolled out of the bedroom and disappeared down the hall. There was something about the witch's attentiveness that made Lucy suspicious. As she adjusted her golden necklace in the mirror, the sensation grew in the pit of her stomach and became much stronger than a regular feeling—Lucy sensed *trouble.*

CHAPTER FOURTEEN

THE SURRENDER

Now look what you've done....

The Righteous King blindsided you....

You walked right into his trap....

You gave him *everything* he wanted....

You should be ashamed of yourself....

Ashamed.

Brystal was living the darkest hour of her life. After fleeing the Southern Kingdom, she returned to the academy and desperately tried to come up with a plan to stop the Righteous Brotherhood. Unfortunately, Brystal couldn't concentrate on anything but her disturbing thoughts, and her negativity did all the thinking for her.

How could you let this happen?

How could you be so *stupid*?

How could you be so *careless*?

How could you *fail* so miserably?

Now all your greatest fears are coming true.

As she paced across her office, word of King Champion

XIV's murder was spreading across the Southern Kingdom. Brystal's reputation was being destroyed, her integrity was being tarnished, and consequently, mankind was beginning to question their relationship with the magical community. She didn't know how to prove her innocence, she didn't know how to prevent the lies from spreading, and she didn't know how to stop the Righteous Brotherhood from succeeding any more than they already had. Brystal was completely powerless and incapable of finding a solution.

You'll never stop them....

You'll only make things worse....

The Righteous King fooled you once, and he'll do it again....

You're not clever enough to defeat him....

You need to *remove* yourself from the situation.

Brystal wished she *could* remove herself from the situation. She would have given anything to just disappear and make all her problems go away, but as she agonized in her office, the Righteous Brotherhood were marching toward the Fairy Territory. In just a few hours, the clan would arrive at the border and expect Brystal to surrender. The Righteous King had promised the Brotherhood she would concede *willingly*, so how would they retaliate when she refused? What sort of attack would they unleash? How was Brystal going to protect the fairies?

Why *not* surrender?

What's the point in resisting?

You'll only cause more damage if you don't....

You'll only put the fairies in more danger if you stay....

They'll be *better off* without you....

The *world* would be better off without you....

Do it for them.

At first, Brystal thought it was a preposterous idea, but the longer she dwelled on it, the more appealing it became. The Righteous King said the magical community would be easy to destroy, but what if he was wrong? What if they *thrived* under different leadership? Without Brystal in the picture, maybe the fairies would have a chance of *winning* the war on magic?

Yes...

That's right....

Surrendering isn't giving up....

Surrendering is the *solution*....

Don't let your pride convince you otherwise....

Surrender to the Brotherhood and all your troubles will go away.

Brystal couldn't deny how tempting the idea of ending all her troubles was. She was so tired her mind and body ached with exhaustion—even her *soul* felt tired.

Surrender and the fairies will be safe....

Surrender and you won't have to fight anymore....

Surrender and you'll be free from fear....

Surrender and the negativity will disappear....

Surrender and all the pain will go away....

Surrender and the nightmare will finally end....

Surrender, Brystal ...

Surrender.

Brystal imagined herself floating in a space of total nothingness—with no worries, no fears, no anxiety, no responsibility, no shame, no guilt—and it gave her the most peace she had had in months. Brystal humored the idea just to feel the serenity, and the more she entertained it, the more she started to seriously consider it. By the time the evening arrived, Brystal wasn't just considering a surrender—she was *longing* for one. And so the decision was made.

As Brystal planned her surrender, she was interrupted by a soft knock on the door. Emerelda stepped inside the office with a cheeky grin.

"Well, you were out pretty late last night," she teased. "How did it go?"

"Which part?" Brystal asked.

Emerelda laughed like she was kidding. "Your date with the prince, of course," she said. "We're all dying to know, but I told the others not to smother you."

Clearly, Prince Maximus's lies hadn't reached the Fairy Territory yet, and Brystal was envious of Emerelda's obliviousness. Brystal had almost forgotten that just a few hours earlier she and Seven had been *laughing* and *enjoying* themselves. She couldn't believe what a dark turn the world had taken in such a short amount of time. Their date seemed like a frivolous thing to discuss at a moment like this, so Brystal changed the subject without an explanation.

"Em, I have something I need to tell you," Brystal said. "It's important."

"Oh?" Emerelda asked with concern. "Did something bad happen on your date? Because if that prince acted like a jerk, I'll kick him right in his crown jewels."

"No, it has nothing to do with him," she said. "It's something I've been giving a lot of thought to lately. This isn't an easy conversation to have, so I'm just going to say it. If anything happens to me, I want *you* to take over."

Emerelda wasn't expecting such a somber topic.

"Me?"

"Who else could do it?" Brystal asked. "You're smart, sensible, extremely organized, and all the fairies respect you. You'll make a wonderful Fairy Godmother when I'm gone."

"*When* you're gone?" she asked. "Are you planning an early retirement or something?"

"No—it's just—life is unpredictable," Brystal said. "All it takes is a single second and the world as we know it could change forever. If something happens, I want you to be prepared. I don't want there to be any confusion over who's in charge. The fairies need to be unified or they'll never survive the days ahead."

"The days ahead?" Emerelda asked. "Okay, now you're starting to scare me. Why are you bringing this up now?"

"Please, just promise me you'll look after the fairies and keep them safe," Brystal said. "It would mean a lot to me if I heard you say it."

Emerelda scratched her head as she tried to make sense of what Brystal was saying.

"All right, I promise," she said.

Brystal closed her eyes and let out a deep sigh of relief. Having an official successor made her looming surrender seem much easier. Emerelda watched her closely and her concerns rose.

"Brystal, you look *tired*," Emerelda said. "When's the last time you slept?"

"Honestly, I don't remember," Brystal said.

"Why don't I give you some time to rest," Emerelda suggested. "Maybe later this evening, I can come back with some tea and we can keep talking?"

"I'd like that," she said.

"Great, I'll see you then."

Emerelda left the office to give Brystal some time alone—but Brystal had no intentions of resting. Sadly, Brystal knew she would be long gone by the time Emerelda returned.

Brystal waved her wand, and stationery appeared on her desk. She wrote Emerelda a letter with all the information Brystal had been keeping to herself. She told her everything she knew about the Righteous Brotherhood—where their fortress was located, the identity of the Righteous King, and his plan to frame Brystal for King Champion XIV's murder. Brystal told Emerelda to keep an eye on the northern lights on the globe, how the Snow Queen was trapped in a cavern deep under the Northern Mountains, and if the lights ever faded from the sky, it meant the Snow Queen had escaped. She confessed part of Madame Weatherberry was still alive and how to find her if Emerelda ever needed advice or guidance. Once the letter was finished, Brystal placed it in an envelope with Emerelda's name on it.

You're doing the right thing....

A lesser person wouldn't know when to quit....

Your sacrifice will ensure the fairies' survival....

Emerelda will be a much better leader than you....

She'll defeat the Righteous Brotherhood....

***She* won't make mistakes.**

It was getting late, and Brystal knew the Brotherhood would be arriving at any minute. She wouldn't need her wand anymore, so Brystal placed it on her desk beside the letter for Emerelda. She slowly made her way to the door and took one final look at her office.

"Good-bye," she said to the empty room. "I'm leaving you in good hands."

Brystal closed the office doors behind her and headed outside. She crossed the academy grounds, went through the hedge barrier, and waited for the Brotherhood on the other side. Shortly after she arrived, all 333 members of the clan appeared in the distance. The men were led by their High Commander and they cautiously approached Brystal with their weapons raised.

Suddenly, Horence charged through the trees atop his three-headed horse. The knight leaped to the ground and drew his sword, placing himself between Brystal and the clan.

"It's all right, Horence," she said. "You don't have to protect me anymore."

The knight was terribly confused. He looked back and forth between Brystal and the Brotherhood but didn't know what to do. Brystal moved past Horence and walked toward the clan, but she wouldn't let the knight follow her.

"I'm not here to fight you—I'm here to surrender," Brystal told the Brotherhood. "But this doesn't mean you've won. On the contrary, my surrender only ensures your downfall. The magical community is much stronger than your Righteous King thinks they are. They'll band together and won't need me to defeat you."

Even though the Righteous King had guaranteed her surrender, the Brotherhood were surprised by how easily Brystal was giving up. They cheered, their victorious roar echoing through the forest around them.

"You see, my brothers, I told you to have faith in the Righteous King," the High Commander said. "The Fairy Godmother is surrendering *willingly* just as he promised—she didn't even need the *extra incentive* he sent us with."

"What extra incentive?" Brystal asked.

The High Commander tossed a book at Brystal's feet. She glanced down and realized it was Seven's copy of *The Tales of Tidbit Twitch*. Her eyes immediately filled with tears at the thought of Seven as a hostage. Brystal should have known the Righteous King would have a backup plan in case she didn't surrender.

"What have you done with him?" Brystal asked.

"Come with us and you'll find out," the High Commander said.

Once again, Brystal closed her eyes and imagined herself floating through the peaceful space of nothingness. She craved the oblivion she pictured, and Brystal was convinced there was only one way to achieve it.

"Take me," Brystal said. "I don't care what happens to me anymore.... I'm tired of fighting.... I'm tired of *feeling*.... I just want it all to end...."

CHAPTER FIFTEEN

THE SHADOW BEAST

Brystal, I made us some tea," Emerelda said. "I hope you're hungry, because I brought some snacks, too. I couldn't find where Mrs. Vee keeps the good cheeses, but these should do."

Emerelda carried a tray of tea, cheeses, crackers, and fruits into the office. She was more than halfway across the room before she noticed Brystal wasn't there. Emerelda set the tray down on the desk and was surprised to find Brystal had left her wand and a note behind. Curious, Emerelda opened the note, but before she could remove the letter from the envelope, the doors swung open and distracted her.

Xanthous, Tangerina, and Skylene staggered inside, covered from head to toe in mashed potatoes. Their hands and arms were wrapped in bandages from all the burns and cuts that were inflicted while cooking. The fairies plopped down on the glass sofa and gave their aching bodies a rest. Emerelda tucked Brystal's note into her pocket to read later.

"How'd dinner go?" she asked.

"The chefs are more whipped than the potatoes, but I think we're getting the hang of it," Xanthous said. "It was the first time I didn't start a fire—you know, while *cooking*."

"I'm sure you're just being hard on yourselves," Emerelda said.

"Oh no, we're *terrible*," Tangerina said. "When Mrs. Vee cooks, it's like watching a conductor leading a symphony—all the cooking utensils float seamlessly around her and create a meal in perfect harmony.

When we cook, it's like watching an earthquake inside a hurricane."

"I think the utensils are starting to hate us," Skylene said. "I didn't realize *pots* could be passive aggressive, but today they wouldn't even hold water!"

"Skylene, you were using a colander!" Tangerina said.

"Oh," she said. "I'm glad it wasn't personal."

"Where's Brystal?" Xanthous asked. "We want to hear about her date with the prince."

"I was just wondering the same thing," Emerelda said. "She mustn't have gone very far—she left her wand on her desk."

"I hope she gets back soon," Tangerina said. "I'm so tired the only thing that could possibly energize me is some good old-fashioned royal gossip."

"*I'm* so tired I'm seeing spots," Xanthous said.

"*I'm* so tired I'm seeing swans," Skylene said.

The fairies gave her a peculiar look.

"Swans?" Tangerina asked.

Skylene nodded. "Yup—*seven* of them," she said. "And they're with a girl, too. And she's flying through the air on a broomstick. And she's got a big sack of something. Wow, this hallucination is very specific. I think the kitchen fumes are starting to get to me."

"I must be delirious, too, because I'm *also* seeing swans!" Xanthous said.

Everyone turned toward the window and realized it wasn't a hallucination. Soaring through the sky, heading straight for the academy, was a flock of swans and a young girl on a broomstick. The birds were tethered to the broomstick like balloons, and the girl carried a bulging bag with her. They flew closer and closer to the castle with no sign of stopping. The fairies dived behind the sofa as the procession crashed through the window and showered the office in broken glass. The broomstick snapped in half, and seven pumpkins burst out from the bag and rolled in every direction. The travelers somersaulted across the floor and collapsed in a pile.

"*Ouuuuuuuch!*" Lucy groaned. "Dang, I could have sworn that window was open!"

She brushed all the glass off her body, released the swans from their tethers, and quickly gathered all the jack-o'-lanterns back into the bag. The fairies immediately recognized her voice but couldn't believe how different she looked.

"*Lucy?*" Emerelda gasped. "Is that you?"

"You look incredible!" Xanthous said.

"What happened?" Tangerina asked.

"Yeah, yeah, yeah—I'm basically a model now," she said. "Where's Brystal?"

"We don't know," Emerelda said.

"Crap! I can't wait for her! I'll need *you guys* to do it!"

Lucy raced to the bookshelves and feverishly searched through the titles. The fairies were confused— if Lucy's new appearance wasn't worrying enough already, her frantic behavior put them all on edge.

"Wait, *what* do you want us to do?" Skylene asked.

"Ooooooh, just a little favor," Lucy said with a nervous laugh. "Think of it as a fun group activity! A great way for us to bond and let bygones be—"

"Spit it out, Lucy!" Tangerina said.

"I need you to help me get rid of a curse!"

"*What?*" Xanthous exclaimed.

"Who's been cursed?" Emerelda asked.

"I have!" Lucy said. "But I don't have time to explain all the details!"

"Then you better make time!" Tangerina said. "You can't disappear for a week and then burst in here with swans, a bag of pumpkins, and a new face and ask us to help you get rid of a curse *without* an explanation!"

"Yeah! Even for you, that's just *eccentric*," Skylene said.

Lucy groaned again and paused her search to fill them in.

"Okay, okay, okay," she said. "Listen up, because I'm going to make this as short as possible. Four days ago, Brystal and I got into a really big fight, so I went to the Ravencrest School of Witchcraft for a couple days to tick her off. *Yes, I know that was a radical move; please hold your comments until I'm finished!* While I was at Ravencrest, I discovered Mistress Mara has been working on a secret plot to kill Brystal and destroy mankind! *Everyone's got a hobby!* I didn't hear all the specifics, but part of her plan involved casting a *curse* on someone. Apparently, Mistress Mara has been trying for weeks to perform the curse but hadn't succeeded yet. Naturally, I wanted to stop her, so I decided to stay at Ravencrest until I learned more. To become a student at Ravencrest, I had to pass four entrance exams—jinxes, hexes, potions, and curses."

Tangerina was appalled. "You did *witchcraft*?!" she asked.

"Lucy, how could you?" Skylene reprimanded.

"Forget the hocus-pocus and *focus*!" Lucy yelled. "Once I finished the exams, I had to participate in an Enrollment Ceremony. All my roommates had completed the ceremony before me, so I didn't think it was a big deal. But *now* I know it was never an Enrollment Ceremony at all—it was a front for Mistress Mara to curse people! She didn't start a school of witchcraft to help people—she opened Ravencrest to find someone to curse for her scheme! And I'm the first person it's worked on! *There, everything's explained! Happy now?*"

After she was done explaining, Lucy turned back to the books and continued searching through the shelves. The fairies were flabbergasted by her account and didn't know what comments to make or which questions to ask first.

"This is insanity!" Xanthous said.

"What kind of curse did Mistress Mara put on you?" Emerelda asked.

"That's what I'm trying to find out," Lucy said.

"And whatever it is, we've got to get rid of it before it puts Brystal and mankind in danger!"

"But you don't *look* cursed," Skylene said.

"No, you've never looked better," Tangerina said. "No offense."

"That's because my necklace hides all traces of witchcraft," she said. "Mistress Mara gave it to me after the Enrollment Ceremony. She told me to keep the necklace on for a couple of days so the enchantment had a chance to settle in. *But that was another fat lie!* Mistress Mara didn't want me to see how the curse was affecting me! Thank goodness my sixth sense for trouble kicked in! If you think I look different now, just wait until you see me without the necklace!"

Lucy became frustrated as she scanned the shelves.

"It's got to be here somewhere!" she said. "I remember seeing it the very first time I was in this office! I was looking through Madame Weatherberry's things while she was talking to my parents. It had such a strange title it immediately caught my—*oh, here it is!*"

Lucy pulled an old book off the shelf and showed the title to her friends:

SO, YOU'VE BEEN CURSED?

A VICTIM'S GUIDE TO DARK MAGIC AND HOW TO STOP IT

BY SHELTER BRIMCOCK

Lucy placed the book on the tea table, and the others gathered around her. She vigorously flipped through the pages, and hundreds of disturbing descriptions and gruesome sketches flashed before their eyes.

"There must be a thousand different curses in here!" Xanthous said.

"How are you going to know which one is yours?" Skylene asked.

"I know the side effects and I know the conditions it was cast under," Lucy said. "Keep an eye out for anything about a moon, music, potion, or excessive bloating."

"Excessive bloating?" Tangerina asked.

"Quit asking me questions and read!"

As she combed through the book, the fairies read over her shoulder and pointed out curses with the similarities Lucy described.

"Could it be a Nightmare Veil?" Emerelda asked. "It says, 'A Nightmare Veil is a curse that heightens and prolongs someone's nightmares. While they sleep, every second feels like a day, and whatever happens to their bodies in the dream happens to their bodies in real life. The curse is performed under a crescent moon and requires a pillow made of albino crow feathers.'"

"No, the Enrollment Ceremony happened under a full moon."

"What about an Infinite Illness?" Tangerina asked. "'An Infinite Illness is a curse that makes someone sick for decades. The person attracts germs and viruses from miles around, and they infect anyone who comes within a hundred yards of them.' It says the curse requires them to drink a green potion that's been coughed on by nine hundred senior citizens."

"No, the potion she gave me was purple."

"Do you think it's the Never-Ending Moisture?" Skylene asked. "It says, 'A Never-Ending Moisture makes someone's undergarments constantly feel wet, causing them to chafe and prune for eternity.' It says, 'The person leaves a puddle on every surface they sit on and a foul smell follows them wherever they go. The curse is performed on an overcast day while the children's song "Good-Bye, Rain" is played on a saxophone.' Oh, I love that song!"

"No—and I don't see how *that* would help Mistress Mara's plan."

"What about a Shadow Beast?" Xanthous pointed out. " 'A Shadow Beast is an entity that enhances a witch or warlock's powers for one, usually very dark, enchantment. The Shadow Beast is grown inside a host like a parasite, and the longer it stays inside them, the more powerful it becomes. To create a Shadow Beast, a witch or warlock must present the host with a potion made from the blood of a hundred different animals. They must drink it directly under a full moon while the percussion of a heartbeat is played. It takes a Shadow Beast twenty hours to reach its full form, and if it isn't removed before then, the host will die.' "

"That's it!" Lucy gasped. "That's definitely the curse she put me under!"

"What time did you drink the potion?" Emerelda asked.

"I'm not sure what the exact time was—I think it was around midnight."

"Then you only have a couple of minutes left before it kills you!" Tangerina said. "It's five minutes to eight o'clock!"

"Xanthous, does the book say how to get rid of a Shadow Beast?" Lucy asked.

"I'm looking, I'm looking," Xanthous said. "Yes, found it! It says, 'Expelling a Shadow Beast is not as complicated as producing one'—well, that's lucky— 'but it comes with its own difficulties'—never mind, spoke too soon. 'First, the host must be placed in a Circle of Purity'—which is a circle of salt, white sage, crystals, and candles. 'Second, the host must be surrounded by a group of loved ones. The loved ones must join hands and chant the phrases *Beast be seen, beast be wrong! Beast be free, beast be gone!* until the entity emerges.' That's all there is!"

"I'll make the crystals!" Emerelda said.

"I'll make the candles!" Tangerina said.

"I'll run to the kitchen and get the salt and the sage!" Skylene said.

The fairies split up to complete the tasks. Emerelda hurried to the snack tray on the desk and transformed the fruit and cheeses into crystals. Tangerina's bees flew out of her hair and used their honey to create a dozen beeswax candles. Xanthous and Lucy pushed the glass furniture to the side of the room and made an empty space in the center of the office. Skylene dashed to the kitchen and returned with an armful of sage and seasonings.

"Everyone ready?" Lucy asked the room.

"I've got crystals!" Emerelda said.

"I've got candles!" Tangerina said.

"And I've got the white sage and salt!" Skylene said. "I also brought pepper and rosemary, just in case!"

Lucy stood in the center of the room while the others made a circle around her with the supplies. Once the circle was complete and all the candles were lit, the fairies held hands—but Tangerina was hesitant to join.

"Come on, Tangerina!" Skylene said. "Lucy needs loved ones to expel the curse!"

"I'm not sure I qualify," Tangerina said. "*Love* is a really strong word."

"*Oh, shut up and find something to love!*" Lucy shouted. "*We only have a minute left!*"

Tangerina rolled her eyes and reluctantly joined them.

"Okay, I'm going to remove my necklace and

expose the curse," Lucy said. "What you're about to see is very disturbing, but whatever happens, keep repeating the chant until the Shadow Beast is gone!"

Lucy took a deep breath and slowly removed the necklace. As soon as the accessory was over her head, Lucy's hair turned back into white feathers, her appearance faded into its regular features, and her body expanded to its normal size. However, Lucy's body then surpassed her original height and weight and kept growing. Her black cloak started to stretch and her striped tights started to rip as Lucy blew up like an enormous balloon.

The fairies were shocked as Lucy swelled before their eyes. They could hear something growling inside her, and occasionally, the face of a ferocious creature would poke out from under her skin and snarl at them.

Lucy never stopped growing and the fairies worried she might explode. After a few seconds, Lucy was too big to stand on her feet and she fell backward. She bounced into the high ceiling and then ricocheted off the walls, knocking books and potions off the shelves as she went. The swans ran for their lives as Lucy bounced around them. The fairies chased after her and rolled her back into the Circle of Purity, but it was hard to keep her in place.

"We'll begin the chant on *three*," Emerelda said. "Ready? *One . . . two . . .*"

"Wait!" Lucy exclaimed, and the room went dead silent. "I've been thinking, maybe what we're doing is wrong? Maybe we should just leave the Shadow Beast inside me?"

"*Whaaat?*" Tangerina asked.

"You're joking, right?" Skylene asked.

"No, I'm being serious," Lucy professed. "I mean, the world is filled with people who have only *dreamed* of having Shadow Beasts, and here I am trying to get rid of mine. What if I regret this decision later? What if this is my last chance to have a Shadow Beast?"

The fairies couldn't believe what they were hearing.

"I think she hit her head while she was bouncing," Xanthous told the others.

"Lucy, if we don't get rid of the Shadow Beast, it's going to kill you!" Emerelda said.

"But who says my life is more important?" Lucy asked. "What if the universe has bigger plans for the Shadow Beast than it does for me? It's my own fault for going to the Ravencrest School of Witchcraft. I knew it was dangerous, I knew something might happen to me, but I went anyway. Why should the Shadow Beast be punished for my mistakes?"

"Lucy, you sound ridiculous!" Tangerina said. "You shouldn't throw your whole life away just because you made *one* mistake!"

"I agree," Skylene said. "Besides, you aren't ready to raise a Shadow Beast! You can barely take care of yourself!"

Lucy tried to roll out of the Circle of Purity but her friends wouldn't let her.

"No, let me go!" she said. "This is my life and I've made my decision! I'm going to keep the Shadow Beast and suffer the consequences!"

The fairies were floored by her abrupt change of heart. They looked to one another with wide, bewildered eyes, but no one could explain what was happening. Xanthous had a feeling Lucy's feelings weren't genuine. He retrieved the copy of *So, You've Been Cursed?* and reread the section about the Shadow Beast.

"Listen to this!" he said. " 'Never trust anything a host says while they're carrying a Shadow Beast. The entity plays tricks on its host's mind, making them believe they want to die for it, so the Shadow Beast will grow to its full size.' That's the Shadow Beast talking—not Lucy!"

"Then let's get this thing out of her before she knits it a sweater!" Tangerina yelled.

"Thirty seconds until eight o'clock!" Skylene cried.

"Quick! Start the chant!" Emerelda instructed.

The fairies grabbed hands and recited the chant in unison.

"Beast be seen, beast be wrong! Beast be free, beast be gone!"

For the first time since she removed the necklace, Lucy's body stopped expanding. The Shadow Beast started to howl from inside her, like it was trying to drown out the sound of the chant. The fairies raised their voices so the chant wasn't silenced.

"Beast be seen, beast be wrong! Beast be free, beast be gone!"

Lucy's body started to twitch and shake, as if the Shadow Beast was trying to find somewhere to hide within her. There were only ten seconds until eight o'clock, so the fairies repeated the chant as loudly and as quickly as they could.

"BEAST BE SEEN, BEAST BE WRONG! BEAST BE FREE, BEAST BE GONE!"

Suddenly, a dark vapor erupted out of Lucy's mouth. The blast was so powerful it knocked all the fairies to the floor. As the Shadow Beast was expelled, Lucy's body deflated and she shrank to her original size. The Shadow Beast whirled around the office like a black cloud, taking the forms of different carnivores as it moved. It smashed through the glass furniture as a bear, it terrorized the swans as a wolf, and it trampled over the bookshelves as a lion. The Shadow Beast leaped off the walls as a frog and then glided through the broken window as an eagle. The fairies ran after it, but by the time they reached the window, the Shadow Beast was out of their grasp. It soared through the sky and disappeared into the eastern horizon.

"Lucy, are you okay?" Xanthous asked as he helped her to her feet.

"My mouth tastes like a wet dog smells—but I'll live," she said.

"Oh my gosh! The Shadow Beast turned your hair into feathers!" Skylene cried.

Lucy pretended she was surprised. "No way!" she said. "That's totally what happened!"

"Look! The Shadow Beast is getting away!" Emerelda said.

"Where's it going?" Tangerina asked.

"It must be headed back to Mistress Mara!" Lucy said. "Come on! We've got to get to Ravencrest before she uses it!"

CHAPTER SIXTEEN

THE RIGHTEOUS REVEAL

The Righteous Brotherhood took Brystal away
from the Fairy Territory and led her into the
Southern Kingdom. They traveled for hours
and the clan kept their weapons aimed at her the entire
time. Brystal had no idea where they were taking her
or what they were planning to do with her, but she
didn't care. She didn't ask any questions, she didn't
keep track of time, and she didn't even look up from

the ground as they moved. Wherever they were going, whatever they did, Brystal knew it would all be over soon.

Brystal assumed the Brotherhood was taking her back to Chariot Hills. She imagined a theatrical arrest was waiting for her in the town square. She imagined Maximus would use the event to publicly condemn his father's "killer" and preach about the "dangerous nature" of the magical community. Brystal knew she wouldn't have a chance to defend herself—she'd probably be executed without a trial—she just hoped her peaceful surrender would make the Southern Kingdom think twice about the lies Maximus was spreading.

As the night turned into the early morning, Brystal realized her assumption was wrong. The smell of salt filled the air, and instead of Chariot Hill's cobblestone roads, *sand* appeared under Brystal's feet. She looked up for the first time since they had left the Fairy Territory and saw the South Sea ahead—*the Brotherhood was taking her back to the fortress*!

Brystal didn't understand the reasoning behind the decision. If Maximus's goal was to make Brystal a public enemy, why would the clan take her somewhere so secretive? How would it benefit them to keep her hidden?

The clan walked Brystal across the drawbridge and into the spacious courtyard at the center of the fortress. When they arrived, the Righteous King was waiting for them on the platform, and he held a loaded crossbow. The High Commander bowed before the Righteous King, and the rest of the Brotherhood followed.

"She surrendered willingly, my lord, just as you promised," the High Commander said.

"*We should have never questioned you!*" a clansman declared.

"*Forgive us for doubting you!*" said another.

"*You have our eternal allegiance!*"

"*Long live the Righteous King! Long live the Righteous King! Long live the Righteous King!*" the clan chanted.

As the Brotherhood showered the Righteous King with gratitude, Brystal noticed he wasn't alone on the platform. Five people were lying in a pile behind the Righteous King, and each of them was as white as snow and as stiff as stone. Brystal recognized the pale faces—they were Maximus's sons, Triumph, Conquer, Victory, Score, and Marvel. She impulsively ran to help them and none of the clansmen tried to stop her. Brystal climbed onto the platform and knelt at the princes' side, but unfortunately, there was nothing she could do—*all five princes were dead*!

Just like their grandfather, there was no obvious sign of what had killed them, but each prince's right wrist was covered in ashy fingerprints.

"You monster!" Brystal yelled. *"How could you kill your own children?"*

"Look closer," the Righteous King said. "There's more to this story."

Confused, Brystal turned back to the princes and discovered a *sixth* body was underneath them. She instantly felt sick to her stomach, and her hands started to tremble. She knew who the body belonged to without looking, but still, Brystal needed to see him for herself. She carefully rolled Prince Triumph onto his side to expose the sixth face beneath. But when his identity was revealed, Brystal gasped in horror because it wasn't who she was expecting—the sixth body wasn't Seven after all: it was *Maximus*!

Brystal was in shock and stepped away from the bodies. She glanced back and forth between the Righteous King and Maximus's body but didn't understand what was happening. If Maximus wasn't the Righteous King, then who was?

"Who are you?!" Brystal shouted. "What have you done with Seven?!"

The Righteous King chuckled at her reaction. He slowly removed his mask and answered both of her questions at once.

"*Seven?*" she gasped.

The discovery was so appalling Brystal's mind rejected it at first. It took her a few moments to realize her eyes weren't deceiving her, but even then, the reality was hard to accept.

"For the most powerful person in the world, you sure are gullible," Seven said.

"What are you doing?" she asked. "Why are *you* dressed like the Righteous King?"

Seven smirked and let out a patronizing laugh.

"Oh dear, you're really in denial about this, aren't you?" he scoffed. "I don't think it could be any more obvious—I *am* the Righteous King."

"No . . . ," Brystal said, and shook her head in disbelief. "This doesn't make sense. . . . You protected me from the Brotherhood at my brother's wedding. . . . We snuck into the fortress to spy on their meeting. . . .

We tried to save your grandfather.... We tried to *stop* them!"

As Brystal listed all the reasons it was impossible for Seven to be the Righteous King, it slowly dawned on her just how *possible* the truth was.

Seven had protected her at the wedding to gain her trust.... He had invited her to the castle because he knew they would end up following a clansman to the fortress.... He purposely slipped away from her during the meeting so he could address the clan as the Righteous King.... He exposed just enough of his plan so they would rush back to the castle to save his grandfather.... He led her directly into the king's chambers to frame her for his murder.... And all the while, Seven had convinced Brystal that Maximus was the Righteous King so she would never suspect *him*.

Brystal was so overwhelmed she almost fainted. The fortress felt like it was spinning around her, and she fell to her knees and started hyperventilating.

"It was *you* the whole time...." She panted. "Everything you said was a lie.... Everything you did was misleading.... You made me trust you.... You made me *care* about you!"

"If *The Tales of Tidbit Twitch* is the key to your

heart, then I suggest getting a better lock," Seven sneered. "I thought it would be difficult to deceive the *great Fairy Godmother*, but you adolescent girls are all the same. All it took was a little smile, a little interest, a little attention, and I had you in the palm of my hand."

"But *why*?" she asked. "What could be worth lying and killing your own family?!"

"You're making it sound so *personal*," Seven said. "Face it, Brystal, I just wanted what everyone wants—*power*. And it doesn't just fall into our laps as easily as it fell into yours. I was seventh in line for the throne—to become king, I had to be *creative*."

"You couldn't have done this on your own," Brystal said. "The king and the princes didn't die naturally! Someone was helping you—someone with *magic*!"

The Brotherhood roared with laughter, as if the idea was absurd. The accusation made an insidious smile grow across Seven's face. He walked closer to Brystal and whispered in her ear.

"Well done, you've *finally* gotten something right," he said. "You won't believe what we have in store next. Sadly, I don't think you'll live to see it."

Seven snapped his fingers, and a net made of bloodstone was thrown over Brystal. The net was so heavy it pinned her to the platform, and she could barely breathe or move beneath it. The bloodstone burned her skin, and the longer she was trapped, the weaker and weaker she became. Brystal had known this moment would happen—she knew surrendering would cost her her life—but she had surrendered because of Seven's false pretenses. Seven was planning something that transcended the Righteous Brotherhood, and not knowing the extent of his plan gave Brystal the will to stay alive and the urge to fight him. Unfortunately, the bloodstone drained so much of her energy that it took all her strength just to stay conscious. All she could do was watch what happened next.

The Brotherhood cheered and applauded as Brystal struggled under the net. While they were distracted, Seven redirected his attention to the back of the courtyard and gestured for someone to come forward.

"It's time!" he called.

"Time for what, my lord?" the High Commander asked.

"Excuse me, High Commander, but I wasn't speaking to any of you," Seven said.

The Brotherhood went quiet. Before they had the chance to question him further, black smoke blew in from the back of the courtyard. The clansmen parted as Mistress Mara strolled inside and made her way to the platform. The witch was followed by the Shadow Beast, which took the form of a panther, then an alligator, and finally an anaconda as it crawled behind her.

"What a delightfully desolate location," the witch said as she looked around the fortress. "I'd say it needs a woman's touch, but trust me, you don't want *mine*."

The Brotherhood couldn't believe their eyes—a woman had never set foot in the fortress before, let alone a *witch*! The clan were outraged and readied their weapons. Mistress Mara was amused by their reaction and cackled as she climbed the platform and stood at Seven's side. The Shadow Beast sat next to her like an obedient dog.

"*My lord, a witch has infiltrated the fortress!*" the High Commander exclaimed.

"Yes, High Commander, I know," Seven said. "I invited her."

The Brotherhood were stunned and erupted in protest.

"*How dare you!*"

"*Her kind isn't welcome here!*"

"You're insulting the Righteous Philosophy!"

Seven raised a hand to silence the angry clan.

"Gentlemen, what I'm about to say is going to shake you to your fragile cores, but try to keep an open mind," he said. "A man's quest for power is pointless unless he sets his sights on *true power*. Ordinary power can be taken away, it can be deceived, and it can be overcome—but *true power* cannot be defeated. No one can achieve true power if they're limited by prejudice, shortsighted by pride, or married to a *single* philosophy. They must be flexible, they must play both sides of the coin at all times, and they must use *all* available resources if they want to become *unstoppable*."

"This is an abomination!"

"We need to kill the witch at once!"

"This is a sacred place!"

"Oh, believe me, I'm well aware of its hallowed origins," he said. "Do any of you know *why* it's such a sacred space? Long ago, your founding fathers used this fortress as much more than a headquarters. Within the walls around us, and deep in the ground below us, lay the remains of the first nine hundred and ninety-nine members of the Righteous Brotherhood. This fortress isn't just the birthplace of your philosophy—*it's a tomb*. And what could make a man more *unstoppable* than commanding an *army of the deceased?* After all, you can't kill a soldier if he's already dead."

The Brotherhood glared at their Righteous King as if he had lost his mind. Seven nodded to Mistress Mara and she nodded back—*it was now or never.*

The witch twirled her arms through the air and the Shadow Beast grew into a massive cyclone. The storm whirled around the courtyard, and the terrified clansmen ran and dived out of its way. The wind was so powerful the Brotherhood dropped their weapons and held on to their masks with both hands. The Shadow Beast split into 999 ferocious animals. The creatures scattered to different parts of the fortress and disappeared into the walls and sank into the ground. Once the animals were gone, the courtyard went dead silent. The frazzled clansmen helped one another back to their feet and anxiously waited for something to happen.

The enchantment was an exhausting exercise for Mistress Mara. The witch hunched over and clutched her chest as she caught her breath. Seven's eyes darted around the fortress, and he grew terribly impatient.

"Well?" he asked. "Did it work?"

Mistress Mara turned to him with a confident smile. "Perfectly," she said.

The fortress began to rumble as if it had been struck by an earthquake. The clansmen moved to the center of the courtyard to avoid the rattling structure. Suddenly, hundreds and hundreds of decaying hands emerged from the dirt and shot out of the stone walls. The Brotherhood watched in terror as 999 corpses clawed their way out from their resting places. The dead surrounded the frightened clansmen and picked up the weapons they dropped. The corpses faced their Righteous King and saluted him, like a platoon of skeletal soldiers.

Seven and Mistress Mara were euphoric as they watched the dead come back to life. Brystal had never seen anything so horrifying in her life, but she was so depleted from the bloodstone she could hardly keep her eyes open.

"*What is this madness?*" the High Commander yelled.

"Gentlemen, just like you, your distant grandfathers made an oath to devote their lives—and whatever may come after that—to serving the Righteous Philosophy,"

Seven said. "For the first time, that *eternal devotion* is being called on today. Allow me to introduce you to the most powerful legion this world has ever seen—I give you the *Righteous Army of the Dead!*"

As the Brotherhood observed the army, it was obvious their ancestors were no longer the same men they once were. The corpses were stripped of all personality and humanity and had returned to life as nothing but cold and soulless warriors.

"My lord, these men will never serve you!" the High Commander declared. "Their oath was to protect and preserve the Righteous Philosophy—and you've defied it by bringing them back with witchcraft!"

"You're mistaken, High Commander," Seven said. "Indeed, they devoted themselves to the Righteous Philosophy—but since the Brotherhood appointed *me* as the Righteous King, the Righteous Philosophy is *whatever I say it is.* And I believe it's time for a few *modifications.*"

"I—I—I don't understand," the High Commander said.

Mistress Mara threw her head back and cackled at him.

"Silly old man," she said. "Don't you get it? He never cared about your Righteous Philosophy. He never intended to restore the natural order or start a war with the magical community. He simply told you what you wanted to hear so we could take advantage of your Brotherhood. And now that we have an unbeatable army, we're going to hold mankind responsible for all the—"

FWITT! Suddenly, Mistress Mara felt something hit her chest. She looked down and saw that a bloodstone arrow was sticking directly into her heart.

"Actually, Mistress Mara, since we're on the topic of dishonesty, I have something to get off my chest," Seven said as he lowered his crossbow. "I never cared about holding mankind accountable either—I fooled you just as much as I fooled them."

The witch dropped to her knees and black blood poured down her body.

"*You—You—You betrayed me!*" she gasped.

"No, I used your *hate* against you," he said with a snide smile. "Turns out, when you stoke someone's hate, you can make them do whatever you want."

Mistress Mara spent her final moments in shock.

Her eyes rolled into the back of her head, she collapsed on the platform, and then the witch became deathly still. Like a dying fire, her body started to smoke, then she slowly disappeared from sight.

Once the witch was gone, Seven moved to the edge of the platform to address the whole courtyard.

"In a few hours, the world is going to wake to the most *dreadful news*," he said. "They'll learn that, after her assassination of King Champion XIV, the beloved Fairy Godmother went on a rampage, killing Prince Maximus and his five children. The world will be horrified to hear the Fairy Godmother also partnered with a witch named Mistress Mara, and together they devised a plan to raise an army from the dead and slaughter all of mankind. But then the world will sigh with relief when they discover that I—the courageous Prince Gallivant—defeated the evil women and took command of the army myself.

"I will march into Chariot Hills, I will claim the throne, and thanks to my invincible new soldiers, I will be the most powerful sovereign the world has ever known. My army will expand the borders of my kingdom until every inch of this planet is under my control.

We will turn this world into one glorious *Righteous Empire*, and we'll destroy anything or anyone that stands in our way.

"Gentlemen, it's time for you to broaden your horizons. Forget the Southern Kingdom and the magical community—this Brotherhood's new objective is *world domination* and obliterating *all species* that threaten us! You can join my army and continue to serve me as your Righteous King—*or* you can stay here and fill your ancestors' graves. The choice is yours."

The Righteous Army of the Dead took an intimidating step toward the Brotherhood with their weapons raised. The frightened clansmen looked to the High Commander for guidance, but there was only one way out alive. The High Commander reluctantly bowed to the Righteous King, and the rest of the clan followed.

"We remain your humble servants, my lord," the High Commander said.

Seven clapped his hands together. "Gentlemen— *brothers*—you've made the right decision," he said. "Welcome to the Righteous Empire."

While Seven gave the Brotherhood their ultimatum,

Brystal's vision started to fade. She had run out of strength and couldn't fight the bloodstone any longer. Her eyes fluttered shut, her mind went blank, and her heart stopped beating. The last bit of life slowly drained from her body and Brystal drifted into the great unknown....

CHAPTER SEVENTEEN

FAMILIAR FACES

The witches and lynxes of Ravencrest were enjoying a relaxing night in the graveyard. Stitches, Beebee, and Pip wore tinted glasses and lounged across three tombs as they took in the moonlight. Sprout was soaking her feet in a jar of fertilizer and pleasantly sighed to herself while her body absorbed the nutrients. The lynxes were gathered around the witches and lazily stretched, scratched, and cleaned themselves.

"I'm so glad Mistress Mara gave us the night off," Sprout said. "It's been ages since we had a Self-Scare Day."

"Why is it called a Self-Scare Day?" Pip asked.

"B-b-because it feels so good it's f-f-frightening," Beebee said.

"I just adore moonbathing," Stitches said. "Can someone pass me the moonscreen?"

Beebee handed her a bottle of blue lotion and Stitches rubbed it on her skin.

"Is there a point to moonbathing?" Pip asked. "I mean, does it actually do something?"

"It g-g-gives witches a nice alabaster g-g-glow," Beebee said.

"Be careful you don't get a moonburn," Sprout advised. "The last time I got one, I glowed in the dark for three weeks."

Pip quickly retrieved the bottle of moonscreen and applied another layer to her skin.

Suddenly, their peaceful night was interrupted by a *boom* in the distance. The witches sat up on the tombs and looked at the horizon. Racing toward the manor at lightning speed were four unicorns with silver horns and magenta manes. The majestic steeds pulled a golden carriage behind them, and they galloped faster and faster as they approached Ravencrest's iron fence. The unicorns smashed into the gate horns first, and it burst open, snapping the chains that kept it locked. Brick and Stone were knocked off the top of the fence, and they hit the ground with two loud *thump*s.

As the golden carriage entered the property, the gargoyles leaped back to their feet and charged after the intruders. Emerelda leaned out the carriage window, and with one snap, Brick and Stone turned into emerald statues and froze in their tracks. After the gargoyles were stopped, a dozen trees pulled themselves out of the dirt and chased the trespassing carriage. Xanthous hopped outside the vehicle, and the flames on his head and shoulders rose several feet. One look at the fiery boy, and the trees backed away.

Stitches, Beebee, Sprout, and Pip were intrigued by the dramatic entrance. The unicorns parked the golden carriage in front of the witches, and Lucy, Emerelda, Tangerina, and Skylene rushed out of the vehicle. Xanthous ran up to join them. The fairies' first glance at the dreary manor gave them the creeps and they huddled closely together.

"So *this* is the Ravencrest School of Witchcraft," Tangerina said.

"It's like a living nightmare," Skylene said.

"Thank you!" Stitches said with an appreciative grin.

"Lucy, what are the fairies doing here?" Pip asked. "I thought you left to find your swans a new home."

"Yeah, yeah, yeah—they're living the dream," she said. *"Where's Mistress Mara?"*

Lucy's sense of urgency concerned the witches.

"We d-d-don't know," Beebee said. "Sh-sh-she left this evening."

"Why? Where's the fire?" Sprout asked. "You know, *besides* the boy who's literally on fire behind you."

Lucy groaned—she didn't have time to break the news gently.

"Girls, what I'm about to say is going to be difficult to hear," she said. "You're going to feel hurt, betrayed, and it's going to turn your whole world upside down!"

"Can't wait!" Stitches said.

"Mistress Mara didn't open Ravencrest to teach witchcraft—she was using it to find a host for a horrible curse!" Lucy declared. "She and the Horned One have been secretly plotting to kill the Fairy Godmother and seek revenge on mankind! She used the Enrollment Ceremony to curse me with something called a Shadow Beast—it's an entity that boosts a witch's abilities for a single enchantment! A Shadow Beast grows inside a host like a parasite, and if the fairies hadn't helped me remove it, the curse would have killed me!"

"W-w-what?!" Beebee said.

"You can't be serious!" Sprout said.

"Mistress Mara would *never* hurt a student!" Stitches said. "Curse one for a hundred years? *Absolutely!* But hurt one? *Never!*"

"For once, Lucy isn't exaggerating!" Emerelda said.

"We witnessed the whole thing!" Xanthous said.

"And I can prove it!" Lucy said. "Obviously, Mistress Mara hasn't turned me into a lynx—but if we went into her study, I bet we'd find a Curse Counter with my face on it!"

Without wasting another moment, Lucy dashed toward the manor, and the witches and fairies followed her inside. She hurried up the grand staircase and led everyone to the tall hallway on the seventh and a half floor. Lucy moved the scaly armchair from the corner and placed it under the door of Mistress Mara's study. She used the chair to climb into the doorway, but when she turned back, the witches were too afraid to join her.

"Come on!" Lucy said. "What are you waiting for?"

"We're not g-g-going in there," Beebee said.

"What if Mistress Mara comes back and catches us?" Sprout asked.

"I don't want to be turned into a lynx," Stitches said. "Not *yet*."

Lucy groaned. "Okay, fine—I'll go in by myself," she said. "Everybody wait here."

She proceeded into the study on her own and headed directly into the closet of jack-o'-lanterns. Lucy searched the shelves and it didn't take long to find a pumpkin with her defiant expression staring back at her. She quickly removed the jack-o'-lantern from the shelf to show the others, but as Lucy headed out of the closet, something peculiar caught her eye.

Lucy passed a pair of jack-o'-lanterns with the faces of a refined couple. The man had a wooden pipe in his mouth, fuzzy muttonchops covered the majority of his face, and a monocle was placed over his left eye. The woman's hair was styled into two buns that resembled horns, a pearl necklace was wrapped around her neck, and she had inquisitive eyes. Lucy was certain she recognized the couple—she couldn't recall from when or where, but she had definitely seen the woman's unique eyes in person.

Suddenly, the sound of a creaking floorboard came from inside the study. Lucy cautiously peered out of the closet and was relieved to see it was just the invisible butler. He was joined by Old Billie, who glared at Lucy from the wall behind the servant. As Lucy gazed into the illustration's inquisitive eyes, it slowly dawned on her *why* she recognized the couple in the closet.

"Wait a second," she said. "The people on those pumpkins—they're *you*, aren't they?"

Old Billie nodded and the invisible butler's monocle bobbed up and down in the space above his collar. Lucy glanced back at the jack-o'-lanterns and noticed that a pendant with the letter R was attached to the woman's pearl necklace and that the man's wooden pipe was *also* engraved with the letter R. Lucy could tell the letter was significant to the couple, and she scrunched her forehead as she tried to think of the reason.

"Holy whodunit!" she exclaimed. "You guys are *Lord and Lady Ravencrest*! This house wasn't a generous donation like Mistress Mara said it was—she cursed you and then stole it!"

Once again, the goat and the invisible butler nodded.

"So *that's* why Old Billie led me to this study," Lucy said to herself. "She wanted me to know Mistress Mara had cursed her and stolen her home. And on the night I got lost, I thought the manor itself was playing tricks on me, but the *butler* was opening and shutting all those doors! I just didn't see him because he's invisible! He purposely guided me to the hallway so I would hear Mistress Mara and the Horned One's conversation! *That also means he was* naked *while he was doing it, but I'll save that concern for another time.*"

Lucy thought she had figured everything out, but based on the couple's somber body language, she realized there was more to the story. Old Billie's gaze drifted past Lucy, and the butler raised his cuff link, both gesturing to something behind her. Lucy turned around, and in the very back of the closet, she saw a jack-o'-lantern that had been placed on its own shelf—it was the pumpkin she had discovered during her first visit to the study. Lucy had trouble recognizing the carving at first, but now that she was looking at it with fresh eyes, it suddenly hit her.

"Oh my God!" she gasped. "It's *Brystal*!"

Lucy grabbed Brystal's jack-o'-lantern and bolted back to the hallway.

"You guys aren't going to believe what I just found!" she announced.

Lucy tossed the pumpkin to Tangerina and Skylene. The girls inspected the carving and then shot her a dirty look.

"Nice try, Lucy, but the witches aren't going to fall for this," Tangerina said.

"Yeah, this pumpkin is *way* too pretty to be you," Skylene said.

"No—that's not mine—*this* is mine!" Lucy said.

She tossed the other pumpkin to Stitches and Sprout. Lucy's likeness was unmistakable and proof that Mistress Mara had cursed her. The witches moaned like their favorite sports team had lost a game.

"Looks like Lucy's telling the truth," Stitches said. "Check the Mara pool. Who had 'kill the Fairy Godmother and seek revenge on mankind'?"

Sprout pulled a rolled-up piece of paper out of her bushy hair and read from it.

"Let's see, I had 'plague the world with exploding bats,' Stitches had 'fill all the rivers with blood and guts,' and Beebee had 'kill a diplomat and seek revenge on mankind,'" she said. "Beebee's was the closest— she wins again!"

"Aw, man!" Stitches griped. "How does she win everything?"

"I was b-b-born lucky," Beebee boasted. "You know the d-d-drill. Give me your m-m-money, witches!"

Stitches and Sprout each begrudgingly handed Beebee a couple of gold coins. The fairies couldn't believe the witches had made a game out of it.

"Wait, you *knew* Mistress Mara was plotting something?" Emerelda asked.

"And you made *bets* on it?" Xanthous asked.

Stitches shrugged. "We knew she didn't open Ravencrest out of the goodness of her heart," she said. "Witches never help anyone but themselves."

Lucy put two fingers in her mouth and whistled to get everyone's attention.

"You guys are missing the important part!" she exclaimed. "Look at the other pumpkin! Recognize the carving? Mistress Mara didn't just curse me—*she put a curse on Brystal, too*! I found that jack-o'-lantern three days ago but I didn't realize it was her!"

"But *how* did she curse her?" Skylene asked. "Brystal doesn't look any different."

"Curses don't always affect someone's appearance," Lucy said. "Sometimes they can disturb a person's health, or their stamina, or their—"

"*Mood*?" Tangerina asked.

The fairies rolled their eyes at her remark.

"What?" Tangerina asked defensively. "I'm not trying to be judgmental, but Brystal's been in a bad mood for weeks."

Everyone went silent as they thought about what Tangerina had said. Brystal's recent behavior had been extremely out of character—they knew *something* had to have been causing her recent mood swings, but they would never have imagined a *curse* could be the culprit.

"Actually, I think Tangerina's on to something," Xanthous said. "If Mistress Mara wanted to kill Brystal, she'd want her to be as vulnerable as possible when she did. Maybe she thought cursing Brystal *mentally* would be more effective than cursing her *physically*?"

"So *that's* why she was so unhappy," Pip said. "Just before I left the academy, Brystal told me she was feeling really negative but couldn't explain where it was coming from."

"Well, now we know," Lucy said. "Brystal has always been so good about hiding her feelings. Remember last year? Brystal knew about the Snow Queen for *weeks* before we did, and we were completely oblivious. She bottled up all her fear and anxiety to spare us from being as worried as she was. The fact that we've even *noticed* Brystal's behavior just shows how miserable she must be! And I'm sure all the stuff with the Three Thirty-Three has only made it worse!"

The comment triggered Emerelda's memory and she suddenly gasped.

"What's wrong, Em?" Xanthous asked.

"Earlier this evening Brystal asked me to take over the academy if anything happened to her," Emerelda said. "I thought she was just tired—I told her we would talk more after she had time to rest—but now I think she might have been *planning* something! When I returned to her office, she had left her wand and a note behind—but I haven't had a chance to read it yet!"

"Do you have it with you?" Skylene asked.

Emerelda retrieved the note from her pocket and read it aloud:

"Dear Emerelda,

> *"By the time you read this, I'll have surrendered myself to the Three Thirty-Three, and you'll be the new Fairy Godmother. This may seem like a drastic decision, but I promise you, it's our best shot at defeating them."*

"No!" Skylene said.

"She couldn't have!" Xanthous said.

"Why would she *surrender* to them?!" Tangerina said.

"Because her mind isn't working like it should!" Lucy said. "What else does it say, Em?"

> *"Before I leave, it's important I pass along all the information I've learned about the Three Thirty-Three so you're prepared.*
>
> *"The Three Thirty-Three call themselves the Righteous Brotherhood and they consist*

of exactly three hundred and thirty-three clansmen. The roles have been passed down from father to eldest son in three hundred and thirty-three families in the Southern Kingdom. Each clansman has devoted his entire existence—life and whatever comes afterward—to upholding something known as the Righteous Philosophy. They believe the world can only function properly if mankind is in control, and if men are in control of mankind. Over the centuries, the Brotherhood have successfully applied their oppressive philosophy to the laws of the Southern Kingdom, and they've eliminated any group that stands in their way.

"The Brotherhood operates from a fortress on the shore of the South Sea. Their weapons are made from a material called bloodstone, but no one knows where the material came from or why it defies magic. The clan is currently being commanded by a man they call the Righteous King, and he wears a suit made entirely out of bloodstone with a matching mask that's shaped like a ram's skull."

"What a coincidence," Sprout said. "That sounds exactly like the outfit the Horned One wears. You think they shop at the same stores?"

Lucy rolled her eyes. "That *can't* be a coincidence!" she said. "Obviously, the Horned One *is* the Righteous King!"

"But that doesn't make any sense," Pip said. "That would mean Mistress Mara is working with the Righteous Brotherhood!"

"Actually, it makes perfect sense," Lucy said. "When I was in show business, we used to have a phrase, 'The enemy of my enemy is the only safe understudy.' It means people can look past their differences and work together as long as they share a common interest. And in this case, *killing Brystal* is their common interest!"

"Beebee, what do you think?" Stitches asked. "You're right about everything."

"I bet he's b-b-backstabbing everyone in a barbaric quest for p-p-power to fill a deep-seated v-v-void caused by a lonely and loveless ch-ch-childhood," Beebee said.

The fairies' eyes went wide.

"Well, case closed," Lucy said. "Keeping reading, Em."

"Don't let the Righteous King fool you, he's actually King Champion XIV's son, Maximus, in disguise. Maximus has recently framed me for the murder of his father to tarnish my name and turn people against the magical community. However, the sooner I disassociate myself from the fairies, the less damage he can do, so I've decided to surrender willingly and hopefully salvage what's left of the fairies' reputation.

"Once I'm gone, the Brotherhood plans to wage war on the magical community. Right now, the clan are convinced that fairies and witches will be weaker without me, but I know my absence will only make them stronger. I've made so many mistakes recently, I know they'll be better off without me—you'll lead the magical community in ways I never could.

"I apologize for how abrupt my departure is and hope you'll learn to forgive me one day.

I must reiterate, this is the only way the magical community can win the war against the Righteous Brotherhood.

> "Please take care of yourself and keep everyone safe,
>
> Brystal

"PS—While you keep track of the Righteous Brotherhood, it's important to keep an eye on the globe in the office. The Snow Queen is trapped in a cavern deep below the Northern Mountains. As long as the northern lights are shining in the sky, the Snow Queen remains a prisoner, but if the lights ever fade from view, it means she's escaped.

"I wish I had more time to explain, but if you ever need advice or guidance, find the cavern in the mountains. Part of Madame Weatherberry still exists within the Snow Queen and she can help you."

The whole letter was shocking, but Brystal's last line

about Madame Weatherberry was the most shocking of all. The fairies expected Brystal to say she was kidding in the next passage—but there was nothing left for Emerelda to read.

"She's not serious," Skylene said. "Is she?"

"Of course not," Tangerina said.

"This is the curse talking—it's made her delusional," Xanthous said.

"Exactly—she doesn't know what she's saying," Emerelda said. "Even if part of Madame Weatherberry *was* alive, why would she exist within *the Snow Queen*?"

Lucy cringed and let out a deep sigh, already regretting what she was about to say.

"Because Madame Weatherberry *is* the Snow Queen," she confessed.

The fairies glared at Lucy like she had said something horribly offensive.

"Shame on you, Lucy!" Skylene said.

"Why would you say such a nasty thing?" Tangerina asked.

"Madame Weatherberry gave us everything we have!" Xanthous said. "How could you be so disrespectful?"

"I'm telling you the truth—I saw her with my own eyes," Lucy said. "Madame Weatherberry thought the only way we could get mankind's approval was by giving mankind a problem that only we could solve. She turned herself into a monster so we could be heroes and win the world's affection. That's why I went to Ravencrest for a couple of days—I was furious with Brystal for not being honest with me."

"Then why weren't you honest with *us*?" Emerelda said. "Why did you run to Ravencrest instead of telling *us* the truth?"

Lucy took a moment to think about it, and the answer surprised her.

"I guess for the same reasons Brystal kept it from me," she said. "When I found out the truth, I was devastated. It felt like everything Madame Weatherberry had taught me was a lie, and it made me question my relationship with magic. I didn't want you guys to go through all that, so I thought I was doing the right thing by keeping it to myself. *I'm sorry.*"

The fairies stared off into space and quietly shook their heads. They didn't want to believe a word of it, but they knew Lucy was telling the truth. Tears came to their eyes as they were bombarded with heartbreak, anger, and a sense of betrayal all at once.

"I know exactly how you feel, but don't make the same mistake I did," Lucy said. "Instead of blaming Madame Weatherberry, I lashed out at Brystal—I didn't understand what an impossible situation she was put in! Living with such a big secret had to have been torture, but she sacrificed her own peace of mind to protect ours. Even while a curse was making her miserable, Brystal never stopped putting us first! And now *she's* in trouble and needs *our* help! So are we going to stand around licking our wounds, or are we going to save her?"

Lucy's message was more profound than even Lucy was expecting, and the fairies didn't know how to respond. They looked to one another for reassurance, but deep down, they were all thinking the same thing. Brystal would *never* abandon them in their hour of need—and they weren't going to lose her without a fight.

"Of course we're going to save her," Tangerina said. "You really think we'd just leave her to die?"

"What are we? *Witches?*" Skylene said. "Oh, sorry! I forgot where I was."

"Compliment accepted!" Stitches said with a wink.

"But how do we know Brystal's still alive?" Emerelda asked. "Does Ravencrest have a Map of Magic we could check before we leave?"

Lucy held up Brystal's pumpkin and peeked inside it.

"We don't need a Map of Magic," she said. "The candle in her jack-o'-lantern is fading, but it's lit! That means her curse is still active, which means she must be alive!"

Emerelda sighed and caressed the pumpkin like it was the real Brystal.

"Hang in there, girl," she said. "Help is on the way."

"We've got to act fast," Xanthous said. "Brystal surrendered hours ago. She could be anywhere by now!"

"I bet the Brotherhood took her to a secret lair inside a volcano!" Stitches said.

"I bet they put her in a hot-air balloon a thousand miles above the earth!" Sprout said.

"I b-b-bet they took her to their f-f-fortress by the sea," Beebee said.

"In that case, we're definitely going to the fortress," Lucy told the others.

"I'm coming with you!" Pip announced. "Brystal tried to warn me about Mistress Mara, but I didn't listen. If I don't make it up to her somehow, I'll never forgive myself."

Lucy was grateful for her support, but the fairies needed a lot more than Pip to stand a chance against the Brotherhood. She turned toward Stitches, Beebee, and Sprout with large, pleading eyes.

"The Brotherhood is really dangerous," she said. "They outnumber us by hundreds and they have weapons that defy magic. I know witches are supposed to think only about themselves, but if you could find it in your dark hearts to help us, we could really use you."

The witches scratched their chins as they considered her request.

"*How* dangerous will it be?" Stitches asked.

"Extremely," Lucy said.

"Will there be violence?" Sprout asked.

"Definitely."

"And c-c-casualties?" Beebee asked.

"Most likely."

The witches smirked at Lucy and cackled with excitement.

"Say no more," Stitches said. "You had us at *dangerous*."

CHAPTER EIGHTEEN

A DEAL WITH DEATH

Brystal opened her eyes....

It was like waking from a deep sleep, but not a sleep she had experienced before.... She wasn't tired or groggy, but surprisingly rested and alert.... Her body wasn't stiff or sore, but unusually relaxed and limber.... She didn't feel anxious or gloomy, but unexpectedly calm and collected....

The temperature wasn't too warm or too cold, just comfortable....

Everything was so comfortable.... And it was a nice change....

Strangely, when Brystal awoke, she was already on her feet. She stood in the middle of a gray field with a perfectly smooth surface. She was facing a magnificent white tree that was engraved with the name *Brystal*. A silver clock was embedded in the center of its trunk, and the hands had stopped turning at 3:33. Brystal heard ticking, and when she gazed up, she saw thousands of pocket watches hanging from the branches on glittering silver chains.

The field stretched for miles around her and was home to dozens of other white trees, but none of them had as many pocket watches as the tree with Brystal's name. In fact, most of the other trees' branches were bare.

As Brystal gazed across the land, she noticed a bright sun hovering over the horizon to her right and a massive full moon hovering over the horizon to her left. Between them was the most spectacular sky she had ever seen. There were hundreds of orbiting planets, thousands of spiraling galaxies, and millions of twinkling stars. Everything was so vivid, the entire universe seemed within reach, and each of the celestial bodies gave off a hypnotic chime—Brystal could *hear* the stars as much as she could see them. Brystal hadn't known such dazzling colors and such soothing sounds *existed*, and she couldn't think of words to describe all the beauty above her.

Brystal wandered through the field, exploring the peculiar place. Something felt oddly familiar about the strange land—like *part* of her had always been there. She wasn't worried or scared as she walked around because, for reasons unknown to her, Brystal knew she was perfectly safe.

All the trees stood at different heights and each of them was engraved with a different name. Their trunks were also embedded with silver clocks, but unlike the clock on Brystal's tree, the others were working and turning at unique speeds. Some of the names she recognized, like *Lucy, Barrie, Emerelda, Xanthous,* and *Celeste*—but there were engravings she didn't recognize, like *John, Lloyd, Alex, Conner,* and *Ezmia*. Curiously, the mysterious names belonged to smaller trees that hadn't been planted, and their clocks were frozen at 12:00, as if their time hadn't started yet.

As she continued through the field, Brystal spotted someone moving nearby. She walked toward the stranger and saw that it was Mistress Mara. The witch was aggressively pacing and her face was tense with worry. She was deep in thought and didn't look up as Brystal approached. After the events in the fortress, Brystal had a million concerns of her own, but the most important question escaped her lips.

"Are we dead?" Brystal asked.

"Not *yet*," the witch said.

Mistress Mara never stopped pacing and kept her eyes on the ground.

"Then what are we doing here? What is this place?"

"We're *waiting*, obviously," she said. "This is the space *between* life and the other side."

Mistress Mara gestured toward the sun and the moon, and suddenly, Brystal realized they weren't what she had originally thought. What she had mistaken for a full moon was actually the *world*, and what she had mistaken for the sun was actually a bright light shining from somewhere *beyond the universe.* Brystal wasn't standing on a field attached to a planet but a strip of land that was floating freely through the cosmos.

"What are these trees?" she asked. "Why are there names and clocks on them?"

The witch groaned as if she had more pressing matters to think about.

"Each tree represents a person you've encountered or a person you *will* encounter if you survive," Mistress Mara explained. "The clocks represent the time each person has left on earth. They spin at different speeds because, well, *time is relative.* Some people need decades to live a fulfilling life, while others can achieve one within minutes."

"Still, it seems unfair that some people have more time than others," Brystal said.

"Everything seems unfair when you measure it with the wrong tools," Mistress Mara said. "Life isn't supposed to be measured by time, by luck, or by privilege. Life is supposed to be measured by *purpose.* Everyone is born with a purpose—whether they choose to believe it or not. Some are meant to learn lessons, some are meant to teach them, while others are simply meant to observe. Naturally, a lot of people resent life when their purpose isn't *easy* or when it doesn't match their *hopes and dreams*, but no one leaves the world without completing exactly what they were meant to do. That's the rule of life."

"And what about the watches?" she asked. "Why are there so many on my tree?"

"The watches represent the lives you've *saved*," the witch said. "Sometime, somewhere, those people became lost—their trees were *unrooted*, so to speak. But because of something you said or did, they found the strength to keep *ticking*. Even though your clock has stopped, your tree will never stop growing because of the lives you've touched."

Brystal glanced back at her tree and was amazed that each of the ticking watches symbolized a person with a beating heart. She knew people liked her, but Brystal didn't know she mattered so much to so many people. It made her ashamed of surrendering to the Brotherhood and giving up her life so willingly.

Mistress Mara was surprisingly insightful about

the space between life and death, and Brystal became curious as to *why* she was so knowledgeable. But before she could inquire any further, the witch became lost in her own thoughts and began muttering to herself.

"I was such an idiot!" Mistress Mara roared. "Seven never cared about anything but *power*! I should have known better! I should have seen it coming! But I was so distracted by vengeance I flew right into his trap like a moth to a flame!"

Brystal sighed with disappointment. "I'm partially to blame," she said. "Somehow, he knew exactly what to say, exactly when I needed to hear it, and I fell for every word."

"Yes, but *you* were cursed," the witch said. "There was no excuse for *my* stupidity."

Brystal did a double take—she was certain she had misheard her.

"Excuse me?" she asked. "What do you mean I was *cursed*?"

For the first time, Mistress Mara stopped pacing and looked Brystal directly in the eye.

"Have you noticed any *changes* lately?" the witch asked. "Have your thoughts and feelings been unexplainably negative? Have you been distancing yourself from the people you love? Has every problem seemed impossible to solve? Has your self-confidence been replaced by self-hate and self-scrutiny? Have you convinced yourself that you're nothing but a failure and that the world would be better off without you?"

Brystal couldn't believe what she was hearing. She had never felt more exposed in her entire life and slowly backed away from the witch.

"How—How—*How did you know*?" she gasped.

"Because *I'm* the one who turned your mind against you," Mistress Mara confessed.

"But—But—*But why*?"

"If you knew we were planning to seek revenge on mankind, you would have stopped us! We had to make you as weak and vulnerable as possible so we could succeed."

"Are you crazy? This is the first time witches and fairies have been *safe* and *respected* by mankind in six hundred years! Why would you jeopardize that?"

Mistress Mara scoffed at her and continued pacing.

"It's complicated—you haven't lived long enough to understand," the witch said.

"And who's fault is *that*?!" Brystal exclaimed. "Thanks to you, I'm stuck somewhere between life and death! The least you could do is explain yourself!"

Mistress Mara tried to walk away but Brystal followed her. The witch rolled her eyes and let out a reluctant sigh.

"Fine," she moaned. "Are you familiar with the story of the Daughter of Death?"

The phrase rang a bell, and Brystal recalled reading a book that mentioned it.

"It's a legend, isn't it?" she asked. "Death sent his daughter to earth, hoping the separation would help him understand human grief. Unfortunately for him, she found a way to stay on earth and live forever. The two never reunited and Death entered a state of eternal mourning."

Mistress Mara gazed at the world with a heavy heart.

"Can you blame me?" she said. "Who wouldn't want to live forever if they could? There's music and food and weather and love and laughter—I was addicted to life from the moment I arrived. Most children like to defy their parents when they're young, and what could be more defiant to Death than a daughter who loved living?"

Brystal assumed the witch was joking and laughed at the remarks. Mistress Mara turned to her with a very grave expression—*she wasn't kidding.*

"You're being serious," Brystal said, and her eyes grew wide. "I suppose it makes sense. Who else could kill people with just their touch? And who else would know so much about *this* place?"

Mistress Mara nodded. "This place has changed over time," she said. "All the clocks used to move at the same speed. Before my father sent me into the world, every soul was given a hundred years to live. But when he lost me, he decided to change the rules of death. Instead of monitoring people's time, my father started collecting souls after their *purpose* was complete. Since *my* purpose was to make Death feel grief, and since that purpose was accomplished, he thought the new rules would unite us. However, when my father created me, he didn't realize I had inherited so many of his traits. Death is *timeless* and his purpose is *eternal*—he's the one thing in existence that can't be killed. And no matter how many times he tried to take my life, I couldn't die."

"Wait a second," Brystal said. "I heard a rumor that bloodstone came from Death—but it's not a rumor, is it? He created it for *you*!"

"Bloodstone, disease, disaster, violence, starvation, plague—*anything* that can end a life was invented for me," Mistress Mara said. "It seems like such a ghastly relationship, but it's actually quite charming when you think about it. A lot of parents do drastic things to reunite with their children."

"I'm confused," Brystal said. "What does being the Daughter of Death have to do with seeking revenge on mankind?"

"I've been around a very long time, and the hardest part about living forever is losing the people I love," Mistress Mara said. "But when those people were *taken* from me in vain, and that savagery went unpunished, the pain *never* went away. For thousands of years I've watched mankind slaughter witches and fairies without consequence, losing friend after friend, and lover after lover. When you legalized magic, you secured peace and acceptance for the magical community, but it didn't erase the crimes committed against us. So when Seven presented me with a chance to avenge the people I had lost, I had to accept it.

"Seven told me his parents were killed by an angry mob, and as a result, he had developed a hatred for humanity that was equal to mine. He said he wanted to create a Righteous Army of the Dead and finally hold mankind responsible. But first, he needed a witch who was willing to partner with him, and like a fool, I believed his intentions were genuine. I opened the Ravencrest School of Witchcraft to produce a Shadow Beast powerful enough to raise the clansmen from the dead. Then I cursed your mind to feel constant misery, but with one very important exception—the curse was temporarily suspended whenever you were in Seven's presence. We knew you'd interpret the breaks as fondness for him, that you'd undoubtedly become attached to him, and you'd never suspect he was deceiving you."

Had Brystal been on earth, the revelation would have made her sick to her stomach. She was furious at Mistress Mara for inflicting such a cruel and manipulative curse on her, but in many ways, Brystal was extremely relieved. Her recent thoughts, feelings, and poor judgment weren't *her fault*—learning that it was all due to a *curse* made Brystal's shame fade away and her self-confidence return.

"If you can't die, then why are you here?" Brystal asked. "Why aren't you back on earth trying to stop him?"

"Because I *can't* stop him," Mistress Mara said. "Seven was honest about one thing—he and I are equally hateful. And you don't fight fire by adding more fire. To defeat the Righteous Army of the Dead, the world will need someone to unite them like they've never been united before. They'll have to convince mankind, the fairies, the witches, and the talking creatures to work together. And there's only *one person* I know of who's capable of that."

"Me?" Brystal asked. "But what if I don't survive?"

"That's why I'm here," the witch said. "I have to ensure you don't cross over. And I'm willing to negotiate whatever it takes."

Before Brystal had a chance to ask another question, the gray field was suddenly engulfed by an enormous eclipse. Mistress Mara eyed the darkness with suspense.

"He's here," the witch said.

"Who?"

"My *father.*"

The eclipse started to recede and the shade collected into a single shadow across the field. The shadow rose off the ground, gaining dimension and texture as it grew, and transformed into a man who was ten feet tall. His face and body were completely hidden under a pitch-black cloak made from darkness itself. Brystal's first sight of Death should have been frightening, but she didn't feel an ounce of fear as she gazed at him. On the contrary, it was like seeing the ship home after a very, very long voyage.

"Hello, Father," Mistress Mara said with a warm smile. "It's good to see you again."

Even though he didn't say a word or move a muscle, Brystal could sense thousands of years' worth of tension between the two. Death ignored his daughter's greeting and walked toward Brystal at a determined pace. The witch stepped between them, placing herself in her father's path.

"She shouldn't be here," Mistress Mara said. "Her purpose is only beginning."

Death acted as if he couldn't hear his daughter and kept moving closer.

"You need her alive as much as the world does,"

the witch said. "Death is an essential part of life—it's what makes people appreciate living—but you forget that *life* is an essential part of *you*. If you don't send her back to earth, the Righteous Army of the Dead will destroy so many lives, you'll become irrelevant."

Death wasn't concerned and proceeded forward.

"I made a mistake," Mistress Mara said. "Someone used my emotions to play me like a fiddle, and I gave them everything they wanted. But if memory serves me correctly, *you* made a very similar mistake once. Someone blinded *you* with desire and tricked *you* into giving them something you regret very much— something that still *haunts* you to this day. Perhaps if you send Brystal back to earth, she can fix *both* of our mistakes?"

Brystal had no idea what Mistress Mara was talking about. *What sort of mistake had Death made?* However, she could tell the witch was getting her father's attention, because his pace started to slow down. When Death was just a few feet away from Brystal, Mistress Mara took a deep breath and offered her father something she knew he wouldn't refuse.

"If you send her back, I'll take her place," she said.

Death suddenly stopped. He and his daughter glared at each other in silence, as if they were communicating telepathically. After a few moments, Mistress Mara nodded, like they had reached an agreement.

"Very well," the witch said.

"What's happening?" Brystal whispered.

"He's made us a counteroffer," Mistress Mara said. "If I take your place, my father will send you back to earth on one condition—you must fix his greatest regret."

"What *kind* of regret?" she asked.

"Many centuries ago, my father was deceived by a woman," Mistress Mara said. "The woman claimed she could kill me with an enchantment from an ancient spell book. The enchantment was as old as the earth, and Death had forgotten such a thing existed. In return for her help, the woman asked my father for *immortality*. By then my father was so desperate to have me back he accepted her proposal with no questions asked. Unfortunately, the moment he granted the woman immortality, she disappeared without a trace and never fulfilled her end of the bargain. This woman—this *Immortal*—still roams the earth, making a mockery of everything life and death stand for.

If you agree to find and terminate the Immortal, my father will send you back to earth."

"But how do I kill the Immortal?" Brystal asked.

"With the same enchantment she intended for me," Mistress Mara said. "My father will give you *one year* to locate and kill the Immortal. But if you haven't completed the task by then, the agreement will expire and your life will end."

Brystal went quiet as she considered Death's offer. It was a huge commitment to make, but what choice did she have? She would have given anything for another chance to stop Seven and the Righteous Army of the Dead.

"This enchantment—if it's powerful enough to kill the Immortal, could it destroy the Army of the Dead, too?" Brystal asked.

Mistress Mara turned to her father, and Death slowly nodded.

"All right then," Brystal said. "I agree."

"Then it's settled," Mistress Mara said. "Congratulations, Miss Evergreen, you've just made a deal with Death."

Suddenly, Brystal was distracted by the sound of

ticking. It was louder than all the clocks in the field put together. When Brystal looked toward the noise, she saw that the clock on her tree had *restarted*. As soon as she laid eyes on it, Brystal was unexpectedly propelled backward. She rose off the ground and flew through the air as an invisible force pulled her back to the earth. Brystal grabbed hold of a tree branch as she ascended, desperate to ask one more question before she returned to life.

"Wait!" she cried. *"What about the curse? How do I break it?"*

"There's only one way to break a curse of the mind," Mistress Mara said.

"What?!"

"With the mind itself."

Brystal held on to the branch with all her might, expecting the witch to give her more information, but that was all Mistress Mara said. The Daughter of Death linked arms with her father and rested her head on his shoulder. He walked her into the horizon and the two disappeared into the bright light of the other side—*reunited at last.*

The branch slipped out of Brystal's grip.... She

flew far away from the field and soared through the universe.... All the colorful planets and galaxies whirled around her.... Brystal started to lose consciousness as she was pulled faster and faster back to earth.... And all the stars faded from sight....

CHAPTER NINETEEN

THE MIND ITSELF

Brystal opened her eyes....

It was like waking from the worst sleep of her life....She was so exhausted she could feel it in her bones....Her head was pounding and every muscle in her body ached....The ocean air was freezing, but she was too weak to shiver....

Brystal awoke to the sound of marching boots and clanking armor. As her eyes adjusted, she noticed there were four dirt walls surrounding her. Brystal looked around and discovered she was lying at the bottom of a deep grave. She could see the fortress's towers stretching into the sky above her and realized she was still somewhere in the courtyard. She heard the living and deceased clansmen moving near the surface, following the commands of their Righteous King.

"Make sure we clear out the arsenal—don't leave a single piece of bloodstone behind," Seven ordered. "After tonight there'll be no need to return to this miserable place ever again. And make it quick—I want to get to Chariot Hills by sunrise!"

Brystal didn't know *how* or *why* she was still alive. The last thing she remembered was her slow death on the platform. As she pondered the mystery, she heard the sound of ticking coming from somewhere inside the grave. Brystal found a silver pocket watch that she had never seen before clipped to the waist of her pantsuit. Her name was engraved on the back of it, and curiously, instead of twelve *hours*, the watch was counting down twelve *months*.

The pocket watch triggered Brystal's memory and she suddenly recalled her time in the gray field. She might have thought it was just a dream, but the watch was proof it had actually happened. Brystal had *made a deal with Death*, and the watch was a reminder of their bargain. She had exactly one year to find and kill the Immortal with an ancient enchantment, and if time permitted, she could use the same enchantment to destroy the Righteous Army of the Dead. However, none of it would happen if Brystal didn't survive the fortress first.

She inspected the dirt walls and didn't know how she'd get out of the grave without her wand. Brystal was in so much pain she could barely sit up, let alone climb.

Don't even bother....

You'll never escape....

The walls are too tall to climb....

You're going to die down here....

You *deserve* to die down here.

For a moment, Brystal thought the disparaging thoughts were right. She was so eager to return to life, but now that she was back in *her* life, her deal with Death seemed pointless. Mistress Mara's curse made her so emotionally and physically depleted she didn't have the energy or the willpower to keep going.

That's it....

There's no reason to continue....

There's no reason to keep fighting....

There's nothing to live for anymore....

So don't.

As she sat in her grave, wounded and heartbroken, the ticking watch reminded Brystal of the space between life and death. She visualized the stars and planets in the sky, the smooth surface of the gray field, and the beautiful white trees. Brystal remembered all the pocket watches hanging from her branches and how each of them represented a living and breathing person. She thought about all the souls she had saved, all the lives she had helped, and all the people she had encouraged. It made her think about all the friends and family members who had inspired *her* over the years, all the love and laughter they had shared, and how she would give anything just to see their smiling faces one last time. . . .

And suddenly, like finding a life raft in the middle of a storm at sea, Brystal found the drive to push through her despair.

Despite what the curse made her think and feel, the world *was* worth fighting for. . . . *She* was worth fighting for. . . . There were people who *cared* about her. . . . There were people who were *rooting* for her. . . . Even if she failed and died in the process, she owed it to *them* to keep moving. . . . She owed it to her friends and family to keep trying. . . . She owed it to *herself* to keep going. . . .

So Brystal kept ticking.

She ignored everything her mind and body were telling her and gradually got to her feet. She slowly walked forward, focusing on one footstep at a time, and moved toward the edge of the grave. Brystal reached up with her aching hands, grabbed two handfuls of dirt, and began climbing. It was difficult, it was painful, and it required strength she didn't know she had, but Brystal did it anyway.

You're wasting your time....

You'll never make it out alive....

Go back to sleep and return to the gray field....

Let Death take you to the other side....

You've already lost.

For the first time, Brystal talked back to the voices in her head.

You're wrong....

It doesn't matter how long it takes me....

It doesn't matter if I fail or die in the process....

They'll only win if I stop trying....

And I'll never give up....

Never!

As if her response had caught the curse off guard, the negative thoughts went silent, and it took them a moment to return.

It's time to face the facts....

The grave is too deep, and you're too weak....

The army is too big, and you're too small....

You'll never defeat them....

It's impossible.

I am facing the facts....

If I were too weak, I wouldn't be here....

If I were too small, I wouldn't have come this far....

The army may be big, and they may be strong...

They may have risen from the dead...

But so have I....

I've already accomplished the impossible....

And I'm not done yet!

Each time Brystal responded to the thoughts, it took them longer and longer to return. She was almost halfway up the dirt wall—just a few more feet and the surface would be within her reach.

Everyone hates you....

The world thinks you're a murderer....

No one will ever trust you again....

You can't stop the Army of the Dead alone....

But that's exactly what you are ...

Hated and alone ...

Hated and alone.

Brystal placed both hands on the surface. She grunted and gritted her teeth as she summoned all her remaining strength for one final heave upward.

You're wrong....

Even if the world loses trust in me ...

Even if we lose mankind's acceptance ...

I'll never be alone....

I have family who love me....

I have friends who care about me....

And they'll always be there when I need them the most!

BANG! Just as Brystal's head rose above the surface, the south wall of the courtyard exploded. The blast covered the fortress in debris and knocked the Brotherhood off their feet. When the dust settled, Brystal saw Lucy standing in the midst of the damage. She was joined by the Fairy Council and the witches from Ravencrest.

Brystal was so overjoyed to see her friends she slipped off the surface and slid back to the bottom of the grave, but she landed with a huge smile on her face. Seeing her friends coming to her rescue validated everything she had said to her disturbing thoughts, and the negativity retreated so deep inside her that Brystal's clarity, her optimism, and her confidence returned at last. The curse hadn't been broken, she knew it was only a matter of time before the disturbing thoughts returned, but Brystal had finally learned how to fight it—not with magic, but *with the mind itself.*

As the fairies and witches entered the courtyard, they were shocked to see the Army of the Dead among the clansmen—the Brotherhood was over four times the size they were expecting.

"Well, *this* was falsely advertised," Emerelda said.

"Is it just my imagination, or do most of those men look *dead*?" Xanthous asked.

"They sure are," Stitches said with a wide grin. "And it's not even my birthday!"

The Brotherhood pointed all their swords, spears, and crossbows at the newcomers and waited for the Righteous King's commands. Seven climbed the platform to get a better look at the intruders and howled with laughter.

"Is this supposed to be an ambush?" he scoffed.

"You bet it is!" Lucy declared.

"They must not teach *math* at your schools," Seven sneered. "There's only nine of you and well over a thousand of us."

The living clansmen chuckled at their commander's remark. Lucy scowled at him and put her hands on her hips.

"Sorry, I can't hear you over that *obnoxiously loud outfit*," she said.

"Archers, prepare to fire," Seven told his men. "I'm going to enjoy this."

"You know, for such a flashy dresser, you sure are dim," Lucy said. "You're not the only one with backup, buddy!"

Lucy whistled into the dark beach behind her, and the fortress started vibrating as something very big approached. Suddenly, all the lynxes from Ravencrest Manor stampeded into the courtyard. The Brotherhood wasn't prepared for such an attack, and they didn't have time to raise their weapons before they were bitten, scratched, or tackled to the floor by the massive felines.

While the lynxes clawed and pounced on the clansmen, Lucy pulled the fairies and witches into a quick huddle.

"So we're a little outnumbered," Lucy said.

"A *little* outnumbered?" Skylene asked.

"We can't beat these guys on our own!" Tangerina said.

"We don't have to beat them—we just have to save Brystal!" Lucy said. "You guys help the lynxes distract the Brotherhood while I look for her! As soon as I find her, we'll get out of here!"

The fairies nodded and followed the lynxes into

battle. The witches ripped off their golden necklaces so their true appearances would help them in the fight.

Beebee buzzed through the air and stung the Brotherhood with her giant stinger. All the archers fired their crossbows at her, but the witch flew so erratically, their arrows whizzed right past her. Xanthous zigzagged through the courtyard and set the clansmen's robes ablaze, sending the men running toward the ocean in a panic. Skylene hit the Brotherhood with watery geysers that erupted from her hands, and she made the ground so muddy the clansmen slipped and slid before they could get anywhere near her.

Sprout kicked off her shoes and sank her toes into the dirt. Her feet grew through the courtyard like large tree roots and tripped the clansmen as they ran about. Once the men were off their feet, Sprout's fingers wrapped around their bodies like vines and kept them restrained. Tangerina sent her swarm through the courtyard, and the bumblebees snatched weapons out of the Brotherhood's hands. The insects also showered the clansmen in honey, sticking their boots and bony feet to the ground.

The Brotherhood's bloodstone weapons went directly through whatever magic the fairies and witches produced, but the clansmen *themselves* did not. Once Emerelda figured this out, she made large emerald blocks appear throughout the courtyard. The clansmen collided with the blocks headfirst and were knocked unconscious. Pip aimed her backside at the Brotherhood and sprayed them with an odor that was so foul it burned the men's eyes and made them vomit.

Stitches snatched a hair off a deceased clansman's head and quickly sewed the follicle onto a knitted doll. After muttering a short incantation, Stitches moved the doll's arms and legs, and the clansman mimicked the motion against his will. The witch played with the doll like it was an action figure, forcing the clansman to fight members of his own Brotherhood. Stitches was thrilled the incantation was finally working and jumped with joy.

"Annnnnd *that's* why they call me Stitches!" she cheered victoriously.

While the lynxes and her friends battled the living and deceased clansmen, Lucy weaved through the action in search of Brystal. Her sense of trouble guided her through the courtyard like a tracking beam, and with every step she took, she knew she was getting closer and closer to her. Just when Lucy was certain Brystal was right under her nose, she suddenly fell into an open grave and landed right beside her.

"Lucy!" Brystal happily exclaimed.

"Oh, thank God!" Lucy cried. "I was afraid we'd be too late!"

The girls gave each other a tight embrace.

"It's so wonderful to— *What happened to your hair?*" Brystal asked.

Lucy waved it off like it wasn't important. "I cursed a bunch of body-shaming ballerinas— but I'll tell you all about it later," she said. "I'm so sorry for getting angry at the cavern! I know you were only trying to protect me and I should have never acted like such a jerk! I'm a horrible friend and I hope you'll forgive me!"

"I'm sorry, too," Brystal said. "I haven't been acting like a good friend either."

"It wasn't your fault! You were cursed!"

"Yes, but I finally figured out how to— Wait, how'd *you* know I was cursed?"

"Because an invisible butler and a goat led me to a pumpkin in a witch's closest! *Wow, that just sounds crazy when you say it out loud.* But the important part is that you're alive and we're friends again! Is there anything I can do to make up for my horrible behavior?"

"Actually, there *is* something," Brystal said.

"Name it! I'll do anything!" Lucy said.

"You can help me out of this grave."

As the battle raged on above them, Seven watched his Army of the Dead from the safety of the platform and was exhilarated by what he saw. While the living clansmen were dropping like flies, it didn't matter what the witches, fairies, or lynxes did to the deceased clansmen, the dead always returned to their feet and kept fighting. They were resistant to Pip's fumes, they weren't bothered by Xanthous's flames, and if their foot got stuck in Tangerina's honey, they'd simply leave the foot behind and continue on.

The witches and fairies were getting tired and wouldn't last much longer. Seven was convinced he and the Brotherhood would be celebrating their first victory sooner than expected—*until* he spotted something that made his blood boil.

Across the courtyard, Lucy emerged from the open grave and then helped Brystal climb to the surface. Even though Seven had witnessed a thousand clansmen rise from the dead earlier, seeing Brystal come back to life horrified him, and it filled the Righteous King with unfathomable fury.

"NOOOOO!" Seven seethed. "That's impossible! I saw her die with my own eyes! I felt her cold flesh with my own hands!"

Lucy and Brystal raced through the courtyard, narrowly dodging the swords, spears, and arrows that came their way.

"I found her!" Lucy told the others. "Let's get out of here!"

The fairies and witches were thrilled to see Brystal had survived, and slowly but surely, they pushed through the clansmen and headed for the giant hole in the south wall.

"ARCHERS!" Seven screamed. "STOP WHAT YOU'RE DOING AT ONCE AND AIM YOUR WEAPONS AT THE FAIRY GODMOTHER! DON'T LET HER ESCAPE!"

The Brotherhood immediately turned toward Brystal and pointed their crossbows at her. The fairies, the witches, and the lynxes formed a protective circle around her, but there were hundreds and hundreds of arrows aimed directly at them, and they didn't know how they could possibly stop them all.

"Lucy, please tell me you have a plan C!" Brystal said.

"Sorry, I thought the lynxes would be enough!" Lucy admitted.

"NOTHING IS GOING TO SAVE YOU THIS TIME!" Seven yelled. "WE'RE GOING TO CRUSH YOU LIKE THE VERMIN YOU ARE!"

"Well, now he's just flirting with us," Stitches said.

"ARCHERS! FIRE ON THREE!" Seven ordered. "ONE!"

The fairies and witches searched for an escape, but they were completely surrounded.

"TWO!"

With nothing to do and nowhere to go, they held one another's hands, closed their eyes, and braced themselves for the end. Only a miracle could save them now.

"THREE!"

Their bodies went tense, expecting dozens of arrows to pierce their skin at once. However, the moment never came.

"I SAID THREE, YOU IDIOTS!" Seven roared.

The fairies and witches opened their eyes and saw that the Brotherhood were no longer focused on them. Thousands and thousands of kitchen utensils flew through the courtyard and began attacking the clansmen like a flock of rabid birds. Sharp knives sliced through the crossbows and cut all the arrows in half, pots and pans whacked the swords and spears out of their hands, and rolling pins knocked their feet out from under them.

"Who's d-d-doing this?" Beebee asked.

"It isn't one of us!" Sprout said.

The fairies knew there was only one person it could be. Everyone turned toward the south wall as a familiar figure stepped through the damage and joined the fight.

"MRS. VEE!" the fairies said together.

"Hey there, kiddos!" Mrs. Vee said. "Looks like you could use an extra *pan*! HA-HA!"

The bubbly housekeeper twirled her arms like a maestro conducting an orchestra as she assaulted the Brotherhood with her kitchen supplies. She smacked their faces with wooden spoons, she beat them over the head with baking sheets, and she poked their eyes with whisks and forks. Mrs. Vee unleashed such a powerful and ruthless attack that the fairies almost felt sorry for the clansmen.

"GET UP AND FIGHT!" Seven screamed at his army. "SHE'S JUST A COOK!"

Mrs. Vee was horribly offended. "Just a cook?!" she asked. *"Just a cook?!"*

The housekeeper pointed at the Righteous King and he was wrestled to the ground by an apron.

"I've seen some bad apples in my day but *that guy* takes the worm! HA-HA!" She laughed.

"Mrs. Vee, what made you come out of your room?" Tangerina asked.

"It sounds silly, but I woke up this morning and was just tired of being afraid," the housekeeper said. "I knew the only thing that would make me feel better was if I *did* something about my fear. When I realized you were all missing from the academy, I had a feeling you might be in trouble. So I found your stars on the Map of Magic and rushed here as fast as I could."

"Mrs. Vee, your timing is as impeccable as your cooking!" Lucy declared.

"Well, don't just stand there like stalks of asparagus!" the housekeeper said. "Let's roll like citrus on a slanted counter! HA-HA!"

While the clansmen fought off the utensils, the fairies, the witches, and the lynxes escaped from the fortress. They hurried down the beach to where the unicorns and the golden carriage were waiting for them. Without Mrs. Vee to conduct the utensils, the kitchen supplies began dropping from the air, releasing the Brotherhood from combat. Seven and the clansmen ran after the fairies and witches but they were too far behind to catch up.

"*THIS ISN'T OVER, BRYSTAL!*" Seven screamed. "YOU MAY HAVE ESCAPED THIS BATTLE, BUT YOU WON'T ESCAPE THE WAR! WE'LL REPAIR OUR WEAPONS AND BECOME EVEN STRONGER THAN BEFORE! MY ARMY WILL SEIZE THIS WORLD AND DESTROY EVERY-THING AND EVERYONE YOU LOVE! MARK

MY WORDS, *WE WILL WIN*, AND THERE'S NOTHING YOU CAN DO TO STOP US!"

Before Brystal joined her friends inside the carriage, she turned back to the fortress and took one last look at Seven. She had every right to *detest* him, she had every reason to *hate* him, but as she watched his eyes bulge with rage and his mouth foam with fury, all Brystal felt was *pity* for the Righteous King.

"People like you will never win," she said. "*Hate* is its own punishment."

· • ★ • ·

The golden carriage raced back to the Fairy Territory with all the fairies safely aboard. The witches flew beside the carriage on their broomsticks, and the lynxes followed on foot. By the time they reached the border and crossed through the hedge barrier, the sun had started to rise. All the fairies and magical creatures were still sound asleep, and the academy grounds were eerily quiet compared with the fortress.

As the fairies climbed out of the carriage and the witches dismounted their broomsticks, everyone was visibly shaken from the battle. Brystal, on the other hand, took advantage of her newfound clarity and immediately planned their next move.

"We've got a lot of work ahead of us," she told the others. "First things first. Emerelda, I want you to surround the territory with an emerald wall—and Xanthous, I want you to surround her wall with a wall of fire. The Brotherhood's weapons may penetrate our magic, but I won't let them set foot in our territory. Tangerina, I need you to send unicorns to the Evergreen house and retrieve my family at once— they won't be safe in the Southern Kingdom. Skylene, I want you to write to King White, Queen Endustria, and King Warworth and tell them Prince Gallivant has killed King Champion XIV and has plans to take over the world with an army of dead soldiers. Don't sugarcoat it, they need to be prepared. And Lucy?"

Lucy was shocked to hear Brystal say her name.

"You want *me* to do something?" she asked.

"Absolutely. Consider yourself back on the Fairy Council," Brystal said. "The Southern Kingdom has been told that *I* killed King Champion XIV and that *I* raised the army from the dead. I want you to create a pamphlet that tells them the truth—use all your show business skills to make it as compelling, as captivating, and as *entertaining* as possible—it needs to grab everyone's attention! Once you're done, I want you and the witches to make as many copies as possible and drop them over Chariot Hills—don't stop until every street is covered."

"Aye, aye, captain!" Lucy said with a salute.

Brystal was practically *cheerful* as she gave the instructions. The fairies stared at her like she was a different person.

"What's wrong?" she asked.

"Nothing—*that's* what's wrong," Emerelda said. "You're acting *normal* again."

"It's good to have you back," Xanthous said.

"It's good to *be* back," she said.

Even though they had a solid plan in place now, none of the fairies or witches leaped into action. All they could think about was the battle they had barely escaped from. They gazed at the border with fearful eyes, knowing they would cross paths with the Brotherhood sooner rather than later.

"I'm really scared," Skylene said. "Is it okay to admit that?"

"Me too," Tangerina said. "We've never faced anything like this before."

"I'm not going to lie to you," Brystal told them. "We're up against some pretty scary and unprecedented times. The world isn't as safe as it used to be, and it may seem like we've lost something, but sometimes you have to *lose* to learn the most important lessons. And if there's one thing I've learned through all this, it's that no one is ever as *alone* or *powerless* as they feel. We can always find someone or something to help us if we're willing to change our perspective.

"The Brotherhood may seem unbeatable, and they may seem frightening, but their greatest weapon isn't their soldiers or their bloodstone—their greatest weapon is *fear*. They want us to believe they're impossible to beat, they want us to think we aren't strong enough to face them, but as long as we don't confuse our fears with the facts, we *can* and we *will* defeat them. The truth is, we *also* have a secret weapon, and it's more powerful than the Brotherhood will ever be. But first, I had to lose it to realize just how valuable it is."

"What is it?" Lucy asked.

Brystal smiled at her friends. "*Hope*," she said.

"And I don't know about you, but I'm tired of letting people use my emotions to control me. So from now on, we're going to starve whatever misery they try to cause us. We're going to fight sadness with laughter, we're going to fight loneliness with friendship, we're going to fight anger with gratitude, and we're going to fight fear with hope. Because as long as we keep fighting, and as long as we keep our hope alive—*the Brotherhood won't stand a chance.*"

ACKNOWLEDGMENTS

I'd like to thank Rob Weisbach, Derek Kroeger, Alla Plotkin, Rachel Karten, and Heather Manzutto for being part of my team.

Everyone at Little, Brown Books for Young Readers, especially Alvina Ling, Megan Tingley, Ruqayyah Daud, Nikki Garcia, Siena Koncsol, Stefanie Hoffman, Shawn Foster, Danielle Cantarella, Jackie Engel, Emilie Polster, Marisa Russell, Janelle DeLuise, Hannah Koerner, Jen Graham, Sasha Illingworth, Angelie Yap, Virginia Lawther, and Chandra Wohleber. A special thank-you to Jerry Maybrook for helping me with the audiobook.

And, of course, to all my friends, family, and readers who aren't afraid to be a little witchy every now and then.